## "Why do _____ darkest secrets?" Gibson asked.

Libby considered. "I guess because we feel comfortable around each other."

"Oh, we do, do we?" His gaze was probing. "Is it just me, or am I the only one who's been doing the confiding in this relationship?"

She stared resolutely at the ground. "I've told you what I could."

He expelled his breath like a man who'd been hoping for more. "You're a hard woman, Libby Bateson. But I guess you've had to be."

Libby felt a shiver travel down her back at the accuracy of that last statement. It was almost as if he knew.

But of course he didn't. She'd told him she had money problems, but he couldn't realize that their situation—hers and her daughter's—had been close to desperate for most of the eight years she'd been away. He had no idea of the hardships she'd faced, yet he spoke as though he did.

Being with this man was more dangerous than she'd thought....

Dear Reader,

By definition, a home is the private living quarters of a family. The true value of a home, however, lies in its intangibles: warmth, love and acceptance. I've been on my own since I was nineteen, but I know that if I were ever in trouble, my parents would be there for me, the door to their home open as long as I needed.

In *A Daughter's Place* I wanted to explore a different scenario. One where a blissful childhood is shattered by a series of tragic events. One where a father turns his back on his daughter and forces her to leave home when she is seventeen. I stacked the deck against Libby Bateson, then gave her two good reasons to persevere: a vulnerable yet stalwart daughter and the love of a gorgeous man who shares Libby's passion for the land.

I grew up in rural Saskatchewan, and writing about the landscape of my youth has been both a pleasure and a challenge. I wasn't exactly a country girl by nature. My brothers will tell you I didn't know where the barn was on our property. (Which is a lie. If I hadn't known, I could never have avoided it so successfully.) But I did enjoy the beauty of the prairie and put in many hours exploring isolated farm roads. I may have moved away, but I admire the people who stay, building their future on the land they love.

I'm always thrilled to hear from readers. Please write to me at Suite #1754—246 Stewart Green S.W., Calgary, Alberta T3H 3C8, Canada. If you have Internet access, you can e-mail me at cjcarmichael@superauthors.com. Or check out my Web sites on http://www.superauthors.com or http://www.canadianromanceauthors.com.

Sincerely,

C.J. Carmichael

# A Daughter's Place
## C.J. Carmichael

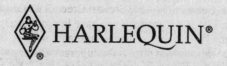

## HARLEQUIN®

TORONTO • NEW YORK • LONDON
AMSTERDAM • PARIS • SYDNEY • HAMBURG
STOCKHOLM • ATHENS • TOKYO • MILAN • MADRID
PRAGUE • WARSAW • BUDAPEST • AUCKLAND

ISBN 0-373-70956-0

A DAUGHTER'S PLACE

Copyright © 2000 by Carla Daum.

Visit us at www.eHarlequin.com

**Printed in U.S.A.**

There is no town called Chatsworth in Saskatchewan,
but there is a farming community by that name.
It is where my parents, John and Kay, raised me,
my two brothers and two sisters.

This book is for them, with love.

# *PROLOGUE*

SEVENTEEN-YEAR-OLD Libby Bateson didn't look out the window as the Greyhound pulled away from the bus depot in Yorkton, Saskatchewan. She was leaving the only home she'd ever known and she would never be back, but she could not risk a parting glance.

Because if she saw even one familiar sight—the old restaurant her mother used to take her to for chocolate shakes after her annual dentist's appointment, or the big-chain grocery store where they "stocked up" every month—she'd start crying.

And she wasn't going to cry. She'd done enough of it the past year and a half and now she was through.

She was on her way to Toronto, on her own. She'd never traveled so far, never even taken a Greyhound, with its plush, high-backed seats that reclined at the touch of a button, so unlike the hard benches on the school bus.

School was another place she couldn't think about, because if she did she'd deeply regret not completing the single year that stood between her and graduation.

The one image she tried to banish from her mind

but couldn't was the look on her father's face at the bus depot that morning. His eyes had been cold and unreachable, his mouth unsmiling. He'd shoved a wad of money at her, not meeting her gaze or touching her hand.

Now she opened her purse and fingered the slick, crisp bills. She'd never seen so much cash. How long it would last in Toronto she had no idea, but she hoped at least a few years.

She didn't want to consider the future, though, not right now. It was off-limits, just like the past. Survival depended on focusing on the present and forgetting she'd ever had a family. A mother with a ready laugh, an elder brother who loved to tease. A father who adored her...

Once.

"Are you okay, miss?" the elderly lady across the aisle gave her a sympathetic smile. "Is this your first trip away from home?"

"I'm fine, thanks." Libby sat straighter, forced her mind to go blank, her eyes to stare at a page in the book she was holding, even though she couldn't concentrate on the words.

The thing was, she couldn't think of *anything*. Not her mother and brother, who were dead, or her father, who never wanted to see her again.

There was only one person, a neighbor, who might have cared about her plight. Gibson Browning had been her brother Chris's best friend. She knew he worried about her and her father. He often dropped by the old farmhouse on one pretense or another. He said he missed Chris and her mother. Said she must be lonely, too. He was so kind that many times she'd been tempted to confide in him.

But shame had held her back. She didn't want anyone to know what had happened on the back country roads in Darren O'Malley's rusted pickup. Especially not Gibson—the hero of all her girlhood fantasies.

There was no way around it. She was alone, and now everything was up to her. To find a new place to live, a new job.

To raise the baby—her baby—who would be born in six months' time.

# CHAPTER ONE

*Eight years later...*

LIBBY BATESON SAT in the chair opposite her daughter's grade two teacher and realized that she herself, not Nicole, deserved the failing grade. What kind of mother didn't know when her kid was struggling and unhappy, suffering from low self-esteem?

"Of course Nicole is capable of doing the work. As you can see, her reading and math levels are only slightly below average." Miss Pendergast put away the assignments they'd just reviewed. Her manner was congenial, yet somehow Libby felt like a recalcitrant student who had been called in for making trouble.

"Her social skills are what I'm worried about," the teacher continued. "In class she's painfully shy. At recess I often see her standing by herself against the school wall, as if she can't wait for the bell to ring."

Libby had to look away from the earnest-faced Miss Pendergast, as tears sprang to her eyes. She focused on the colorful pictures taped above the children's coat hooks. Nicole's drawing of her family stood out. Two tiny, black-and-white stick people in the center of a large white sheet of paper. No father, no brothers or sisters, no pets…

"What do you think I should do?" Libby strove for dignity, when all she felt like was crying.

Miss Pendergast's smile was sympathetic. "Perhaps you could invite some of Nicole's classmates over to play after school. It might help her develop friends."

Libby said nothing. With her work schedule, that was impossible. Her shift at the Fashion Warehouse on Spadina Avenue was over at three. That just gave her enough time to pick up Nicole from school and take her to the Westwinds Seniors' Home by four. The manager there was very accommodating about Nicole hanging out in the lounge while Libby cleaned until seven every week night. By the time they got home on the Bathurst streetcar, there wasn't time for much besides dinner and a bath, maybe a story or two.

"Anything else?"

"Well, you might want to consider an after-school activity. Many children take gym classes or music. If you could find something Nicole enjoyed, it might help build her confidence in herself."

Another excellent idea Libby had zero chance of implementing. Even if she could find the time, she had no room in her budget for extras. As it was, she barely had enough money for clothing and food.

Libby often felt tired. Now exhaustion made even speaking a struggle. "I'll definitely consider your ideas. I appreciate your concern about my daughter."

"I'm sure you'll do your best."

Miss Pendergast's smile, which had seemed kind, suddenly appeared condescending. Libby wondered if possibly the university-educated woman knew that Libby didn't even have her high school diploma.

"Yes, I certainly will," she replied. Then, her back stiff with self-consciousness, she exited the classroom.

Once in the hallway, Libby paused to blot her eyes. She'd worn mascara for the interview, something she rarely bothered with, and now she saw traces of the black dye on her tissue. Down the hall was a washroom. She slipped in the door and turned on the light. Checking herself in the mirror, she was relieved to see she didn't have raccoon eyes. She pulled up her panty hose, which had been sagging, and smoothed down her dress, then washed her hands and splashed a little cool water over her cheeks.

She'd tried to dress nicely for the interview with Nicole's teacher, but the minute she'd walked into the classroom and seen Miss Pendergast's beautiful knit sweater and pleated linen slacks, she'd known her own outfit screamed "discount merchandise" and "secondhand."

Of course, her appearance wasn't the important thing. Nicole's education and happiness were what mattered. She reflected on her conversation with the teacher, and how they'd both just danced around the real issues: lack of money, lack of time and an absence of support from other family members.

Libby wondered if she was just making excuses for herself. Other single mothers somehow managed. Why couldn't she? She'd promised Miss Pendergast she would do her best for Nicole. Yet she was already doing her best. The problem was, it just wasn't good enough.

THE SECOND Libby stepped off the streetcar, she could see there was a problem. Because of the meeting with Miss Pendergast, she'd arranged for Nicole to go to a neighbor's house after school. But Nicole now stood at the landing to their basement apartment. Three bigger girls, on the threshold of adolescence, crowded around her. Libby had seen the trio before, usually hanging around the local corner store, in their high platform boots and flared jeans. Now she was concerned at the way they'd circled her daughter, like wolves moving in on a sickly calf.

Libby's dress shoes were an encumbrance as she hurried to cross the street. The wind was cold, the sun hidden behind thick cloud cover. Spring had yielded to one more cold snap this week, so she'd bundled Nicole well this morning. What had happened to her hat?

A young mother pushing a stroller crossed in front of her. Libby waited, then rushed forward. The taunting of the older girls became audible.

"Hey, Nutty," the tallest girl sneered. "Don't you know you've got snot dripping down your nose? Don't you know how disgusting that is?"

A second girl groaned. "Oh, yuck, look at that! She's wiping it on her jacket. How gross!"

"Nicole?" Libby's voice startled the three girls, and they scattered like trash in the wind. Libby moved in, scooping her daughter into a warm, tight hug.

"Sweetie?" She pulled back a bit to check Nicole's face. She was smiling now, however tremulously. "Why are you standing out here? Why aren't you at Mrs. Spitzel's?"

Nicole shook her head, unable to choke out a word of explanation.

"Never mind. Let's talk later. You feel as cold as an icicle. How about I run you a nice, hot bath?"

Inside, Nicole stripped down as Libby put the plug in the bathtub drain and turned on the taps. The tub was small; it didn't take long before it was half-full and Nicole could step in.

"Those girls live up the street, don't they? Have they bothered you before?"

Nicole sunk low into the warm water, and finally stopped shivering.

"They were being cruel, weren't they?" Thinking of her daughter's tormentors made Libby wish she'd run after them and demanded to speak to their parents. But her first instinct had been to comfort Nicole, and they'd disappeared so quickly.

"I don't care about them," Nicole said.

"And what happened to your hat?"

Nicole wiggled her toes. "I lost it."

Libby perched on the edge of the tub and asked pointedly, "Did someone take your hat from you?"

Her daughter took a small washcloth and covered her face with it. "No," she said. "I just lost it."

Right. Libby peeled the cloth away. "Look at me, sweetie."

Nicole did.

"You know what I see on your face?"

"Dirt?"

It should've been funny, but Libby couldn't laugh. "No. Not dirt. Resignation. You don't complain because you know you can't expect anything better."

Of course Nicole didn't understand what she meant. She still thought she'd done something wrong.

"Was Miss Pendergast mad at me?"

*Oh, Nicole!* "No, Miss Pendergast isn't mad. Not at all."

"Then why did she want to talk to you?"

"We'll discuss it after dinner, okay?"

LIBBY HAD BEEN sixteen when she'd realized that, despite what her mother had told her, every cloud did not have a silver lining. Two times events outside her control had shattered her world.

Now her life was poised for devastation a third time.

Of course she'd seen signs that Nicole wasn't happy. Libby hadn't needed to talk to Miss Pendergast to know there were problems, particularly in terms of friends. Nicole was never invited to play with the other girls in her class. That wasn't normal. The scene with those girls on the street simply confirmed that her daughter was in some sort of trouble.

Standing at the fridge, Libby stared at the leftovers from last night's dinner. Everything was distorted and blurry, thanks to the tears that she could no longer hold back.

Never would she forget the beaten, hopeless look on Nicole's face just before her daughter had spotted her on the street. Libby was certain it wasn't the first time those girls had tormented Nicole, yet the little girl had never complained.

Of course, Nicole never did. And that was a big part of the problem. She probably knew her mother could do nothing to help....

Libby took out several plastic containers and tossed the contents into a frying pan. As she stirred, she dabbed at her eyes with a tissue.

She'd do anything for her daughter, but her choices were few. She couldn't afford to quit either of her jobs, since both paid only minimum wage. A better education would lead to more opportunities, but night classes would just mean less time for Nicole and more exhaustion for her. If only there was somewhere to turn...

As the pasta-and-vegetable stir-fry began to steam, she called to her daughter. "Time to get out of the tub."

"Okay, Mom."

A second later, Libby heard the water swooshing down the drain. She turned down the heat under the pan and set plates on the table.

From the moment of Nicole's birth, all she'd known was struggle. Libby had never managed to do much more than provide shelter and food. The money from her father had run out all too quickly, forcing her to put Nicole in government-subsidized day care when she was only three months. Soon after that, the ear infections had started.

Libby couldn't count the number of times she'd had to phone in sick to work because Nicole was too feverish to go to day care and, later, school. Many times, those absences had cost her the job. Nor could she count the number of different grungy basement apartments she and Nicole had lived in over the years.

Nicole came out of the bathroom dressed in her pajamas, a towel wrapped around her head. "Should I pour the milk?"

"Yes, please." Libby peeled a couple of carrots, then dished out the warmed-up pasta. The sad meal was a reminder of how she'd failed as a parent. The fact that Nicole didn't complain but just picked up her fork and started eating made Libby want to start crying again.

How different life had been for her at Nicole's age. Mealtimes had been full of conversation and laughter as well as good old-fashioned farm cooking, featuring garden-fresh vegetables in summer and her mother's home preserves in winter.

She'd taken those occasions for granted, never guessing a day would come when Chris wouldn't be around to tease her or her mother wouldn't be available for a hug.

Too bad Nicole could never know that life... Or could she? Returning to the farm had never been an option she'd considered. Maybe she'd been wrong. Speaking quickly, before her courage faltered, she posed a question to her daughter.

"Sweetheart, what would you think about us moving to my dad's farm in Saskatchewan for a few months?'' It was the only possible solution, and yet it wasn't a solution at all. Her father had made it clear that he never wanted to see her again. Which was just the way Libby wanted it, too. Small-town Chatsworth, Saskatchewan, held nothing for her except a bunch of painful memories.

But Nicole had no painful memories of the place.

"I thought you said you and your dad had a big fight?'' Nicole sounded cautious, but Libby could see a spark of interest in her eyes.

"That's true.'' Libby fiddled with her silverware. "I was thinking it would be good for me to finish school. And a change of scenery might be nice for you, too. Unless you'd rather finish out the school year with Miss Pendergast?''

"No.'' Nicole shook her head vehemently.

If Libby could stay at the farm rent free, she'd be able to complete high school by correspondence. Then she and Nicole could move to a smaller town, where the cost of living wasn't as high as in Toronto. Maybe with her high school diploma she'd be able to get a decent job.

"I'd like to visit the farm where you grew up.''

She'd told her daughter so many stories. "You know it'll be different from when I was little.''

"That's okay. I could still see the attic bedroom where you used to sleep and climb the poplars at the back of the house and...do you think there'll still be kittens in the cow barn?''

The longing in her daughter's voice cinched matters. At that moment Libby vowed to set aside her differences with her father, for Nicole's sake. What was she really sacrificing, after all, except her pride?

Nicole read from one of her favorite picture books, while Libby did the dinner dishes. For once Libby couldn't concentrate on her daughter's words. She kept thinking about her plan to return to Chatsworth.

She wouldn't just have her father she'd have to deal with. She'd grown up among the farmers in that area. All of them would wonder where she'd been the past eight and a half years. They'd especially wonder about Nicole and who her father was.

Libby didn't want to face any of that. Still, she and Nicole wouldn't need to stay long. She'd make some calls tomorrow and find out about those correspondence courses. Then she'd contact her father.

AFTER HER FIRST job the next day, Libby used a pay phone to call the high school she'd attended in Saskatchewan. They gave her a number to phone for information about correspondence courses. Then she called the bus depot to inquire about tickets to Yorkton. Now for the hardest part.

It was almost two in Toronto, which meant it would be one in Saskatchewan. Her father's usual lunchtime. Libby knew she had to act quickly before she lost her nerve. After digging more change from her purse, she dialed "1" for long distance, then punched in the area code and the seven-digit phone number.

She'd vowed on the day her father kicked her out that she'd never go back. But here she was, about to renege on that vow. She listened to the rings, counting them; she reached seven before a slight click signaled someone had answered the phone.

"Hello?" The man's voice was so hoarse it wasn't recognizable. Yet it had to be her father's.

She hesitated a moment. The last time they'd spoken, he'd said he would rather she was dead than pregnant, with not even a boyfriend willing to accept responsibility. The passing years had not made her father's rejection any more understandable, or forgivable, to her. Now the hurt, the pain, the bitterness and anger, choked up her throat, and she found it difficult to say the words she knew she had to speak.

"It's me, Libby," she finally managed to say. And then, because she sensed he was going to hang up, she continued in a rush, "Nicole and I need a place to stay—only until September." Four months would be long enough to get her diploma. Once she had that, somehow she'd make a future for her and Nicole.

There was a long pause before her father spoke again. "Well, don't think you'll be staying here."

Libby was stunned. She'd often wondered over the years if he felt remorse for the way he'd treated her. His answer proved the opposite was true. She closed her eyes and tried to picture the kind, quiet father of her childhood. "How can you say that? Are you going to deny your own granddaughter?"

"I don't have a granddaughter. My family are all dead. Killed."

To discover the pain could still strike with such flaming heat was a shock. "That was Mom and Chris who died in the car accident. Not me."

Although she'd often wished it had been her. Anything to not have been the one standing at the door the day the Mounties came to bring them the news.

"You're wrong. They're dead. They're all dead."

"We have no place else to go," she said. "We're coming—we've got to."

"Don't come. The door will be locked." And he hung up the phone.

Seconds ticked by before Libby could follow suit. Once the receiver was back in position, she realized she'd stopped breathing. Now she filled her lungs deeply. That had been way worse than she'd imagined. To think she'd hoped time had made her father repentant, even sorrowful, for what he'd done to her.

But clearly he hadn't spared her a single caring thought. He'd never worried how she was making out. Probably never even wondered whether her child was a boy or a girl, or if it was healthy.

The truth was painfully obvious. She was nothing to him; she might as well have perished in that car crash.

More tears. Libby brushed her cheeks. At least this time she didn't have to worry about streaking mascara. She stood straighter and squelched the pain and hurt, emotions she couldn't afford.

Her father wanted to turn his back on her, and that was fine, but she wouldn't let him deny Nicole. If he chose to lock his door against them, then they'd crawl in a window if they had to. It might not be pleasant, it might be downright ugly, but she and Nicole were returning to the farm and they were going to stay for as long as they needed.

But not, she promised herself, a second more.

# CHAPTER TWO

"HOW MANY KIDS can I invite to my birthday party this year, Daddy?"

Gibson Browning smiled at his daughter in the passenger seat next to him. "You don't turn eight for over three weeks, Allie. Isn't it a little early to worry about guests?"

He was bringing her home from school. She'd been chattering the whole way, a sound Gibson liked.

"Well, I have to invite Ardis and Jenny and Violet...."

Headlights, surrounded by a cloud of distant dust, warned of an approaching vehicle. Gibson eased up on the accelerator, then steered his truck over to the side of the graveled road, wondering who could be coming. The only other farmer sharing this access road was Old Man Bateson, who lived up a half mile. He was practically a hermit, his big monthly excursion a trip into town to pick up his mail and supplies and go to the bank.

The old man didn't receive visitors, either. The only traffic Gibson ever saw going in and out was the Co-op fuel truck and the occasional farmer interested in buying seed grain.

As the vehicle passed, Gibson was surprised to see

it was a Yorkton taxi. Taxis were a rare enough sighting in rural Saskatchewan, but on this particular road spotting one was downright alarming.

Concerned about the old man, Gibson ignored his own driveway. Instead, he drove the extra half a mile to Bateson's. He himself had traveled this stretch of road countless times as a boy, then later as a young man. Back then, the Batesons' farm had been like a second home.

But much had changed since those days.

The old man had changed. Gibson remembered a patient, kind father, the sort of man who spoke rarely but stood up for principles he believed in. Now he was ornery and unreasonable, turning down all offers of help or friendship from the neighbors around him. And he'd developed a litigious streak that was wearing out what little sympathy remained for him within the community.

Even Gibson, his closest neighbor, rarely saw him, and, when he did, couldn't get a civil word out of him. Still, he felt sorry for the old coot. He'd lost a son and a wife. Then Libby, his only daughter, had left town and never looked back. Whatever that taxi from Yorkton meant, Gibson hoped it wasn't more bad news.

"Where are you going?" Allie asked, peering over the dashboard. "You missed our corner."

"Just checking on Mr. Bateson," Gibson said. He pulled into the top of the Batesons' driveway and stopped. Through the line of crooked pine trees that stood on either side of the dirt road, he could see a woman and a child in front of the old farmhouse.

The woman was tall and slender, and had a mass of brown curls, as did the youngster sitting at her feet.

Good God. He felt a strange, prickly sensation between his shoulder blades. He hadn't seen hide nor hair of Libby Bateson since she'd run off when she was seventeen. He hadn't heard of her since, either, certainly no word about her having had a baby. But with that head of curls, the child had to be hers.

The woman had turned at the sound of his truck and now she stared down the lane, one hand shielding the sun, the other reaching for the young girl beside her. He was too far to see her features clearly or to read her expression, but, certain it was Libby, he raised one hand in salute. After a few seconds she gave a faint response, a mere nod, before turning back to the house.

What could have brought her back after all these years and what did she think of the place now? Would it bother her conscience to see how badly everything had deteriorated in her absence?

He was half tempted to get out of the truck and talk to her, but her body language wasn't inviting. Hell, maybe she'd forgotten all about him—she'd been gone long enough. He ground the truck into reverse and backed out of the lane.

As he headed home, the rearview mirror showed him nothing but the cloud of dust kicked up by his own tires. He wondered about Libby and her daughter. They had to have been standing like that for several minutes, ever since the taxi had let them off. Why hadn't they gone inside the house?

"WHO WAS THAT, Mom?" Nicole asked, grinding her foot into the dirt of the road.

"Gibson Browning." The truck was different, but Libby would know that shock of blond hair anywhere. "His family has the only other farm on this road. He was my brother's best friend."

The truth of the matter was that Gibson and Chris had been inseparable, and she, eight years their junior, had looked up to them both with almost worshipful admiration. Those boyhood ties had loosened only slightly with Gibson's marriage. He and his bride had moved into the Brownings' farmhouse when his parents had retired to their home in town.

Strangely, Libby couldn't picture the woman Gibson had married, although she remembered a halo of perfect blond hair. The little girl in the truck was obviously their daughter, with coloring just like her parents'.

Funny that Gibson hadn't stopped to talk, but she was just as glad he hadn't. It was too soon to face the neighbors. Right now she was having enough trouble adjusting to being back here where she'd grown up, a place that held both the happiest and most painful memories of her life.

"My uncle Chris?"

Libby nodded, fighting the tears that had threatened ever since they'd come within sight of her old house. It was hard not to picture her mother running out the front door to greet them, or her brother glancing up from under the hood of an old car to crack an insult at her.

Living in Toronto, facing the daily grind of survival, had put her out of touch with her grief. Now the pain was raw and fresh, her losses unrecovered. Just as on the day they'd heard the news, her father and her, standing together in the doorway.

The day the laughter died.

Libby took a few steps forward. The verdant land was spongy underfoot; it must have been a wet spring. Mint-green leaves danced in the breeze; heavy purple blossoms scented the yard with the fragrance of lilac.

Everything was new and fresh and clean. Even the clouds appeared just laundered, puffed out to dry in the blue crystalline sky.

"It smells good here," Nicole commented.

"Fill up your lungs, sweetie. This is the air God meant us to be breathing." Only now that she was back home did she realize how suffocating she'd found the city. For some reason, maybe the humidity or the pollution, Toronto had always seemed shrouded in haze. Here the light was sharp, allowing her to see far across the green pasture to the plowed black fields waiting to be seeded.

Amid all this springtime beauty, the farm itself was a disgrace. The place Libby remembered had been a showcase; now paint was peeling from the house, the barn and the old machine shed, and weeds had taken over her mother's prize flower beds in the front yard and the vegetable garden around the side.

"Is my grandfather at home?"

"I think so. The truck is here. And so's the tractor." Both were parked near the two fuel tanks—one for diesel, one for regular gas.

"Should we knock on the door?"

"Not yet." Libby sat on the suitcase they'd brought with them. The same suitcase she'd taken with her when she left. Her sixteenth birthday present.

Once again, Nicole sank down by her feet, and Libby examined her daughter's upturned face. "I told you about that fight I had with my dad when I was seventeen, right?"

Nicole nodded.

"Well, he may be angry that I've come back here. He may say some nasty things. I want you to remember that he isn't mad at you. He doesn't even know you."

Nicole nodded again. Libby had explained all this on the bus ride here. They'd talked about her mother and Chris, too. She'd never before told Nicole the details of the accident that had claimed their lives. It had seemed an unnecessary burden for a little girl. Even now there was so much she had to leave out.

Like the identity of Nicole's father.

"Did you really live here when you were growing up?"

"I sure did. It didn't look like this, though, way back then. The house was always a lovely pale yellow and your grandma grew the most beautiful flowers in that garden over there."

It was so easy to picture her there, dressed in her usual white shirt and slacks, hoeing weeds or maybe staking the delphiniums.

"Did I ever tell you that your grandma used to wear white shirts every day? She told me farm women had to have their standards, and she used to bleach and iron those shirts until they were perfect.''

Libby scooped Nicole's hand in hers and pulled her to her feet to more closely examine the house. The sun had bleached most of the pale-yellow paint. The dormer windows that peeked out from the gray-shingled roof were dull with grime. A dilapidated wide veranda spread across the house. Once it had been screened, and Libby remembered her parents drinking tea there after mealtimes. Now the wire netting had so many holes it might as well be taken down.

"What are we going to do, Mom?"

"I'm not sure," she admitted.

Letting go of Nicole's hand, Libby advanced farther. She opened the screen door of the veranda and stepped onto plank boards, rough and dry from lack of paint, then crossed to the front door. She'd remembered it as being white, now it was yellowed and dirty. Libby curled her hand into a fist and knocked firmly. After several seconds, she knocked again. This time a voice answered from the open living room window.

"Get out of here!"

The glare of the midday sun prevented Libby from seeing her father's face, but the words, and the venom they held, were enough to let her know that he hadn't softened in the days it had taken her and Nicole to bus halfway across the country.

She glanced at Nicole. Her daughter was walking backward, her gaze glued to where her grandfather's voice had come from.

Had the old man not seen her? Or was his heart so completely hardened that he would frighten a small child this way?

"Look, we have no place else to go, as I explained on the phone. Do you think I'd be here if I had a choice?"

"I told you not to come." The window slammed shut. Libby's hand curved round the dull brass door-knob and she gave a hard turn. It didn't move. When she'd been growing up, they'd never bolted their front door.

So he was locking her out, was he? Well, she'd see about that…. The kitchen was at the side of the house. Just as she'd suspected, the window over the sink was open. The cotton curtain with its eyelet trim was brown with dirt and flapped in the slight breeze from the west.

"You may as well let us in," she said. "We aren't going anywhere. We'll stay out here all night if we have to."

*Slam!* Her father crashed the window down, then briskly closed the grimy curtains. Her anger churned into bitter determination. If he thought he could block her out that easily, he had another think coming. She marched around back, past the small, closed-in porch that led to the kitchen—she didn't bother trying that door, assuming it, too, would be locked—and continued around to the other side of the house, past the main-floor bedroom window, then the larger living room window. She could hear her father closing more windows and curtains.

She'd circled back to Nicole, who was staring at

her with wide, frightened eyes. Libby sighed and
stooped to open the large shopping bag she had used
as a carryall during their journey. She removed the
ham sandwich and a carton of juice she'd picked up
at the Yorkton bus terminal and handed them to her
daughter.

"Here's your lunch, sweetie. Eat up. He's a stubborn old man and it may be a while before he lets
us in."

"What if he doesn't?"

"Oh, he will." Just saying the words gave Libby
a confidence she hadn't felt moments before. She returned to the front door and tried it again. Still
locked, of course. She leaned against the warm
wood, her mouth inches from the small crack between the frame and the door.

"Are you going to call the police? Because that's
what you'll have to do to get rid of us, I promise."

There was a crash in the house, followed by the
splintering of glass. Libby looked back at Nicole and
held up her hand reassuringly. Let him think about
what she'd just said for a while. She rejoined her
daughter. Nicole was gnawing on the crusts of her
sandwich now. The scared look in her eyes was beginning to fade. Maybe she'd sensed her mother's
newfound courage. Libby smiled and ran her hand
over the curls so like her own.

"Don't you worry, sweetie. He'll give in soon.
And if he doesn't, we'll make up a bed in his truck
over there." She pointed to the old red Ford standing
like a faithful steed.

A forgotten piece of information came to mind.

"On second thought, maybe we'll just drive into town and buy some groceries." She trotted over to the truck and looked in the open window. Sure enough, silver keys dangled on the other side of the steering column.

Feeling slightly light-headed, Libby waved at Nicole to get in the other side. She ran over to the house and shouted at the stubbornly closed door. "I'm just taking the truck into town to pick up some groceries. We'll be here in time to make supper."

She didn't wait to hear the reaction—be it another smashed item of furniture, or the old man hollering. She just ran back to the truck, jumped into the front seat, turned the key and started to drive.

She had a young child to take care of, no home and only eighty-three dollars left to her name. At this very moment her father was probably phoning the police to report a stolen vehicle.

Yet, for some strange reason, she felt happier than she had in a long, long time. She was behind the wheel again, choosing her own route for a change. Outside the dirt-streaked windows was the landscape of home: acres of soil waiting to be plowed, the expanses of brown dirt relieved here and there by willow fringed sloughs and long lines of poplars dividing one field from another.

Occasionally there was a pasture, bright green from the moisture of newly melted snow, populated by cattle and a smattering of new, rubber-legged calves. The black vinyl seat was warm behind her and the breeze from the open windows was refreshing as she gathered up speed.

LIBBY SHOPPED QUICKLY, not wanting to run into anyone she knew, face questions she had no idea how to answer. She bought groceries to last several days, and a good supply of cleaning products, which she suspected would be desperately needed.

When she pulled into the driveway for the second time that day it was three o'clock. Nicole had fallen asleep and was slumped against the passenger door. Libby rearranged her daughter so that she lay the length of the bench seat, then took a deep breath and steeled herself for phase two of her house invasion plan. At least her father didn't appear to have called the cops on her. She supposed she could take that as a good sign. Once out of the truck, she headed for the front door, and was surprised to see that it stood wide-open.

"Hello?" she said cautiously as she planted her hands on the wooden frame and leaned inward.

Dirt and dust were everywhere—on the furniture, the carpet, even hanging in the air. She sneezed, then took one step inside.

This couldn't be her home. God, she and Chris had sat on that sofa and watched TV together every Sunday night. Now the fabric was filthy. The houseplants were dead and decaying. Clutter littered the table beside the leather recliner—her father's favorite chair and the only piece of furniture that seemed to have been used.

Her mother's chair, next to it, was just as dirty as the sofa. A broken lamp lay on the carpet beside it—the source of the earlier crashing noise, Libby assumed. She ignored the closed door in front of her that led to her parents' bedroom and walked to her left, toward the dining room. Here, she found the table and chairs gray under years of undisturbed dust.

So many special meals had been enjoyed in this room. She remembered birthdays and Christmas, her father always sitting at one end of the table, her mother at the other.

At the doorway to the kitchen she paused, catching her breath at the squalor. The smell was stronger here; she could see the accumulation of grease on the stove, and the crust of dirt around the kitchen faucet and sink. Used dishes were strewn over the table, and flies buzzed around odd bits of uneaten food. Putting a hand to the door frame to steady herself, Libby fought an attack of nausea.

She'd expected the house would need a good cleaning. But nothing could have prepared her for such a disgusting sight.

Her father had been a neat man, tidy and clean. He, more than her high-spirited mother, had been responsible for the immaculate state of their house and outbuildings. In the winter, when outdoor work was minimal, he'd often invented little housekeeping projects for himself to keep his hands busy.

How could he be living like this?

Libby went back to the truck to get the cleaning supplies. She left Nicole sleeping with the windows to the truck wide-open, then returned to the house. This time she went up the stairs to the bedrooms. Seeing these rooms completely unchanged by the passage of years was a shock.

She wondered if her father had even stepped foot

up here since the day she'd left. Judging from the dirt on the floor, she doubted it.

The miscellany in the rooms triggered so many memories. From the trophies on Chris's bureau to the dried-flower arrangement that she'd made with her mother, which was now nothing more than a heap of dust on her old nightstand. But if she allowed herself to get sentimental, to start thinking about the past, nothing would get done. Fighting the urge to give in to tears, she stripped the beds, hers and Chris's.

At the bureau she paused, peering in the mirror as she tied back her hair. The last time she'd stood here, at the age of seventeen, she'd felt more scared than any young woman should ever have to feel. Now she was no longer frightened. Just determined to make things right for Nicole.

Libby ran back downstairs to the kitchen. First she emptied the fridge, throwing absolutely everything into a large garbage bag. She scrubbed for half an hour before deciding the fridge was clean enough that she could restock it. Nicole was still sleeping; the poor thing was exhausted. It was already four-thirty, but Libby couldn't start dinner because the kitchen was still much too filthy.

She bleached the counters and table while the dishes soaked in water she'd boiled on the stove. Then she washed the stove elements as best she could, leaving the oven for another day. The kitchen floor was next. She swept, vacuumed, then got down on her hands and knees to scrub the old linoleum. It took five buckets of water before she felt satisfied.

As she was drying the last rack load of dishes, the kitchen door opened.

In walked her father.

The dishrag fell from her hands as she turned to face him. He was smaller, his shoulders stooped, his features sharper than she remembered. The past eight years had aged him twenty. Dressed in dark-blue coveralls and a gray, long-sleeved T-shirt, he appeared as dirty as any street person she'd seen in Toronto. His face was grizzled, his hair bushy and unkempt.

He didn't look at her, just set a pail with eggs in it by the door and walked through to the living room. His dirty boots left prints on the freshly washed floor.

Libby stared after him, the rehearsed sentences of blame and anger frozen at the back of her throat. That man couldn't be her father. It was impossible. She remembered a stocky, fit man with short dark hair barely touched with gray. He'd always been clean-shaven and particular about his clothes, just like her mother. His pants had to have a crease and his shirts a collar, even if they were only work clothes.

And how could he have walked past her like that, as if she wasn't even there? For a moment she was tempted to march into the living room and force a showdown between them. All the while she'd been cleaning and scrubbing, bleaching and scraping, she'd been planning her strategy. Polishing up the angry thoughts and bitter recriminations she'd accumulated over the years. Of course she'd expected him to start the argument by trying to kick her out of the house.

The last thing she'd anticipated was silence.

Hearing him settle in his chair and flick on the television, she changed her mind. If this was how he wanted to handle the situation, then so be it. Libby made supper, and, after a moment's consideration, set three places at the table before going out to the truck to get Nicole.

She found her daughter rubbing her eyes and stretching. "Where are we?"

"Back at the farm. Supper's ready. Do you feel hungry?"

Nicole sat up and yawned. "I think so."

"Come on in and wash your hands, then."

At the back door Nicole hesitated. "Is he there?" she asked, her eyes fixed with dread on the old farmhouse.

"Yes. Watching television. Don't worry. It'll be fine."

Once Nicole was seated at the table Libby took a deep breath and called out to her father, "Supper's ready."

He didn't reply.

Libby shrugged when Nicole gave her a questioning glance. The two of them ate, hungrily and quietly, with Libby setting aside a serving for her father. Maybe he would eat it later. She didn't know. At any rate, she intended to earn her room and board while they were staying here.

When the dishes were done she and Nicole went

upstairs. Nicole was in a happy, playful mood as they made the beds together.

"Was this my uncle Chris's room?" she asked, bouncing on the bed as Libby unpacked pajamas and toothbrushes.

"It sure was. See this trophy? That was for a ball tournament he won when he was about your age. One of his first, I think."

"Wow! Is it real gold?"

Wouldn't that solve all their problems! "I wish. Now let's go downstairs to brush your teeth."

As they passed the kitchen Libby noticed the plate of food she'd left on the table was gone. Her father's boots were propped up by the back door, and his dirty footprints had been mysteriously erased from the linoleum floor.

## CHAPTER THREE

LIBBY TIGHTENED her hold on Nicole's hand as they stood gazing up at the three-story, brown-brick, elementary schoolhouse. She had happy memories of this place, and hoped it would prove a similar haven for her daughter. With two months to go to finish out the school year, Nicole wouldn't have much time to adjust. But at least she wouldn't have to deal with those bullies who'd lived down the street. Libby still felt sick when she thought about that scene in front of their basement apartment in Toronto.

Nicole had never told her the whole story, although Libby was positive that hadn't been the first incident. This time, Libby was determined to help her daughter fit in. It was probably too late in the year to join any after-school activities, but they could invite friends to the house.

"Ready?"

Nicole's expression was serious and more than a little fearful. Libby squeezed her hand, trying to impart courage, while wishing she'd been able to afford to buy her daughter some new school clothes. The ones Nicole was wearing were clean, but the jeans were almost two inches too short, and the colors on her sweatshirt were dull.

However, there was no money, so no point in wishing, Libby supposed. Their financial situation wouldn't improve, either, until she found a job, something part-time so she'd have lots of time to study. School had never come painlessly to Libby, but with effort she'd managed to do okay. After so many years away from books, she acknowledged she'd have to work even harder. The end result, though, would be worth it.

As for finding a part-time job, it wouldn't be easy in a rural community, but it hadn't been that easy in the city, either. Somehow, she knew, she'd find something.

"I spoke to the principal on the phone," she said, attempting to reassure Nicole. "Mrs. Jenkins. She was the principal when I went to school, and she's very nice. I think you'll like her. We're supposed to go to her office, then she'll take you down to the grade two classroom to meet your teacher, Mrs. English."

Nicole nodded, not saying a word. Libby could detect a faint trembling in her arm as they began to walk toward the main door.

"Libby."

It was a man's voice, coming from the street. Libby turned and recognized Gibson Browning, stepping out of the same truck she'd seen pulling around into the driveway the day they arrived.

Her first thought was that he hadn't changed. He was still handsome, with hair sun-bleached almost white, eyes a pale, clear blue and skin the color of sun-ripened wheat. Faded jeans emphasized his long, lean legs and a plaid shirt stretched across his muscled shoulders.

A closer look, however, revealed subtle, but unmistakable changes. He'd lost the smooth skin of youth, acquired a few lines around his mouth and eyes. And while his body was still lean, his chest was broader, more powerful.

Not the same young man who'd alternately teased and tolerated, ignored and tormented his best friend's little sister.

"Libby Bateson. Is it really you?"

She put her hands on her hips, inwardly preparing herself for the encounter. "Well, who else would be driving my father's Ford? I presume you recognized it, since you parked behind it."

"Still cheeky after all these years. I guess it's Libby Bateson, all right." He squinted into the morning sun as he checked her over. "Grown up a little, though," he declared. Then his gaze dropped to her daughter and Libby could see the questions accumulating.

Quickly, before he could ask one of them, she said, "No school bus anymore?"

"There was. Bonnie Wright delivered her ten-pound son last Friday. She won't be driving for a few months, maybe longer." He opened the passenger door of his truck and held out his hand to the little girl inside.

"Come on, pumpkin. I want you to meet an old friend of the family's."

The young girl who came out of the truck was about Nicole's age. She had the same coloring as her father, but her features were delicate, her mouth small and bow shaped. She was wearing designer jeans decorated with sequins and ribbons around the pockets and at the cuffs, a pretty pink top with a ruffled collar and a pale-blue sweater over top. Even her little canvas running shoes had sparkles and bows—in short, everything that a little girl would deem beautiful.

"This is Allie," Gibson said, pride and love underscoring the introduction. Libby wasn't surprised to see Gibson was a doting father. He was probably a doting husband, too. He'd certainly never been like her brother, who'd chosen and discarded girlfriends depending on his mood at the moment. She remembered Chris's indignation when Gibson had announced his engagement, the year she'd turned fifteen.

"You're throwing away your life, man," Chris had said. But Gibson had only smiled, oozing a serene confidence in his decision.

"It's nice to meet you, Allie," Libby said. "This is my daughter, Nicole. She's joining the grade two class today."

"Hi, Nicole," Allie said. "We'll be in the same grade. I can show you around if you want."

"Hi," Nicole mumbled, staring at the ground.

Libby's heart ached at her daughter's obvious shyness. But here at last was the opportunity she'd hoped for. Allie lived so close it would be easy to get the girls together to play.

"We have to stop at the principal's office first,

Allie. But that's a very nice offer. Maybe you girls can play at recess?''

Nicole nodded, still staring at the ground.

Libby glanced back at Gibson and saw him watching her daughter, a puzzled expression on his face. She put a protective arm over Nicole's shoulders and pulled her toward the school. ''Well, we'd better get going. Nice seeing you, Gibson.''

She was turning to leave when his touch stopped her cold. ''How about a cup of coffee at the café before you head back?''

''I don't think so. Dad might need his truck.''

Gibson withdrew his hand. ''Yeah. He goes out a lot, your father.''

Libby blinked. Was that a note of blame in Gibson's sarcastic comment? ''Well, he's a grown man. I guess he does what he likes.''

''As does his daughter.''

No doubt about it this time. Gibson was blaming *her*. ''Care to tell me what you're driving at?''

''Wouldn't mind. But apparently you're not free for coffee.''

''That's right.'' Head high, she turned her back to him.

WHEN LIBBY CAME OUT of the school fifteen minutes later, slightly reassured by Mrs. Jenkins's calm, caring manner, she found Gibson leaning against the cab of his truck. He watched her approach, making it obvious he'd been waiting for her. He was also looking at her as if he were as startled by the changes in her as she was by the changes in him.

She remembered him as she'd remembered him years ago, teaching her to ride his horse after she'd begged him to for months. He'd held Curry's bridle with one hand and cupped the stirrup with the other. Once she'd slid her foot inside the metal holder, he'd put his hand under her arm and helped her settle into the hollow of the saddle.

"Don't let the reins go slack," he'd told her. "Sit up tall, but allow your hips to flow with the saddle."

She'd been eleven or twelve at the time. Life had stretched out before her like a pleasant walk through a prairie pasture: flat and serene, with no trouble in sight. Of course, the prairie always looked different on closer examination. That was when you saw the gopher holes that could trip you and the wasps' nests hidden in the tall tangles of grass.

She'd trusted Gibson back then to warn her of the dangers. He'd kept her in the pasture, leading her around the perimeter of the old wooden fence until she had her confidence. She could still remember the smell of the horse, mingled with the scent of dried hay and the perfume from a nearby field of ripening clover. When he'd finally let go, he'd talked her through every step, and when she was tired, he'd helped her dismount.

Now his expression was charged with questions and she wished she could run in the opposite direction. Instead, she just slowed her pace and shoved her hands in the pockets of her worn jeans. She was well aware that her own clothes were in even worse condition than Nicole's and that her unkempt hair hadn't seen a pair of professional scissors in a long,

long time. Still, she tossed her head as though she had all the confidence in the world and gave him a challenging look.

"What's the matter? Truck won't start?"

He laughed, showing off white, even teeth. There'd been a period of braces, she remembered. Chris had teased him unmercifully.

"Didn't seem like we'd finished our conversation, earlier. Lord, but you have changed...." His gaze skimmed the length of her. "I'd forgotten how much you resembled Chris."

As a child, Libby had heard the similarities remarked upon frequently. She and Chris had both inherited the dark curly hair and brown eyes of their mother, and the strong bones of their father.

"Why has it been so long, Libby? I was beginning to think you'd never come back."

And she wouldn't have, either, if she'd had a choice. "We aren't here for good. Just until fall, I think." She'd have to leave come September. Wherever they ended up, she wanted Nicole to start the school year at her new school.

"Then what? Moving back to Toronto?"

She shook her head. When she was seventeen, the big city had promised excitement. Eight years of living there had brought nothing but disillusionment. Better to stay in Saskatchewan this time, though far enough away from Chatsworth that she wouldn't be hobbled by the tragedies of the past. "Maybe Regina, or Swift Current."

"I see."

"Where's Allie's mom?" she asked, calling up

her vague recollection of a blond, slim bride swathed in white.

Gibson's expression turned grim. "Rita's dead. There was an accident when she was unloading grain."

His gaze drifted to the sky, and on his face Libby saw an expression she'd seen hundreds of times, on the faces of a hundred different farmers: assessing, watchful. But she knew he wasn't checking out the weather. She was familiar with the way people in this part of the country dealt with tragedy. Stoically, balling up the pain inside.

"I'm sorry."

"It was a long time ago. Five years."

"Allie would have been a toddler," she said softly. She saw his lips tighten with pain and felt bad she'd brought the subject up.

"How come you didn't know?" Gibson's hand was on her arm, stopping her from walking away. "Didn't your father tell you?"

His question caught her off balance. She had no prepared response. That only left the truth. "No, he didn't. My father and I aren't exactly on speaking terms."

No mistaking the censure in his eyes this time. "You don't say."

Libby immediately regretted her candor. The problems between her and her father were best kept private. Gibson had been like one of the family at one time, but that was before Chris and her mom died. She had to remember to keep up her guard.

''What about Owen?'' Gibson asked. ''Why didn't he come back with you?''

This conversational curveball also caught her by surprise. He had to be talking about Owen Holst, the boy she'd gone to school with. But why?

''Come on, Libby. You must have known we'd figure it out. Or did you think we'd all find it an interesting coincidence that you and Owen Holst took off from Chatsworth on the same day?'' His expression suddenly softened. ''He didn't leave you, did he, Libby?''

Libby stared at him, amazed. So people thought she'd run off with Owen, did they? But the two of them had been friends, nothing more. His dream had been to move to the city and study music.

''No,'' she said slowly, giving herself a chance to think. ''No. He didn't leave me.''

Gibson registered disbelief, but not, she suspected, for the right reasons. ''I've often thought about you two over the years, wondering how you were making out in the city. We'd heard you'd gone to Toronto, but no details beyond that.'' He waited as if he expected some answers, and when she didn't speak, he added, ''Owen's parents are gone now, retired to Arizona about six years ago. Sold all their land. But I guess you know that.''

A feeling of fate settled over her. If Owen's parents had left the district, Owen would never be back. Maybe she should let people think what they wanted about the two of them. If people believed Owen was Nicole's father, it would never occur for them to consider other possibilities.

"So are you and Owen still together?"

Gibson was obviously not going to let this go. Her back to the wall, Libby made her decision. "I haven't seen Owen in years." It was the truth. Gibson could make what he liked out of it.

Gibson started to speak, then changed his mind and was silent. Libby avoided his gaze and focused, instead, on the trees surrounding the schoolyard, noting how much they'd grown.

She was being evasive, and Gibson realized it. Thankfully, he didn't press the subject. But she knew it was only a matter of time. If not him, then someone else would ask the same questions. And what would she say then?

"How was life in the big city?"

"It was okay." Here again, it was better to avoid the truth. She didn't want anyone finding out how truly desperate she and Nicole had been, or how she struggled to afford the bare necessities.

"I hear the winters are warm."

"Yes, though the humidity in the summer can be hard to take. But I'd better get going. I've got work to do."

Libby went to the truck with relief. The cab was warm with the trapped heat from the sun. She twisted the key and was about to shift into drive, when she heard a vehicle pull up on her left. It was Gibson, motioning for her to roll down her window.

She cranked the handle. "Yes?"

"I was thinking maybe we could car-pool until they hire a new bus driver."

The idea made sense. It would save both time and gas. "Sure."

"If you could pick the girls up this afternoon, I'll take them in tomorrow."

"Okay." She nodded, then waited for him to leave ahead of her. This time, when she shifted the truck into drive, her hand was trembling.

Behind Gibson's questions, she'd sensed his disapproval. He thought it was her fault her father had turned into a recluse and let his home go to pot.

The injustice of it made her stomach burn. But that was something she'd have to get used to. She wasn't about to spread the word that her father had kicked her off the farm because she was pregnant.

Of more concern to her were the questions Gibson had asked about Owen Holst, because those questions involved Nicole. It was fine for Libby to let Gibson believe Owen was Nicole's father. She hadn't had to be untruthful to leave him with that impression. But could she keep the deception up over several months? And what would she tell Nicole if someone mentioned Owen Holst to her?

GIBSON TOOK A BITE of his ham-and-cheese sandwich and stared out the large kitchen window. From here he could see the top corner of his property, all tilled and ready to seed. He felt the usual buzz of anticipation in his veins. The fall was wonderful; there was a lot of satisfaction in watching his wheat crop stream by the bushelful into the back of the grain truck. But for some reason he still preferred the spring. So full of hope and possibilities.

Moira, his part-time housekeeper, was standing at the other end of the large harvest table, folding towels fresh from the line. She wore her usual work uniform: a pair of jeans and a baggy old T-shirt. Moira was so thin the outfit made her look like a scarecrow, an illusion furthered by her flyaway gray hair and the smattering of fine wrinkles on her sun-weathered face.

"If you're planning to start seeding this afternoon, I guess I should pick Allie up from school," Moira said.

"No need." Gibson took a gulp of his tea. It was hot and sweet, the way he liked it. "Libby Bateson's going to bring her home."

Libby. Just saying her name gave him a funny feeling in his chest. There was no denying he had felt a shock at seeing her at the school this morning. He'd always thought of her as a kid, his best friend's little sister. To suddenly view her as a woman, with all that beautiful, wild hair and those soulful brown eyes, had about knocked the wind out of him.

As a child she'd had a sweet candor about her that had always pulled at his protective instincts. One glance at her expressive little face and you knew exactly what she was thinking.

The woman he'd seen today was so boarded up she might as well have a No Trespassing sign pasted on her forehead. Maybe he'd asked too many questions, but given the relationship he'd had with her brother—and with her—he'd felt entitled. And he still couldn't see why she'd been so secretive.

Perhaps she felt guilty for having deserted her father. Yet she'd seemed more defiant than remorseful. He couldn't understand it. The Batesons had been such a close family. To have up and left the way she did, not coming back, not even once, in all those years...it was damn near criminal.

Still, he couldn't be quite as angry with her as he'd like to be, because clearly the years she'd spent away hadn't been easy on her. There was a sadness in her eyes, a sense of great tiredness. Life had kicked Libby around, and it showed on her young face. And on the face of her daughter.

Her leaving Chatsworth the way she had had never made sense to him. People talked about Libby and Owen's romance, but while he'd seen them together occasionally, he'd never had the impression it was anything hot and heavy. He must have been wrong.

He could imagine what had happened. Owen Holst had lured her to the city, then left her. Libby claimed he hadn't, but he intuited that she wasn't telling him the truth. At least not all of it.

Maybe it had been worse than Owen just leaving. Maybe he'd hurt Libby, or even Nicole. That might explain Libby's carefully guarded responses to his questions.

Yet Owen hadn't seemed like the violent sort. Gibson remembered him as quiet and well mannered. But weren't those just the fellows you had to watch?

"I heard the Bateson girl was back in town. They say she brought her daughter with her. How old is she?" Moira asked, interrupting his reverie.

"Libby?" Gibson said, deliberately misunderstanding. "About twenty-four, I think. Maybe twenty-five.'' He stood and took his dishes to the dishwasher. Moira would find out soon enough that little Nicole was the same age as his Allie. Which meant Libby had to have had her shortly after she'd left Chatsworth. Which, in turn, would lead to the conclusion that Libby had been pregnant when she'd left. Not such a big deal these days, but still news worth talking about, for some people, anyway.

"Well, I hope her return knocks some sense into that father of hers," Moira said, snapping the creases out of a large bath towel.

Gibson took the thermos off the shelf and filled it with the remainder of the tea. "I don't know, Moira. I hope so, too." But all those years of silence was a big barrier to overcome.

As his closest neighbor, Gibson had witnessed the slow changes in the older man. They'd started after the accident, with him becoming quieter, more withdrawn. Understandable, surely. However, it wasn't until Libby had left that he'd become such a cantankerous soul. He'd stopped taking care of himself and his home, although he still seemed to do a decent enough job of looking after the farm and the animals.

Libby's departure must have broken Henry's heart. That was the way Gibson had it figured. And he still couldn't understand how she could have done it. Owen Holst didn't strike him as the sort of man to inspire such drastic action as that. But maybe it hadn't been Owen. Maybe Libby had just seen him as her ticket to the big city.

"I hear Henry's suing the Tylers now," Moira

said. "Over drinking rights to that slough between their properties."

Gibson shook his head. Both farmers had used the slough to water their cattle ever since he could remember. The slough was deep; there was water enough for all. The only thing Henry could possibly get out of a legal action like this one was another enemy to add to a growing list. It saddened Gibson to think of it. And at the same time, he couldn't help wondering if, in some perverse way, that was exactly what Henry wanted.

"DO YOU HAVE a CD player in here?"

"No, we don't, Allie. But you can turn on the radio if you like." Libby grinned, thinking there wasn't much chance they'd hear the music under either scenario. Allie hadn't stopped talking since Libby had picked the two girls up five minutes ago. She was a real contrast to her Nicole, who had barely spoken a sentence.

"That's okay." Allie bounced a little in her seat between Libby and Nicole. "Did I tell you I got to take Nicole around the school? I showed her the gym, the library, the bathrooms, everything. We missed almost the whole math lesson!"

"Is your new teacher nice?" Libby asked Nicole, but Allie was the one who answered.

"Oh, Mrs. English is the greatest! She lets us pick our own groups when we're working on projects, and there's no assigned seating. I always sit by Ardis, and now Nicole has the desk on the other side of me."

"Isn't that lucky."

"Ardis has been my friend since kindergarten. She has the longest hair in the whole class. You wouldn't have noticed today because it was in braids," she said in an aside to Nicole, "but when it's brushed out, it reaches her *bum*. Amazing. Daddy says I can grow my hair that long, too, but it's taking a long time." Allie twisted the end of her blond ponytail.

"What's your favorite thing about your new school?" Libby asked, in yet another effort to draw some sort of comment out of her withdrawn child.

Nicole just shrugged. Then, before Allie could get them started on a new topic, she said in her usual quiet way, "Mrs. English sent home a note about school supplies. I need a bunch of things—pencils and glue and stuff like that. Also, there's a fee that has to be paid to the school. Twenty-five dollars, I think."

"Right. Mrs. Jenkins mentioned something about that. I guess I just forgot." Libby spoke lightly, but she knew Nicole would not be fooled. Although Libby tried to keep her financial worries to herself, Nicole had picked up on this all-consuming obsession with making ends meet.

Observing Allie in her pretty clothes, Libby felt a tightening in her chest. She was willing to bet Allie hadn't given a second thought about where the money would come from to pay for her school supplies. In all honesty, neither had she at their age.

No denying, the fees presented a real problem. Libby wondered if she could delay payment to the school until she found a job. She couldn't ask her father for the money. They still weren't speaking, and did their utmost to avoid each other. It was sort of like living with a ghost; she knew he was there, but she almost never saw him.

Thankfully, she was too busy to worry much about the situation. She'd never done such a thorough housecleaning in her life as in the past four days. She'd washed down walls, laundered curtains, scrubbed windows until they gleamed. The house still wasn't perfect, but it was certainly livable.

Libby eased off the accelerator as they neared the Brownings' turnoff. She could see Gibson on his tractor, heading up the field toward the house. He must have finished seeding for the day. She felt a flash of nervousness at the prospect of seeing him again. Nervousness and something more. Unaccountably she pictured the look in his eyes when she'd come out of the school after dropping off Nicole. He'd made her feel as though she was under a microscope or something.

"There's Daddy!" Allie crawled over Nicole's lap and bounded out of the truck, rushing past an older woman who had come out from the back of the house, a basket of laundry in her arms. The woman's face was familiar, but for the moment Libby couldn't think of her name. She slid from behind the steering wheel reluctantly and went to say hello.

"Hi. I'm Libby Bateson. Just bringing Allie home from school."

"Yes. Gibson told me you were back." Now Libby was scrutinized again, this time by sharp gray eyes rather than blue ones. "It's been many years since I've seen you. Maybe you remember my daughter, Colleen. She was a couple of years younger than you. She's in university now."

"Colleen Plant." Libby vaguely recalled the girl and now was able to place her mother, too. Mrs. Plant had always been very involved in the activities of her three children.

"That's right. I've been housekeeping for Gibson and his young miss ever since poor Rita's accident. I suppose you heard about that from your father."

Libby longed for the sanctuary of her truck. However, turning away now would be rude, and she had to start facing people sooner or later. "A terrible tragedy," she said, avoiding the question. "But I'd better be going—"

"And what brings you and your little girl back to Chatsworth?" Moira continued, ignoring Libby's attempt to escape. "Obviously not just a visit, or you wouldn't have enrolled your daughter in the school. How old is she? She's just a speck in that truck."

Libby turned back to look. Sure enough, Nicole's head was barely visible above the dashboard.

"Nicole is seven. We'll be staying till the end of summer…." Libby trailed off as Gibson came within speaking range. He had his daughter up on his shoulders, and their beautiful border collie romped at his feet.

"Libby," he said, his gaze meeting hers. "Thanks for giving Allie the ride."

"No problem." She watched as he walked over to the passenger side of her father's truck.

"Hey there, Nicole. How was the first day? Did

Allie show you around and introduce you to her friends?''

Nicole nodded and almost smiled.

Gibson eased his daughter back down to the ground. ''Why don't you run up to the house with Mrs. Plant and get started on those cookies she took out of the freezer for you. I'll join you in a minute.''

At the mention of cookies, Allie sped off, dragging Moira with her, not bothering to say goodbye or thank Libby for the ride. Gibson didn't seem to notice, and Libby supposed that a mother was more in tune with those breaches of etiquette.

She hadn't planned on seeing Gibson again—had hoped for the opposite, in fact—but now that he was here, she decided to make the most of it. ''About that bus driver problem you mentioned—''

''Yes?'' He turned to face her, a hand on his jeans-clad hip, and she noticed a streak of dirt running in a straight line down his leg.

She tried not to sound nervous. ''I was thinking I might like the job. Driving the bus, I mean.''

Gibson ran the hand that had rested on his hip over his chin, dragging a bit of the dirt from his jeans across his jaw. The smudge should have looked ridiculous, she thought; instead, it added to his rugged appeal. ''No reason you shouldn't. I know you've had experience driving the grain truck. Shouldn't be too hard for you to manage your class two license. I could put in a word for you at the school board if you like.''

''Would you?'' Libby tried to sound grateful but not desperate. She didn't want Gibson, or anyone else in the community, to know how badly she needed this job.

"Not a problem." Gibson looked back into the truck at Nicole. "As for you, how would you feel about joining the girls' soccer team for the under nines? I'm the coach, and since I have to take Allie anyway, I could give you a ride. We play Tuesdays and Thursdays from six-thirty to seven-thirty."

Libby knew Nicole did not like new situations, so she was shocked when her daughter nodded her agreement.

"Good." Gibson checked with Libby. "Okay with you?"

"Of course it is." In fact, it was perfect. Odd, how easily the pieces were falling into place, almost as if she'd been *meant* to come back. She hesitated a second before asking, "I suppose there's an entry fee."

"Nah." Gibson shook his head. "We provide the T-shirts, though you have to return them at the end of the season. Shin pads are a good idea, but I think Allie has a spare pair Nicole can borrow."

"Great."

"Our next game is tomorrow night. I'll pick you up at six o'clock," Gibson said to Nicole. Then he nodded at Libby. "And I'll give you a name to call if you're serious about that bus driving job."

"I'm serious."

"Good. By the way—" his voice lowered, took on a husky tone that gave her pause "—I've figured out why you look so different. It's your hair. You always wore it short before."

Libby pushed her long brown curls behind her

ears, very conscious of how unkempt she must appear. She'd always preferred her hair short, but then, it had been a long time since she'd had a spare twenty to spend on a luxury like a beauty salon cut.

She didn't say anything, just got behind the wheel, closed the door and turned the key. She was about to shift into reverse when Gibson touched her shoulder through the open window.

"I like it this way." She felt his hand brush against the back of her head, lighter than the prairie wind. Then he stepped back and waved as she turned around and headed up the drive to the main road.

She could still see him in her rearview mirror when he walked toward his house and his waiting daughter. Her scalp tingled from the touch of his hand on her hair, and the sound of his parting words floated around her head with the breeze from the open window.

## CHAPTER FOUR

GIBSON BLEW HIS WHISTLE. "Out of bounds!" He
signaled one of the forwards. "Ardis, you throw it
in." Weaving between the players, he pointed out
proper positions. "Give her someone to pass to.
That's right, Nicole. Try to get out in the open if you
can."

It was a clear spring evening, warm with very little
breeze. Soccer fields had been marked out on the
large green space behind Chatsworth High School to
accommodate four different age groups. Gibson
watched the throw-in, checking his impatience when
Ardis tossed the ball to a member of the opposing
team who promptly scored a goal.

As the players repositioned themselves for the
kickoff, Gibson called out more instructions, then
stood back to observe. Only a quarter to seven, and
still a couple of hours until sunset. He loved the
lengthening days of the prairie spring. Especially in
the evening, when the diffused angle of the sun's
rays, so harsh during the height of the day, brought
out all the different shades of gold and green in the
grass and trees and surrounding shrubs.

In the distance he could see the silver thread of
the highway connecting Chatsworth to Yorkton, and

beyond that the undulating fields that stretched to the horizon, where the blue sky was already softening to mauve.

As if excited by the approaching evening, flocks of house sparrows gathered on the electrical wires that lined the street, squawking constantly. A couple of robins took turns pulling at tufts of dried grass to collect for some hidden nest. Across the street, a dog watched the running children eagerly, as though he wanted to share in the fun but wasn't sure which team to join.

As he'd promised, Gibson had driven over to the Batesons' at six o'clock, and found Nicole and her mother waiting on the front porch. He'd noticed that the torn screening was gone.

Nicole had beamed when he handed her the neon-green soccer T-shirt and a pair of shin pads. It had felt great to see that little girl so happy. Still, he hoped Libby never found out he'd submitted the entry fee on their behalf. He knew she was as proud as she was obviously strapped for cash.

"How do I look, Mom?" Nicole had proudly paraded in the new shirt, which she'd quickly pulled on over her sweatshirt.

"Great," Libby had said, smiling.

Seeing Libby had given him that funny feeling in his chest, and reminded him of how he'd felt as a kid before an important hockey game, knowing a lot was at stake and people were counting on him to perform. Not that Libby would be counting on him for anything. From her perch on the front step, her eyes held a hint of wariness, as if she expected him to whip the T-shirt off Nicole's back and drive away without them.

She was wearing jeans, the same jeans—if he wasn't mistaken—that she'd been wearing every time he'd seen her. They were so faded they were almost white, and had started to fray at the knees and around the seams.

Those jeans had seen a lot of hard living, just like their owner.

Did Libby have any idea how much she'd changed? She'd been one of the happiest kids he'd known. A real tomboy, who loved animals and couldn't stand to see any creature suffering. He remembered a runt calf she'd had once. Libby had fed her every morning and night, carrying out a half pail of milk, then staying with the animal, talking and petting, until Chris was sent out to call her in for dinner. He could close his eyes and picture her coming into the kitchen, her cheeks glowing, her brown eyes warm with laughter and love.

Was Owen Hurst responsible for turning that happy, carefree child into a cautious, sad woman? The very idea made his gut burn, even though he knew better than to judge. He had experienced firsthand how a man could ruin a woman's life. Sometimes without even realizing what he was doing.

Libby had on a different shirt with her jeans today, though, a clean white blouse that contrasted with her honey-toned skin. Her long hair was pulled back in a tidy ponytail, a style that emphasized her darkly lashed brown eyes and wide, full mouth. Something about her appearance had sparked a remembrance in him. But before he could be sure what it was, Nicole had jumped into the back seat, obviously eager to go.

"Hurry up, Mom," she'd said impatiently from the open window.

Libby had looked uncertain. "I wasn't sure if the invitation extended to me."

He'd taken for granted that she would come. "We can always use a little help in the cheering department. And we have lots of room." When she continued to hesitate, he'd added, "I'm sure Nicole would like you to come." And wondered what she would have said if he'd admitted that he wanted her along, too.

It hadn't taken any more persuasion than that and she'd climbed in the vehicle to share the back seat with her daughter. Allie had talked most of the way into town, although Gibson had worked to squeeze a sentence or two out of Nicole. Something about that kid got to him, made him feel as though a giant hand had taken hold of his heart and given it a hard squeeze. She was so serious and quiet he figured she hadn't had much in the way of fun in her life.

They'd parked at the soccer field, and Gibson had taken Nicole aside to explain the rules. Watching her on the field now, he could see that she'd caught on to the game quickly. In fact, he thought she had the look of a budding young athlete. Which was kind of interesting, considering her parents.

Libby had never liked team sports much, preferring to concentrate on her gardening and caring for the various pets she'd raised over the years. Owen had shunned outdoor pursuits to focus on his music.

Gibson remembered him playing in the school band, as well as performing the male lead in the annual high school musical three years running.

The Chatsworth team had another throw-in. Gibson sprinted to the sideline to give his instructions. This time Ardis managed a perfect throw to Nicole. The new player maneuvered her body to block an opponent, even as she kicked the ball to Allie, who unfortunately fumbled, letting another girl wrest the ball from her.

"Good, Nicole! Forwards, move up into position!"

Gibson jogged slowly behind the action, observing as the girls tried to keep the momentum going. Passing Allie, he patted her on the shoulder. "Pay attention, pumpkin." Allie loved soccer and hated to miss a game, but sometimes, Gibson noticed, she had trouble concentrating on the field.

Nicole had the ball again. She feinted to her left, then switched suddenly to the right, before passing to a teammate standing close to the goal. The other girl got the pass but hesitated a moment too long before aiming the ball into the goal. The opposing team was in control now, and Gibson called the defense players to the alert.

Shooting a glance at the sidelines, he saw Libby standing slightly apart from the other spectators, even though she must have known at least half of them. Certainly his mother who came out to all the home games to cheer on her granddaughter. Libby had her arms crossed over her chest, apparently oblivious to everyone and everything but the game.

It was obviously the way she wanted things, but there was an aura of loneliness about her that called out to him. That and her beauty.

She *was* beautiful. No other way to put it. Chris Bateson's little sister had left home a fresh-faced teenager and come home a woman. And a very desirable woman at that.

By halftime the little soccer players were tired, their faces red and brows sweaty. They rushed, delighted, to the sidelines, where one of the fathers passed out chunks of juicy watermelon. Gibson went to join Libby. "Nicole's doing great. She's a real natural."

"I can't believe it. She's never played soccer in her life. She's never played any sport before."

Nicole trotted up, her mouth full of melon. "Did you see me, Mom? I almost scored a goal!"

"I know, I saw. You were great, Nicole."

"It's so much fun. Soccer is the coolest thing I've ever done. I wish we could play every night. Don't you, Allie?"

Allie was slightly behind Nicole, carefully picking the dark seeds out of the fruit, then dropping them to the ground. "It's not *that* great, Nicole." Carefully she bit into the pulpy flesh, then chewed slowly. Once she'd swallowed, she eyed Nicole critically. "The juice is running down your chin. It looks disgusting."

"That's half the fun of eating watermelon," Gibson said, embarrassed by his daughter's rudeness. He looked apologetically at Libby, and was surprised to see that her face had turned as pink as the fruit and her usually full lips had drawn into a hard, thin line. She whipped a tissue out of the front pocket of her jeans and cleaned Nicole's face quickly.

Nicole was oblivious to it all. She tossed the gnawed semicircle of rind into a nearby garbage bag and gestured impatiently at Allie. "Let's practice." Without waiting to see if Allie would join her, she kicked a ball over to a corner of the field where several of the other girls were passing back and forth to one another.

After a momentary pause, Allie threw her half-finished watermelon into the garbage and reluctantly followed.

Gibson shoved his hands into his pockets and checked Libby's expression. Her color had returned to normal and she was smiling again.

"You're good out there," she told him. "You give them direction without being too demanding."

"It's a fun league. Nobody cares about winning. We're just out to have a good time. Although with Nicole on the team, we may start winning more than we used to."

Libby smiled. "Thanks for thinking of inviting her to play. It never would have occurred to me to put her into something like soccer. Yet watch her. I've never seen her so happy."

The natural flow of words halted, and Libby bit at her lower lip.

"Starting a new school can be tough," Gibson said, venturing an explanation for the change in Libby's mood. "But kids make friends easily at this age. She'll be fine." As he spoke, Nicole was kicking the ball toward Allie—a strong, straight effort that sailed between Allie's legs.

To see Nicole push a strand of brown curly hair out of her eyes in a gesture so like her mother's made Gibson smile. Nicole resembled Libby in many ways, but her heart-shaped face, with the delicately pointed chin, and her fine, turned-up nose must have come from her father.

Except that Owen had a long, narrow face. Gibson slanted a look at Libby, remembering how uncomfortable she'd seemed when they'd discussed Nicole's father the other day. Was Owen still in touch with them? he mused. Did he send any support payments? Gibson wished he could ask Libby, but he guessed she wouldn't interpret his interest as concern; she'd see it as an intrusion.

At the moment, Libby's attention was focused once more on her surprising young daughter. Gibson fought an urge to gently tuck her hair behind her ears so that he could see her face more clearly. If Libby's smiles had become rather rare, if her expression often seemed strained, he thought he could understand why. Being a single parent was tough; sometimes it seemed that all he ever did was worry about Allie. And it was lonely, too. He wondered if Libby ever felt the same aching emptiness that often plagued him late at night after Allie was asleep.

"Libby..."

She turned. "Yes?"

He realized he'd been about to ask her out. To a movie, or maybe for dinner in Yorkton.

This time, *he* bit his lip. "Time to start the last

half,'' he said, instead, filling in the blank of that unfinished sentence. He whistled and called the girls to a pregame huddle, all the while unclear what had come over him back there.

Certainly Libby had grown into a beautiful woman, and undeniably the sadness clouding her brown eyes all too often got to him.

But he wasn't sure asking her out was such a good idea. She probably still thought of him as a brother. Even if she didn't, they'd be better off sticking to being friends. He figured Libby could use a good friend. Truth be told, so could he.

LIBBY STARED resolutely at the soccer field, ignoring the other parents and grandparents standing beside her on the sideline. She wished she wasn't so uncomfortable. This was her hometown; these were people she'd known all her life. Why did she feel as if there were some wide, unbridgeable gap between them?

Because there was. No matter how firmly she kept her eye to the future, nothing could erase the past. It wasn't that she was afraid any of them knew what had driven her from town. Her father wouldn't have said anything. And Darren O'Malley wouldn't have, either. His ego wouldn't stand up to the admission that he'd found a female who wasn't willing to have sex with him, so he'd had to force her.

If only she'd known better than to go out driving with the older boy. But she'd been so proud to be singled out by the handsome star hockey player from nearby Sledgewood. He'd been good-looking, confident, able to take his pick of the girls. And he had asked *her* out. Even though she was still in school and only seventeen.

His attention had helped divert her from the huge void her mother's and Chris's deaths had left in her life. Growing up, she'd idolized her mother. Virginia Bateson had always known what each of them needed. She'd respected Libby's love of animals, never getting impatient with all the stray pets, or the mess they brought into the house. She alone had been able to curb the wild impulses of her feckless son, and bring out the best in her sometimes introverted husband.

Virginia Bateson had been the glue that had held the family together. Without her, Libby and her father had been like two orphaned calves. If only they could have found comfort in each other. But perhaps they were too similar, both withdrawing when they should have come together.

In some ways Darren had reminded her of her brother, Chris. She'd loved his energy and confidence. They'd gone out a few times and she'd been gratified by the obvious envy of the other girls. They'd stayed out late—curfews were no problem for her; her father neither knew nor cared how she spent her time. Since the accident he'd hardly noticed she was still alive.

It seemed there had been no limit to what she would have done to impress Darren. She'd never smoked or drunk very much, but with him she did both, eager to appear sophisticated. On their third date she'd ignored the warning voice in the back of

her head and given in to his suggestion that they go
for a drive down a deserted farm access road.

That was when she'd discovered there *was* a limit
to what she was willing to do to impress Darren.
Only, he was past the point of listening to her ob-
jections. Maybe it was his ego. Maybe it was the
alcohol. Probably it was both of them together. But
that was the night Nicole had been conceived.

If Libby could have confided in someone at that
point, maybe her and Nicole's lives would have
turned out differently. But her father's only reaction
when she showed up at four in the morning, her
clothing torn, the side of her face bruised, was anger.
*What were you doing? Have you no sense of de-
cency?* Judging from his reaction, Libby had decided
that no one would take the side of one inconsequen-
tial young girl against the popular, widely admired
Darren O'Malley.

So she'd kept her secret and never told anyone.
Not any of her girlfriends, not her teachers, certainly
not the police. If her own father didn't care, why
would some stranger?

Now, of course, she knew that had been a mistake.
She should have at least attempted to tell someone
her story—

On the field Nicole suddenly broke away from the
crowd and raced toward the goal. "Go, Nicole!"
Libby focused on her daughter's small arms pumping
furiously as she guided the ball. Nicole was so co-
ordinated, so agile, and her kick, once she got close
enough to the goal, was bang on target.

"Hooray!" Libby cheered as the ball sailed over

the goalie's right shoulder. Nicole's teammates swarmed her, patting her back and slapping her hand. All except Allie, that is, who hung back on the edge of the group, her shoulders slumped and expression downcast. Gibson trotted into the ring of girls and picked Nicole up to whirl her high in the air. Nicole looked startled at first, then she laughed.

"Way to go, champ!" Gibson said, setting her feet back on the ground. He gave her a high five, then blew the whistle. "Fifteen minutes left, girls. Let's see if we can score another goal to win the game. Maybe it will be you this time, Allie. Why don't you play forward for a while. You've been defense all game."

Allie muttered something; Libby couldn't make out the words. Her attention returned to Gibson, who, dressed in his shorts and soccer cleats, still had the physique of an athlete, including highly developed muscles in his thighs and calves. The bright color of his T-shirt contrasted with the gold in his skin and his bleached-out yellow hair. Every now and then he would shoot her a quizzical look and on those occasions Libby could almost feel little goose bumps break out along her arms.

Was she attracted to him? The question seemed to pop into her mind out of nowhere, and she instantly dismissed it. Of course she found him attractive. She always had. So had all the other eligible girls in Chatsworth. He and her brother, Chris, had never had a shortage of girlfriends.

The thing was, she was Chris's little sister. Gibson would never give her a second glance. Or was that true? She'd noticed him watching her from the field during the game. Of course it didn't have to mean anything. Most likely he was just curious about her. What she was doing back in town and what she'd been doing these past years.

"Hello, Libby."

She turned to see Gibson's mother approaching from the side. Connie Browning was a small, spry woman, with skin like a dried apricot and hair now more gray than blond.

"Gibson told me you and your daughter were back in Chatsworth." Her smile was friendly and accepting.

To smile back wasn't as hard as Libby had thought it might be. "Hi, Mrs. Browning. How are you enjoying living in town?" Gibson's parents had moved into Chatsworth after Gibson's marriage. There'd been plans for Gibson's new wife to remodel the old farmhouse, and Libby wondered whether that had ever come about.

"Getting used to it. I'll be the first to admit it's been an adjustment. When Rita died, I was tempted to move back home and help take care of the wee one, but Stan insisted we stay out of it. Now I think he was probably right, but I tell you, it's been hard watching the two of them on their own." Connie shifted her gaze to the soccer field. Allie was scuffing her foot in the ground, not paying much attention to the game.

"I heard about Rita's accident. What a terrible tragedy."

"We've all had our sorrows, haven't we, Libby?"

She straightened her back. "But you must call me Connie now. You're a grown woman, and beautiful, although a little on the thin side. Must come from living in the city. Looks like you could use a batch of those raisin tarts you and your brother were so fond of."

"I remember those tarts." Libby smiled, thinking about the many times she'd ridden her bike to the Brownings' farm, hoping for a couple of the pastries.

Gazing out on the soccer field now, where Allie was still visibly pouting, Connie said, "Poor Allie. She just doesn't have a talent for soccer, although she wants so badly to be good at it. It doesn't excuse her rudeness, of course. Gibson tries hard with her—his intentions are honorable—but sometimes I think he overcompensates for the loss of her mother. He isn't doing Allie any good, pampering her the way he does. Of course I can't tell him that."

Libby thought of the little signs she'd noticed—certain indulgences, a bit of a blind eye. Connie's explanation fit in with what she'd observed. "Why don't you feel you can talk to Gibson about it?"

"It's a long story. I made some mistakes, right from the beginning, when Gibson got married. I wasn't all that keen on Rita. I didn't see her as a farm wife, and unfortunately I had no hesitation in telling Gibson he shouldn't marry her. Of course he went ahead and did it anyway, and my disapproval drove a wedge between us.

"Then that accident—well, Gibson blamed himself for having expected a city woman to adjust to country living. I would have given anything to take back the words I'd said before they were married."

"But accidents can happen to anyone. Even the most experienced farmers..."

"True, Libby, but my policy now is to make no judgments, or at least to keep quiet about them if I do. Slowly my relationship with Gibson has been improving. But I do feel that my hands are tied when it comes to Allie."

As Connie told her story, Libby remembered a few of the details she'd known about Gibson's wife. "Gibson met her at a ball tournament, didn't he? Rita was from Yorkton?"

"That's right."

A vague memory sparked. "I remember that tournament. Chris played, too, but he came home in a snit, complaining that Gibson had been no fun at the windup party because he'd spent all his time with just one girl."

"That would have been Rita. 'Course Gibson and Chris brought back the trophy that year—thought they were real heroes."

"It galled Chris to admit it, but Gibson's batting pulled them through."

"Yes, well, Gibson always was athletic...."

"Wasn't he offered a chance to try out for the Melville Millionaires once?" The invitation to play minor hockey was an opportunity most boys would have jumped at. Certainly Chris had been as jealous as could be.

"Yes, but he turned it down. Gibson's always known what he wanted."

The words struck a chord with Libby. Once she, too, had known what she wanted. Growing up, she'd never seen farther than the wire fence that went around the pasture where they kept the cattle. For her, life on the farm had been perfect. Those days seemed so far away now.

"Look. Nicole has the ball." Connie grasped Libby's arm and pointed toward the opponent's goal.

"Go, Nicole!" Libby called out, then watched as her daughter maneuvered the ball into an opening and passed to Allie, who was positioned right in front of the net.

Caught off guard, Allie fumbled the ball, and a member of the other team capitalized on her mistake. A moment later, Allie let out a cry and fell to the ground. "She kicked my ankle!"

The referee blew the whistle and Gibson ran for his daughter. After a few moments of conversation he scooped up the little girl and hurried toward Connie and Libby. The rest of the girls huddled together, watching uncertainly. Although Libby had her doubts about the severity of Allie's injury, she couldn't help but empathize with the worry she saw in Gibson's face.

"Hello, sweetheart," Connie said, as her son set her granddaughter down on the grass in front of them. "Did you hurt yourself out there?"

"I didn't hurt *myself*," Allie protested, indignantly. "That girl *kicked* me." She wrapped both hands around her ankle and moaned loudly.

Gibson stroked his daughter's forehead comfortingly, then consulted with the other coach. "Maybe we should call it a game. There were only a few minutes left anyway.''

''Sure. No problem. I hope she's okay. I know Lisa wouldn't have kicked her on purpose.''

''I didn't kick her at all!'' the girl in question protested.

''Enough, Lisa.'' Her coach held up his hand for silence.

''Thanks,'' Gibson said as he bent down and picked up Allie once more. ''We'll see you girls on Thursday,'' he said to the rest of the team as the players began to disperse. To his mother, he asked, ''I wonder if I should take her into Yorkton to get her ankle x-rayed?''

Connie shrugged. ''It's up to you.''

He hesitated for a moment, then as Allie let out another moan, he made up his mind. ''Maybe I'd better.''

''I'll drive the Batesons home,'' Connie volunteered. ''You give me a call when you find out the results of that X ray.'' Under her breath, she added to Libby, ''And if it isn't perfectly normal, I won't bake another raisin tart for a month.''

THE NEXT MORNING, Gibson drove into the Batesons' yard at eight-thirty, as usual, to pick up Nicole for school. Libby was clearing the breakfast dishes from the table when she heard his truck. She peered out the front window and saw Allie sitting beside her father. Obviously the injury to her ankle hadn't been severe enough to prevent her from attending school.

''Your ride is here, Nicole!'' she called, drying her

hands on a tea towel tucked into the waistband of her jeans. She was wearing another one of her mother's white shirts, which she'd found hanging in one of the upstairs closets.

She still hadn't stepped foot in her parents' bedroom—her father kept the door closed, and she could only respect his privacy. Clearly he'd decided to cope with their presence by ignoring them. The emotional distance he maintained was so great Libby wondered if he'd ever loved her. She couldn't imagine any circumstance that would warrant her treating Nicole the way her father was treating her.

But when she thought that way, it hurt too much. It was easier just to be angry.

"Coming, Mom." Nicole emerged from the bathroom, tucking in her T-shirt as she spoke.

"Here's your lunch. And your coat." Libby passed the articles in question while Nicole slipped into her well-worn sneakers.

"Thanks, Mom. See you later." Nicole turned her cheek for a kiss, then ducked out the back door. Libby listened to her footsteps in the tall grass that surrounded the house. Now that the cleaning was finished, it was time to tackle the yard.

But first she had some business to take care of. Earlier in the week she'd phoned the number Gibson had given her to apply for the job of driving the school bus. In Yorkton she'd updated her driver's license and registered for her class two license. She'd had to borrow money from the stash of twenties her father still kept in the china candy dish of his mother's that sat on the dining room buffet table. In its place she'd left a written IOU. Maybe her father had noticed and been upset that she'd taken the money. If so, he hadn't said anything.

For the license she'd have to take a written test and a road test, then pass a medical. She'd brought home a booklet to study, but first she wanted to phone the high school and arrange to borrow textbooks for the correspondence courses she would be taking.

She went upstairs to use the phone in Chris's room, which was now Nicole's. No sooner had she picked up the receiver than she heard the kitchen door open. It would be her father, in from feeding the cows and gathering eggs. She paused before dialing, listening as he opened the cupboard door, then scraped oatmeal from the big aluminum pot.

This was how it had been each morning since she and Nicole had arrived—her father's every movement orchestrated to avoid contact with the both of them. In a way Libby was relieved. She didn't want angry, ugly scenes to disturb Nicole. On the other hand, his ability to totally block them out stung. She was his daughter. Nicole was his granddaughter. Did they really mean so little to him?

Focusing on her goals, Libby dialed the number. Moments later the arrangements were made. She smiled at herself in the mirror as she gathered her hair into a ponytail. Nicole had made a friend and was enjoying playing soccer. She herself had a job lined up and would soon be working toward her last grade twelve credits.

Libby finished with the elastic, then stepped back

and frowned at the result. Maybe when she started working once more she'd splurge and get her hair cut at a salon. That was a cheerful thought. She turned to making the beds, keeping up her implicit pact with her father, putting in time as she waited for him to leave for the fields.

As she puttered she heard him scrape out his bowl, then run water from the tap. Finally the kitchen door banged shut, and she knew he was gone.

She went downstairs and out to the garden. It was located on the west side of the yard, screened from the house by a long hedge of common lilacs now in full bloom. Libby breathed in the sweet perfume with pleasure as she surveyed the tangle of weeds that had taken over one of the finest vegetable patches in the district. It hadn't been touched in years. She wasn't up to planting anything the spring after her mother and Chris had died, and obviously her father hadn't done anything in the years that followed.

The weeds grew thick, many as tall as her knees, despite the earliness of the season. She pulled on an old pair of gardening gloves and began the job of clearing them out. Some she pulled by the roots; others she had to dig out with a pitchfork. The work was hard, but the sky was clear and the sun shone warmly on her back. After an hour she was hot and thirsty. She went inside to change into shorts and a sleeveless T-shirt and grab a big glass of cold water.

She didn't know how much time had passed since her short break, when she heard a vehicle in the drive. Sweat gathered on her brow and in the hollow between her shoulder blades as she rose slowly, working the kinks out of her neck and back. Hand to her forehead, she glanced out to the lane and felt a jolt of apprehension when she saw Gibson's dark truck winding its way toward the house.

## CHAPTER FIVE

LIBBY WAVED as Gibson stepped out from the cab, not sure if he'd spotted her. He paused, then took off his cap and tossed it in the truck. In the bright sunlight, his hair gleamed.

"Hi there!" He was carrying a package.

"How's Allie's ankle?" She propped the pitchfork in the dirt, then peeled off her work gloves.

Gibson stopped a few feet away from her, suddenly sheepish. "Fine. We didn't get the X rays after all. By the time we reached Yorkton she said it had stopped hurting, and there wasn't any swelling or anything. I guess I overreacted."

Libby held back her smile. "Easy to do when your kid's health is at stake. All Nicole has to do is sneeze and I'm off to the medical clinic to get her ears checked." She was curious about the package he held. Approximately the size of a shoe box, it had pieces of waxed paper peeking out from around the lid.

"Does Nicole get a lot of ear infections?"

Libby nodded. "We had to have tubes put in her ears when she was only five. It didn't seem to help much, though."

"By the way," he said, handing over the box,

"these are for you. From my mother. I stopped in after taking the girls to school. She said to tell you they were fresh."

Libby accepted the container, then peered inside. "Raisin tarts," she said, and laughed, remembering Connie's vow from the previous night. "Want to join me for a couple? I'll put on some coffee."

He gazed off to the side for a moment, as if considering some previous commitment, then nodded. "Sure. That sounds great."

Following Libby into the kitchen, he tried not to stare at her long, slim legs or notice the way the faded denim of her cutoff shorts clung to the curves of her gently rounded bottom. The top she was wearing fell just short of the waistband, leaving a delicious spare inch of flesh open to view. That inch of skin kept drawing his eyes in a most annoying way. Heck, this was Chris Bateson's little sister, he reminded himself again. He shouldn't be noticing these things.

Any more than he should have observed that she wasn't wearing a bra.

Sitting back in the wooden kitchen chair, Gibson watched as she measured coffee, then added water to the machine. Funny how her every little movement compelled his attention. Was he losing his mind that he found the sight of her finger pressing on the little plastic switch somehow erotic? When she turned away from him he could see the hollow in her back, just above the denim waistband of her shorts, and that, too, struck him as unbelievably sexy.

Reluctantly, he forced his eyes to the plate and

coffee mug that she set down in front of him. How many times had he seen Libby in a pair of shorts and a T-shirt and never given her a second glance?

But she'd been a girl back then, not a woman.

That didn't matter. Libby might be a woman, but she wasn't a woman he had any business being interested in. If they were going to be neighbors for the next couple of months, he'd just have to immunize himself against the appeal of her soft curves and long lines.

Libby held out the box of tarts. "Want one?"

"Sure." He took a pastry, not willing to admit, even to himself, what it was he really wanted. As for ignoring Libby—fat chance.

It was her skin that drew his gaze now. He could swear she was already tanned from her morning in the sun. Just like their mother, Chris and Libby had always turned brown quickly and deeply. Something he, with his fair complexion, had envied in his youth.

The thing that was so unfair, he realized, as he bit into his mother's baking—holding a hand underneath to catch the crumbs—was that Libby fit into her surroundings so perfectly. If she'd come back in fashionable clothes, wearing tons of makeup and sporting nails like red talons, it would have been easier for him to keep his distance, easier for him to see her for what she really was. A city girl.

Where had she said she was moving next? Regina or Swift Current. Both were far cries from Toronto, but as far as he was concerned, any city was too big for him.

"Funny how life turns out, isn't it?" He leaned

back in his chair, unable to take his eyes off her. "I remember what a little tomboy you were growing up. Who'd have thought you'd get the itch for the big city?"

She lifted her chin and regarded him with eyes full of suspicion. "Who says I did?"

"Isn't it obvious? Eight years in Toronto. That's way more than I could take. Why'd you leave in the first place, Libby? Was Owen really that irresistible? Or was it because you were pregnant?"

Libby's dark eyebrows rose dramatically. "Don't be shy. If you have any questions, just shoot."

"I never was shy. But thanks for the invitation."

She just shook her head and took a bite of her pastry.

He softened at her defensive posture. "No shame in being an unwed mother, Libby. Is that what the problem was? Were you afraid we would judge you?"

"You don't give up, do you?"

"I just want to understand." He paused, watching while she poured the fresh steaming coffee into their cups. Once the pot was back on the burner, he switched topics. "Are you and your father getting along these days?"

"Not exactly."

Somehow Gibson wasn't surprised. Henry had turned into a hard man. He wouldn't easily forgive his daughter for running off so long ago. "He's older than his years, your father. You may not have much time left with him."

Libby's eyes flashed resentment. "No lectures,

please. They don't go well with your mother's raisin tarts.''

Anger fired up his blood pressure a notch. Surely she had to care, at least a little. If not, she had no business being here. ''Don't forget whose home you're living in, whose food you're eating and truck you've been driving...''

''Do you have any idea what a trash heap he'd turned this place into?'' Libby swept her arm through the air dramatically. ''I've paid for my keep, even if I can't afford groceries at the moment.'' Her face flushed. ''At the moment,'' she repeated, with emphasis.

Confirmation of her dire financial situation made him regret his hard words. ''Libby, I didn't mean—''

''I know very well what you meant. And I resent the implication. My relationship with my father is none of your business.''

Gibson's sympathy cracked at that point. ''You don't think it's my business? As an old family friend and your father's closest neighbor, I might take exception to that.''

''Is that right.'' He'd really made her mad now. ''And I take exception to getting the third degree from a guest in my own home.'' She stood with a jerk, scattering pastry crumbs over the kitchen table.

He jumped up in front of her, blocking her from the door. ''*Your* own home? Have you forgotten that this house belongs to your father, a man you haven't seen, written or called in over eight years? Did you even let him know that you'd had a child, that he was a grandfather?''

Libby gave a bitter laugh. "What makes you think he would've cared?"

"Come on, Libby. Henry was a good father to you and Chris. Even if you don't want to admit it."

"A good father? Maybe once..."

"He didn't deserve to be left on his own, especially so soon after the accident. I guess that's the part I just can't understand."

Libby bowed her head. Damn it, he wished she'd answer him, but she angled her body away from his, to face out the kitchen window. "You may be the only friend my father has left, and Lord knows he can sure use one."

"I want to be your friend, too."

The offer didn't seem to impress her. "I have a lot of work to do, Gibson." She picked up the work gloves she'd tossed on the counter earlier. "I think it's time you were leaving."

"That's *your* specialty, isn't it?" He hadn't intended to sound bitter, but she just ignored him anyway. Gibson stared at her as she downed the rest of her coffee in one swallow, then pulled on her gloves. Who was this woman? Right now he felt he barely knew her.

"Why did you come back, Libby? Just answer that one question for me."

Libby stopped in her tracks, the color in her face rising. "You're never going to give me a moment's peace, are you? Isn't it obvious why I'm here?"

"It was the money...." Not her father, not the farm. Not any desire to see Chatsworth again.

"Damn right it was the money. I couldn't take

proper care of my daughter, couldn't get a decent job. All because I never managed to finish my grade twelve." She looked at him with bitterness. "Now that you know, I hope you're happy."

He stepped forward, but she was too fast for him. She slipped out the back before he realized what she was doing. The screen door slammed, and he was alone in a room suddenly too quiet. He wanted to go after her, but not yet. Better to calm down first. Settling both hands on the edge of the counter, he bowed his head over the sink. Arguing was rarely the answer, yet he'd felt driven to defend Henry. It was still inconceivable that she could have distanced herself so completely from her own father.

She'd come home because she had to. Exactly what he'd guessed. There was no reason to be surprised, but every reason to be disappointed.

Brushing his hands against his pants, Gibson pushed his way past the screen door, then headed toward the garden. He found Libby yanking out weeds and breaking up huge clumps of dirt into fine, fertile soil with the pitchfork. She ignored his presence and he considered leaving without saying anything more. He'd never been one to start a fight.

But he just couldn't make himself go.

"No sense putting in a garden if you don't plan to stay for harvest."

She grunted as the pitchfork hit a rock, then she shifted position and dug in again. "I'll be here for most of it. I'm not planning to leave until the end of August." Libby bent to pick up a cluster of weeds, which she tossed in the general direction of the compost heap. Pausing for a moment, she leaned against the pitchfork, clenching the handle.

"Have you ever considered staying?" he asked.

"No."

Gibson was not amused, but for some reason, his reaction was to laugh. "Well, you're not alone. Most of my graduating class moved away from Chatsworth years ago. And I don't blame them. It's hard to make a decent living on a farm, and the work is exhausting. You know all that."

"Yes, I do."

"But at least here you have family and friends. If you get that bus driving job you'll have a regular income."

"Family? Friends? I don't have either. I'm surprised you haven't noticed."

"You're right. I haven't noticed. What am I, if not a friend? And my parents? As for family, you have your father." He reached for her slender shoulder. "Don't turn away, Libby. Maybe you don't need him, but have you considered that he might need you?"

She appeared to find that concept incredulous. "My father can watch out for his own interests, thank you very much."

Something inside him snapped at this assessment. "That's news to me, but then, I'm the one who's had to stand by and watch him deteriorate more and more with each passing year, while you're living half a country away, too busy to spare the old man so much as a couple of minutes of your time. Did you think you could come back here and no one would say anything? Well, maybe your father's willing to take it all in silence, but I'm sure as hell not. Probably won't even bother visiting him again when you leave this time, will you, Libby?''

She pulled the pitchfork from the earth, clearly having had enough. ''I don't need you to tell me what I should have done, and I sure as hell don't need you to tell me what I ought to be doing now. I had a brother, Gibson, and just because he died doesn't mean I'm in the market for another one.''

LATER THAT WEEK, Libby took a trip to Yorkton while Nicole was at school. On the way home, she drove the truck with confidence, every now and then sneaking a glance at the textbooks she'd picked up for her high school correspondence courses. On top of the math book was her class two driver's license.

She'd done it. She'd passed the written test and the road test, and the doctor had given her a thumbs-up medical. Today was Friday. She would get the school bus tomorrow, and begin driving on Monday. Just the thought of having a salary again eased half the troubles on her mind. She anticipated the day she'd open her new savings account and start work on her courses. If she stuck to her schedule, she would complete the requirements for grade twelve by the end of August.

And then she could leave. Pack her suitcase, take her daughter and never look back. Just the way she'd planned.

Of course, Gibson would then feel justified in concluding that every rotten thing he thought about her was true. That she was deserting her father; that she didn't care about the farm.

Libby cranked the window open a couple more inches until the breeze was whipping her heavy curls back from her neck. She could defend herself if she wanted and tell Gibson her side of the story.

But that solution didn't sit right with her. After all, in four months she'd be gone, while her father would live on the farm for the rest of his life. The people in the community already thought he was strange. Why make the situation worse by letting it be known that *he* had booted her out, not the other way around?

No. That was private family business, and no one had the right to know. Not even an interfering neighbor with delusions of being her elder brother.

Gibson as a brother. Despite his meddling, his bossiness, the role didn't quite fit. There were occasional flashes in Gibson's eyes that were far from brotherly. Libby didn't have a lot of experience with men, but she had enough to recognize when a man felt attraction. And enough to know when she felt the same thing back.

Driving past Gibson's farm, she wouldn't let herself check if his truck was beside the house, signaling that he was home. She proceeded to her own driveway, then turned in and coasted to the side of the house. Surveying the yard, she saw the results of her past week's labor: grass cut around the house, vegetable garden tilled and ready to plant, bushes and shrubs pruned into manageable shapes. As she allowed herself a moment's satisfaction, something

caught her eye—white against the green back-
ground...

She parked the truck by the fuel tanks, then walked
around to the backyard, where a couple of large bed-
sheets and one pillowcase flapped in the warm prairie
breeze.

A typical sight, all right, except she hadn't done
any laundry before she'd gone to town. She stepped
closer, fingered the thin white cotton, and found it
completely dry. Had her father actually washed his
own bed sheets?

Automatically, she pinched a clothespin, then
pulled the line toward her to remove the bedding,
which she then folded over her arm. The fabric was
stiff and smooth to the touch, and smelled like Nicole's hair when she came in from playing outside.

Libby carried the sun-warmed linen into the house,
not sure what to do next. The door to her father's
bedroom was still closed. Staring at the bedding in
her arms, she thought she should probably just lay it
on the sofa, but somehow she felt driven to recip-
rocate her father's effort.

Tentatively, she walked toward the door, thinking
that she could make up his bed and that would be a
sign...of what, she didn't know. She wasn't seeking
a reconciliation. There could be no excuses for what
he had done to her. Still, she reached for the door-
knob, and found the door unlocked. It swung inward
and she stepped across the threshold.

The room was almost dark; only a pale light came
through the drawn curtains, revealing small particles
of dust suspended in the air. Coughing slightly,

Libby reached for the curtains and pulled them to the side. The action released yet more dust and Libby sneezed. Needing air, she tried to open the east-facing window.

She had to struggle with the pane. "Heavens," she said to herself. "Has he never even—" The wood gave all of a sudden and she just missed catching her fingers. As she turned to face the room in the sunlight, words failed her. She saw the double bed, two night tables on either side, a bureau and a dressing table on the opposite wall and two wooden chairs in the corners. The same as always.

*Exactly* the same.

A glass still sat on the table on her mother's side of the bed. As did a novel, placed facedown to save the page. The flowery cover identified it as one of Rosamund Pilcher's bestsellers—definitely not a book her father would read. On the floor were her mother's slippers, strewn as if kicked off and not thought of since. On one of the chairs had been flung a housecoat and a silky nightgown. Both were covered in dust.

As clear as day, Libby could picture her mother in those clothes. Scurrying around the kitchen on school mornings, packing Libby's lunch as Libby searched for her coat and mittens.

"Hurry, sweetie. I think I hear the bus."

*Oh, Mom!* Libby's jaw and throat tightened; her eyes flooded with tears. She dropped to the bed, now noticing that when her father had stripped the sheets, he'd left the pillow on her mother's side of the bed intact.

Libby reached out to stroke the soft cotton, her eyes sliding up to the table with the glass—water long since evaporated—and the chair with the clothes. Her attention shifted to the bureau and the framed photographs.

In the center of the arrangement sat a formal studio picture of her parents' wedding. There were also hospital pictures of her and Chris as newborns. And a family portrait that had been done when Libby was thirteen. *How young we all seem,* she thought. *How young, and how happy.*

Chris had been movie-star handsome at twenty-one, his dark hair thick and curly, his grin engaging and his eyes sparkling with his exuberant personality. Her mother had a similar appeal; from her had come all the laughter in their family. At her side, her husband gazed down at her, his expression pure devotion.

A devotion that hadn't faded in all the years her mother had been dead. She pictured her father, lying on his side of the bed, staring at her mother's pillow, her empty glass of water, her unfinished novel.

*Mom, you shouldn't have left. We needed you....*

Libby suddenly felt overwhelmed by the need to cry. She turned away from the bureau, a movement across the room startled her. She gasped in the instant before she recognized her own image in the full-length mirror that hung on the door. The flash of the white shirt—her mother's white shirt—was like seeing a ghost.

She decided against making the bed after all. Instead, she shut the window and pulled the curtains closed again. Then she left the room. She set the folded sheets on the sofa, as she'd originally planned, before she went upstairs to change into gardening clothes. But she'd no sooner removed her one pair of good pants and her mother's white shirt than her energy fizzled. She sank onto the edge of her bed and stared at the wall.

In front of her were pictures of animals, mostly kittens and playful little puppies, that she'd taped to her walls when she was young. The tape was dry and yellow now, but still it held. Libby stared at a calendar photo of two gray kittens tumbling inside a wicker basket. After a few minutes she realized tears were pouring from her eyes.

Her mother had always said there was nothing wrong with a good cry. Libby remembered arriving home from school to see her mother in front of the television, watching *Marcus Welby* while she ironed, a tissue box close at hand.

She'd laugh at herself when Libby came into the room and quickly turn off the iron to get out cookies and milk.

The house might not be spotless, the beds might not be made, but her mother always ironed their clothes so they looked brand-new, and she almost always had home-baked cookies on hand.

Maybe Libby hadn't allowed herself time enough to cry: maybe that was the problem. Now she was making up for lost opportunities.

For eight years.

People were expected to get over the loss of a loved one. A year, maybe two, was allowed for the grieving period. But her father hadn't stuck to the schedule.

Her mother and Chris had left too big a hole. They'd taken a chunk of her father with them, and somehow what had remained of the man was getting smaller and smaller with each passing day.

The past few days were enough to convince Libby that he was only going through the motions of living, that he might have given up completely if not for his obligation to his land and livestock.

Libby understood her father's pain. But the little girl inside her couldn't help but wonder, *What about me?* Wasn't she worth anything? Why had her father's love for her died with the others?

# CHAPTER SIX

THE SOUND OF Gibson's truck in the lane signaled Nicole's return from school. Libby ran downstairs to the kitchen, where she splashed her face with cold water to erase the evidence of her crying jag, knowing the action was too little, too late.

While she waited for Nicole to come in, the horn of Gibson's truck blared once, then again. Peering out the living room window, she saw Nicole, Gibson and Allie by the truck, obviously waiting for her. Resigned, she practiced a big smile, then stepped out onto the veranda. Maybe, if she didn't get too close, Gibson wouldn't notice....

"Didn't you pass, Mom?" Nicole bounded over to her and flung her arms around her neck, then stepped back to examine her face. Gibson's hand was on Allie's shoulder, his expression almost as anxious as Nicole's.

Libby smiled. She'd forgotten about the good part of the day. "Yes, I passed. I'm going to be your new school bus driver."

"Hooray!"

Gibson took a few steps in her direction. "Congratulations. That's great news."

"No more car pooling," she said, as if it were a

good thing, when the truth was she would miss seeing his truck pull up in their drive.

"No more car pooling," he agreed. Then, struck by an idea, he snapped his fingers. "Hey, we should celebrate."

"We should?"

"I'm not a great cook, but I can throw together a decent barbecue. What do you say?"

The girls had been trying to pet the old tabby that lived in the barn, but tuned in quickly to the prospect of a party.

"Great idea, Daddy," said Allie. She faced Nicole. "He makes the best burgers—with no little bits."

Libby glanced at Gibson. "Little bits…?"

"Onions."

She should have known. Distrust of all things vegetable in nature was a universal trait in kids.

Allie, impatient at the interruption, began speaking again. "We'll have lots of time to play and—say, Dad, could Nicole sleep over tonight? It *is* Friday."

Both girls turned pleading eyes to their respective parents. Libby couldn't help feeling apprehensive. Nicole had never spent a night away from home. But clearly from the longing in her daughter's eyes she felt no concern about doing so.

"It's fine with me," Gibson said. "How about it, Nicole? Would you like to stay the night?"

She nodded shyly and smiled at Allie, who was by this point dancing wildly around the truck. "Yay! Yay! We get to have a sleepover!"

"Thanks, Gibson," Libby said, warmed by her

daughter's quiet happiness. This was just what she'd wanted for Nicole. Friends and sleepovers and the feeling of belonging.

"They'll have a blast. And I'll try to make sure they spend at least a portion of the night sleeping." He moved closer, touching a finger to the collar of her blouse. "I've been meaning to talk to you about the other day. I was out of line—"

Libby shook her head. "No. It's okay. I shouldn't have said—" she hesitated, then began again "—that thing about not needing another brother. I'm really sorry...."

"Hey. Forget it."

She was very aware of his fingers—so near her skin. And she wanted to touch him, too. To put her hand over his, pinning it against her body. She knew it didn't make sense. She'd been so angry with him earlier. And he'd been so angry with her.

But his offer of a celebration party had caught her off balance. It was neighborly and thoughtful—she didn't dare read more into it than that.

"Can I bring a salad?"

"That would be great." Gibson let his hand drop, then moved back to his truck. "Come on, pumpkin. We better go home and start getting organized. Six o'clock okay?"

"Perfect." Libby put one arm around her daughter's shoulders and waved at the departing truck with the other. A celebration party. For her. Whatever Gibson's motives, she was looking forward to the evening. A lot. And that scared her more than anything else.

MOIRA PLANT WAS in the kitchen, whipping cream for strawberry shortcakes, when Libby walked into the house with her bowl of potato salad. She'd left Nicole outside, by the barbecue pit with Gibson and Allie.

"Hi, Moira," she said, speaking loudly over the motor of the hand beater. She slipped her salad into the spotless fridge. "Need any help?"

Moira turned off the mixer and put the whipped cream in the fridge beside the salad. "You could clean the strawberries." She handed Libby a knife. "I hear you're going to be the new school bus driver."

"That's right."

"Better you than me. I couldn't take the screaming and yelling...."

Libby shrugged. She was sure it couldn't be worse than the noise levels at some of the factories she'd worked at in Toronto.

"So how are you enjoying being back in Chatsworth? I bet your dad is glad to have you."

Bet again. "It's nice to be home. Nicole is settling in all right."

"Having a friend close by is a good change for Allie. I often worry about her. This farm's so isolated. If only she had her mother, even a brother or sister...but I guess you know what raising an only child on your own is like." Her shrewd gray eyes assessed Libby knowingly. "Owen been gone a long time?"

Libby's fingers slipped, and she hacked off the end of one of her fingernails. She should have known better than to offer to help. Should have known Moira would seize the opportunity to subject her to more questions.

"Yes...yes, he has," Libby replied. He'd been gone as long as she had, hadn't he? It wasn't really a lie. She sliced out the green top from the strawberry in her hand, then dropped the red berry into the glass bowl on the counter.

Of course it was a lie, Libby's conscience asserted. Here she was, letting the whole of Chatsworth believe that she'd run off with Owen, that he was Nicole's father and that he'd deserted them both, when the truth was Owen and she had been nothing but friends.

So it was a lie. No one would be hurt by it, least of all Owen. He and his parents were gone; they had no ties left to the community. She doubted Owen would care what anyone here thought of him.

That still didn't make it right.

Moira rinsed the sink and hung up the dishcloth. "Spoon those berries onto the biscuits, will you, Libby? I've got to get going. It's bingo night, and I've still got to feed Fred. I've got the stew all ready to be heated in the microwave, but do you think he can transfer the bowl from one place to another and press a few buttons?"

Libby sat in one of the plush, swivel kitchen chairs, relieved at the sudden quiet once Moira left. Was this what the next few months were going to be like? Everywhere she went she was met with questions. Some well meaning, others less so. How long could she continue to dodge the issue of Nicole's parentage?

Gently she removed the tea cloth and split the golden biscuits into halves, then spooned berries generously on each. As she worked, she glanced around the kitchen. Rita had remodeled, all right, and she'd done a good job of it. Libby admired the pale-oak cupboards, butcher-block counters and blue and yellow decorative accents. The kitchen was both attractive and practical, though it bore little resemblance to the cluttered, homey room she remembered from childhood. All the appliances were supersize, and the stove even had a wood-burning component that added to the farm atmosphere. Maybe Rita hadn't been much of a country girl, but she'd certainly nailed the look.

The kitchen door opened again and in came Gibson.

"Time to put on burgers. Would you like a beer?"

She covered the dessert and accepted a can, refusing his offer of a glass.

Gibson had changed out of his work clothes into a fresh pair of jeans and a yellow cotton T-shirt. The yellow contrasted nicely with the blue of his eyes and drew out the gold highlights in his hair. The jeans suited him, too, molding his lower body and legs like a comfortable second skin.

"How are the girls doing?"

"They're feeding the bunnies. I told them the burgers would be ready in about twenty minutes. Do you mind grabbing that for me?" He nodded toward a large wooden tray laden with fresh buns, condiments, napkins and utensils.

"Sure." She followed him to the back patio and set the tray on the outdoor table, then joined him by the fire. He was carefully lifting the patties, which sizzled as he placed them on the freshly cleaned grill.

"You've always had a way with flames, haven't you?" She sat on a chair near the pit, enjoying the heat radiating from the red-hot coals. "Didn't you and Chris start a little grass fire one year down by the slough?"

"You would have to remember that, wouldn't you? At least we had the sense to start it close to a good source of water."

"Yes, very thoughtful of you."

"That's just the kind of kids we were." He pulled up a chair next to hers and popped the tab on his own can of beer. "Thoughtful, considerate…"

"Fortunately you could run fast, too. As I recall you and Chris made it home in record time, yelling for water and buckets."

"At least we didn't need the fire department."

"Only because Dad called half the neighbors."

"True. Chris and I had to work a month of Saturdays to repay them." If he'd resented the punishment then, he sure didn't now. She hadn't seen him looking so at peace since she'd returned.

The sound of the girls' laughter floating from across the yard added to the air of relaxation. "Seems like they're having fun," Libby said.

"They always have a good time together. Just like—"

He didn't say, but Libby knew he was thinking of Chris.

"Hell, it's good to see Allie happy. I don't know about you, but this being a single parent—it's a lot of pressure. I keep worrying I'm screwing up somehow."

"It is tough. At least Allie talks to you. Nicole is so quiet I never know when she has a problem."

"She's a serious little girl."

Libby nodded. It was true. She'd tried to keep the worries of managing as a single mother to herself, but she'd obviously failed. So often when she looked at Nicole's face, she saw every one of her own insecurities reflected there. It wasn't right, but Libby didn't know how to fix it.

"My deepest fear," Gibson said, "is that something will happen to Allie when I'm not around to protect her. Even letting her go off to school was a struggle for me. Dumb, right?"

"Maybe a little overprotective. But understandable." Especially given the way he'd lost his wife. "What was Rita like? I can hardly remember her."

Gibson's gaze shifted to the field he'd just finished seeding that morning. "She was pretty. And talented. You saw what she did with the kitchen."

"Nice enough to be in a magazine. But comfortable, too."

"Yeah. And practical the way a farmhouse ought to be."

"I must admit I miss that old wallpaper of your mother's."

"The vegetables?" Gibson grinned. "Chris used

to complain that seeing all those carrots and broccoli dancing on the walls ruined his appetite.''

''I thought they were cute. I especially liked the little radishes.''

Gibson flipped the burgers. ''*Cute* wasn't the word Rita came up with.'' He glanced back at the house, hesitated for a moment, then said, ''Sometimes days would pass without Rita coming outside except to hang the laundry or put out food for the cats. She never did get the hang of gardening, wasn't keen about farm life in general. That's what was so maddening. Why did she have to wait until I wasn't around…''

Libby didn't want to hear the details of the accident, but she thought maybe Gibson needed to talk about it. ''What happened?'' she asked quietly.

''I was out combining in the northeast section.'' Gibson's eyes traveled across the fields, as if he could actually see himself there. ''I'd left the truck loaded with grain in the yard, and I guess when Rita got Allie down for her afternoon nap she decided she'd unload it into the granary for me. She'd seen me work the auger many times before, although she'd never done it herself.''

Gibson ran his hand over his face. ''She was wearing a loose dress—sort of a granny style, which she favored because she still hadn't lost all the weight from her pregnancy.''

Libby shuddered. Loose clothing and an auger. She was enough of a farmer's daughter to know it was a deadly combination.

''Later they figured her dress must have caught

and she hadn't been able to slip out of it fast enough.''

Libby had known it was coming, but that didn't make it less dreadful to hear. ''Oh, Gibson...''

''When I came home, I could hear Allie crying as soon as I got out of the pickup. I gave her a bottle, then called for Rita. There was no sign of her inside, which was strange enough. So I went out in the yard....''

Libby stared at the grass by her feet, knowing what he must have seen. His wife's body, mangled and bloody.

An auger was just a machine; it wouldn't have reacted to Rita's screams. Without someone to throw the switch, it would have pulled on Rita's dress, then on her body, the blade curving like a corkscrew, driving whatever it held in its grasp upward, until finally, overloaded, the engine would have broken down and stopped.

Rita had probably died from loss of blood. It wouldn't have been quick, and would definitely have been painful. The poor woman.

''Harvest was slow that year. We'd had a wet fall and I was getting desperate to get the crop off. Rita was feeling bad that she wasn't much help. She knew most wives worked hand in hand with their husbands during combining.''

''But you never asked her to unload the grain.''

''Of course not. I guess she wanted to surprise me. To prove something.''

He blamed himself. Of course, someone like Gibson would. Just as his mother blamed *herself* for the pressure she'd put on Rita. Poor Connie. No wonder she was so reluctant to offer her opinions to her son.

Finally, it seemed that the space between Gibson and her was intolerable. Libby went to stand by him and placed a hand on his shoulder. "Don't blame yourself, Gibson. I know you feel it's your fault, but Rita used really poor judgment, and you can't hold yourself accountable for that."

Gibson pressed her hand against his cheek. "Thanks for listening, Libby. I've missed Chris for many reasons over the years, but when Rita died, that was when I almost went crazy."

Somehow Libby was pulled into his arms, her cheek tight against his chest as he buried his face in the softness of her hair. Libby allowed her hands to wrap around his broad back. Gibson was so big, tall and thick around the chest that she almost felt lost in his arms. It was a nice feeling. Safe and warm.

"Libby."

His breath was in her ear, and suddenly she wasn't sure who was doing the comforting anymore.

"You know all about heartache, don't you, Libby? You were crying this afternoon." He tipped her head up. Gently his thumb stroked her chin, then glided down her neck to rest at her collarbone. "Did Owen hurt you very badly?"

She closed her eyes, tired of the lie. She couldn't be in Gibson's arms like this and continue to pretend that she'd run off with Owen Holst.

"Gibson, I never—" Words died on her lips when she saw the way he was looking at her. She felt a pressure in her chest that had nothing to do with the strength of his arms around her but was more of a yearning for something she wasn't even aware she wanted.

How long had she known Gibson? All her life. And although there'd been a period—quite a long period, between early adolescence and Gibson's engagement—when she'd daydreamed of Gibson falling in love with her and the two of them getting married, she'd never seriously believed she would one day be in his arms, wanting nothing more than for him to kiss her. And having him look at her as if that were all he wanted, too.

Kissing Gibson Browning was beyond the realm of possibility. Yet it was happening. His head was lowering, his mouth moving toward hers. She could feel her heart ballooning, and the impulse to tilt up her face and close her eyes was undeniable.

Gibson was a strong man, but he touched his lips to hers gently. The scent of his skin was subtle, sunshine and prairie wind rolled together. She rubbed her face against his cheek and smelled the charcoal in his hair, the fabric softener in his shirt.

He whispered her name, so quietly she could hardly hear him.

And then, from the corner of her eye she caught a movement from the barn. And in the next second, the cry of a panic-stricken child. "Mommy!"

In an instant they were apart.

"Gibson! Mommy!" Nicole called. "Allie fell off one of the ponies!"

Fear flashed across Gibson's face in the split second before he turned to dash for the barn.

They found Allie lying in a mound of straw on the barn floor, alternately crying and yelling at the ponies to stay away from her. The two gray Shetlands seemed in no danger of doing otherwise. They were huddled in the far corner of the stall, looking just as unhappy as Allie about the whole situation.

"Are you all right?" Gibson jumped the wooden gate and bent over his writhing daughter.

"Sporty bucked me off! All I did was slide onto her back from the side of the stall, and she started rearing!"

Libby glanced at Nicole and could tell that there was, perhaps, a different version of the story, but both of them stayed silent, watching as Gibson gently probed his daughter's limbs.

"You aren't supposed to ride the ponies unless I'm around to supervise."

"I know, Daddy. I'm sorry." Allie held out her arms and her father lifted her and carried her outside.

They were halfway toward the house when the smell of burning meat rose up to meet them. "The hamburgers!" Gibson ran, but it was too late. Four charred black disks sat on the grill, obviously inedible.

"Never mind. More where those came from." Gibson settled his daughter comfortably in one of the chairs, then scraped the burned burgers off the grill and added four fresh patties.

He glanced sympathetically at Allie. "Feeling any better?"

She shook her head, bottom lip thrust out, eyes red with the threat of more tears.

"Next time you want to ride the ponies, please remember to call me for help, okay?"

Maybe the scare of the fall would be enough to teach Allie her lesson, but something in the little girl's expression when her father turned back to the grill made Libby doubt it. She was only seven, but Allie knew how to pull her father's strings in order to get her own way. Which was exactly what Gibson's mother had been talking about the other day at the soccer game.

Libby checked out her daughter, who was sitting quietly at the patio table, legs swinging, hands folded neatly in her lap. What must she think of these ploys of Allie's? Or of the little girl's wealth of possessions?

Maybe this new friendship was not as ideal as Libby had initially supposed.

Just then, Allie piped up with a new line of conversation. "Can Nicole come to my birthday party, Daddy?"

Gibson was just flipping the new batch of perfectly cooked burgers onto a platter. "Well, of course she can. It's next Saturday." He looked at Libby questioningly. "If it's okay with her mom."

"Oh, yes!" There was no doubting Nicole's excitement. "Can I, Mom? Please!"

Libby couldn't say no; it would be Nicole's first party. So she nodded assent, but in her heart she had grave reservations. For Nicole to see all the gifts Allie would get, the fuss and celebration, when her own birthdays had always been such quiet affairs, would be hard. Libby sighed, thinking that if Allie had been overindulged by her father, the exact opposite was the case for Nicole.

"Don't look so sad." Gibson was speaking. He'd given the girls their burgers, and they were eating together happily on a small plastic picnic table made for children. "I didn't burn them this time."

Libby gave her head a mental shake. "They smell great." She loaded a bun with tomato, lettuce and barbecue sauce, listening as the young girls chattered about the details of the upcoming party. There would be a birthday gift to buy, she realized, and her heart sank as she wondered how she could ever meet the expectations of a little girl who already had everything she could possibly want.

"Pass the lettuce, would you, Libby?"

She slid the plate across the table and Gibson reached out at the same time, his tanned, work-roughened fingers brushing against hers as she let go. The touch reminded her of what had been happening between them earlier, before the incident with the ponies. She raised her eyes, to find him watching her, his gaze on her mouth as she bit into her burger. She chewed self-consciously, aware of the smile teasing his lips.

When she swallowed she noticed he hadn't even started eating yet. "Aren't you hungry?"

"To be honest, I'm having a difficult time thinking about food right now," Gibson admitted, his voice too low for the girls to hear.

Libby focused on her burger, feeling her cheeks redden. Gibson Browning had kissed her, and it was the most amazing thing she'd ever experienced. Who would have guessed being kissed by a man could be so gentle and warm, yet totally engulfing? She could have been standing on hot coals and not even have noticed.

"Eight years' difference isn't so much at this stage of our lives. It seemed unbridgeable when I was fourteen and you were only six. Do you remember me walking you off the bus to the classroom your first day of grade one?"

She laughed. "Chris was too cool to be seen with his younger sister. Yes, I remember." She had a lot of memories of Gibson. And just a few minutes ago they'd made another one. She knew Gibson's kiss was something she'd never forget.

"This is so strange. Only the other day we were so angry at each other," she said.

"I know. But you've got to admit, the argument was all your fault."

"What?"

"Just kidding. I'm sorry I allowed myself to get so worked up." He paused, watching Nicole as she scooted up Allie's wooden playground center. Then he focused back on Libby. "But it wasn't idle curiosity. I care about you, Libby, always have."

"Like a brother, you mean?" She slapped away a hovering mosquito—they were always worse in the evening—and waited for his answer.

"How can you say that after what just happened? Libby, I still care, but it's different now."

She knew exactly what he meant.

Gibson brushed his hands down her shoulders,

along her arms. "What's happened to you, Libby, these past eight years?"

She shook her head. The impulse to tell him the truth about Owen was still there, but she had to be careful. After all, if he knew Owen wasn't Nicole's father, his first question would be, then who was? And what would she say to that?

Gibson's mouth tightened. He was frustrated by her silence and she didn't blame him. He'd been so open with her, and she hadn't reciprocated. But she really wished she could.

"Gibson, can't we be...*friends*...without all these details? The past isn't something I enjoy talking about. I'd like a chance to think of the future for a change."

"I'm interested in the future, too. But is friendship really all you want from our relationship? Personally, I think the potential is there for something a whole lot more."

Libby was so caught up in his words she almost jumped when he suddenly swatted her arm. Lifting his hand, he revealed a squished mosquito. "These critters are getting bad," he said. "Let's go inside for dessert."

LIBBY RETURNED from the barbecue alone and went straight to the kitchen table to work on her first mathematics assignment. She felt lonely without Nicole, and kept thinking of Gibson, wondering how he passed the time while the girls snuggled into their sleeping bags, laughing and talking.

His wife had been dead five years now. He had to be lonely. Just like her…

Libby read the first problem, then frowned over the fact of two trains on the same track, racing toward each other from opposite directions. The object of the exercise was to determine, based on the distance and speed of each train, the exact moment that they would collide. This type of question had always annoyed her. What kind of twisted mind had thought it up?

She tapped her pencil on the notepad in front of her, then got up to make herself a cup of tea. Math had never been her favorite subject. It was easy to allow reliving the moment of Gibson's kiss to distract her.

She knew her feelings were dangerous, but that didn't stop her heart from lifting every time she remembered Gibson saying he was attracted to her.

It seemed so impossible. She didn't feel like a woman who would be attractive to a man, especially not one as handsome and appealing as Gibson. Instead, she felt that every worry and concern she'd ever had were etched in lines across her face. And even though she knew men didn't pay as much attention to clothes as women, by now he'd undoubtedly noticed that she always wore the same pair of jeans—and that they were barely hanging together. The bottom line was, she didn't feel twenty-five. She felt forty-five.

Libby sat back at the table, cradling the warm mug in her hands, suddenly aware of the sound of the television from the other room. She could readily picture her father reclining in his favorite leather chair, watching the Friday-night programs. Libby tried to imagine eight years' worth of evenings spent exactly the same way, night after night. Alone in that room. The idea was depressing. No, more than that. It was pathetic. Maybe even tragic.

But most of all it was confusing. She didn't know what to think of her father anymore. With the perspective of an adult, she could understand how her mother's death had derailed her father. But as a mother, she couldn't understand how a parent could abandon a child the way he'd abandoned her.

She'd always suspected that her pregnancy had been just an excuse. The truth was her father couldn't stand to have her around the house. He'd simply wanted to be alone. And that was exactly how it had turned out.

She wasn't going to feel sorry for him.

And she wasn't going to feel sorry for herself, either. What was the point? It was too late to change anything. The future demanded her concentration now. This high school diploma meant everything to her and Nicole's chances of making it on their own again. She had to keep her thoughts focused, her energy on track.

How fast were those trains going...?

SINCE RITA HAD DIED, Gibson had found nights tough to face. He didn't like lying alone on the big queen-size bed, tossing and turning on the 280-count cotton sheets that Rita had made such a fuss about. Recently, he'd begun to think he should marry again.

But the task of choosing the right woman nearly scared him to death.

Because he hadn't chosen the right woman the first time. It hurt him to admit it, especially since Rita had paid the price for his mistake. In exchange, the least he could do was keep a loving memory of her in his heart. And it wasn't hard, because she'd had wonderful qualities. She'd been lovely to look at, talented and fun to take out to a party or a dance.

Yet she hadn't made him a partner in the way he'd hoped. And it had been his fault. You couldn't take a woman used to city life and city pleasures, a woman who didn't particularly like animals or have any feeling for the land, and transplant her into hard, isolated country life, expecting her to dig in her roots, deep and strong.

He thought of a lawyer from Yorkton he'd dated for a while a year ago. She'd been attractive, smart and good company. Despite himself, he'd been tempted. For several months he'd ignored the differences in their backgrounds and interests, but finally the relationship had progressed to the point where he'd been forced to make a choice. He'd broken it off, and even on his loneliest nights, he knew he'd done the right thing.

Not that he necessarily assumed that a woman who lived in the city wouldn't love living in the country. No more than he would assume that a woman who lived in the country took the same delight and fulfillment from it that he did.

Libby, for instance. She'd grown up on one of the most prosperous farms in the district, but that hadn't stopped her from running off to the city. He still didn't understand why she'd left, but then, he'd never been able to comprehend the lure of city life. It had never held any attraction for him.

Libby Bateson did, though. There'd always been something a little bit untamed about her. As a child she'd gravitated to the outdoors, just as he and Chris had. Sometimes she'd been a pest; often, however, she'd been content to play on her own, with her animals, or to help her mother in the garden.

In those days he'd felt a fondness for her, as well as a sense of obligation to look out for her. Now he found it difficult to reconcile those protective instincts with the desire she brought out in him.

She'd been an attractive child, but who could've guessed her beauty would explode so lushly? It was hard for him to imagine that any man could look at her without wanting her—he sure couldn't.

The impulse to kiss her had been undeniable. The way she'd responded proved the attraction wasn't one-sided. So much for his plans to only be friends.

He supposed he could pull back, try to pretend that kiss had never happened and just avoid being alone with her again. But it wouldn't be easy. Not when all his instincts were driving him to spend *more* time with her, to explore the attraction between them and break through that wall of reserve she'd built around herself.

Her stubborn silence about her past was driving him crazy. Was she afraid he would judge her and blame her for her mistakes? Probably. He'd given her every reason to think exactly that.

Maybe he needed to be more sympathetic. After all, she'd only been seventeen, still suffering the loss of her mother and brother. He knew firsthand what grief could do to a person.

If only Libby would talk to him. He felt certain that was the next step. But would Libby cooperate?

# CHAPTER SEVEN

"DO I LOOK LIKE A QUEEN?" Nicole paraded in front of the long mirror in her grandma's old sewing room. She had on Allie's birthday present, which was a costume her mother had made from fabric remnants and bits of old-fashioned jewelry. There was a fancy red velvet cape with a pretend fur collar, and a tiara they'd concocted by gluing pieces of sparkling glass and colorful sequins to a plastic hair band.

Her mom bowed in front of her, extending an empty wrapping paper roll spray-painted a sparkling gold. "The royal scepter, Your Majesty."

Nicole swirled the cape, then swooshed the scepter on top of her mom's head. "Well done, handmaiden. I crown you, Sir Bateson." She twirled in front of the mirror one more time. "Can a woman be a *sir*?"

"No, I believe *lady* is the right term. So do you think Allie will like the present?"

"Why not? I'd like it."

Her mom looked happy. "Well, we can make you one if you want. But now you have to take Allie's off and wrap it in the paper you decorated. Then put on your new dress and I'll do your hair."

"Okay." Her mom had had this really neat idea of cutting shapes out of potatoes, dipping them in ink, then stamping the shapes on a sheet of brown wrapping paper. They'd left the paper drying on the kitchen table. Now Nicole ran downstairs to get it.

She paused just before rounding the kitchen and steeled herself for the possibility that her grandfather might be in the room. Usually he worked on Saturday, just like any other day, but you never knew...

The couple of times Nicole had accidentally stumbled across her grandfather had only made her more nervous of him than before. He never talked to her; he didn't even look at her.

Even on the few occasions her mom had actually spoken to him or asked a question, he just acted like she was invisible. Sometimes Nicole wondered what he would do if *she* tried to talk to him. Would he ignore her, too? So far she'd been too scared to try. Maybe one day...

The paper was dry, so Nicole put the cape, tiara and scepter into the large box her mother had found, then wrapped the paper around it, using tape to hold it in place. When she was done she glued the birthday card she'd made to the top of the package, then went upstairs to change.

This was the moment she'd been waiting for. Her mother had sewn her a new dress from a bolt of pretty blue cotton that they'd found in her grandma's sewing supplies. What made the dress extra special was that her mom had had a dress cut out of the exact material when she was a little girl. They'd even found the same pattern.

Now Nicole swirled in front of the mirror again, this time in her new outfit. She felt beautiful, but as lovely as the new dress was, she knew Allie would be wearing something much nicer. That was just the way things were. Allie had the prettiest clothes of all the girls in their grade. And Nicole had never met anyone with as many toys.

She wasn't sure why this was so. Maybe because Allie's dad had finished high school and they had more money. She'd have to remember to ask her mom if that was it. But not until she'd passed her courses.

"Can you do my hair, Mom?"

"Sure. Come here." Libby felt her heart lighten as Nicole entered her bedroom. The dress looked wonderful on her daughter; thank goodness styles for little girls weren't as quickly outdated as those for older women.

If only there'd been time to sew something for herself to wear to the party, but she had enough to do, what with planting the garden, driving the bus, studying and taking care of the house. No one would notice what she was wearing, anyway. All the focus would be on the children, which was exactly how it should be.

Besides, she thought she looked just fine in her good pair of pants and white blouse. Her hair hung in a long French braid down her back, and she'd even applied some mascara and a little lipstick.

"I want my hair like yours, please."

"Sure, sweetie. Pass me the brush." She'd made a bow from some of the leftover fabric, and now she used that to fasten the end of Nicole's braid.

"There. You look like a queen yourself. Go check it out in the mirror."

"Thanks, Mom." Nicole ran out the door to the sewing room. After a few seconds she called out, "It's great! Are you ready to go? I don't want to be late."

"Don't worry, we'll be on time. Take the present to the truck and I'll be right there." Libby turned back to the mirror, fussed with her hair a few more minutes, then went outside after her daughter. She was just walking around to the front of the house when she saw that the tractor was in the yard. Her father climbed down from the cab and started toward the house.

Libby froze in her footsteps, automatically glancing at Nicole, who was standing outside the truck, jumping from foot to foot impatiently. Nicole hadn't yet noticed her grandfather, but he'd seen her. His footsteps slowed; his eyes were riveted on the seven-year-old.

"My God...it's little Libby." His voice was deep and low, but Libby heard the words clearly—the first he'd spoken since they'd moved in almost a month ago now. Libby felt her throat tighten; even the muscles along her jaw ached. It was the dress, she realized. And the hairstyle. Just the way her mother had done it for her when she was little.

"Grandpa?" Nicole had stilled the moment he'd spoken, and now she turned eyes filled with uncertainty toward her mother.

"Remember I said that I used to have a dress just like the one you're wearing?" Libby tried to speak naturally, as if nothing out of the ordinary had occurred. "I guess your grandfather was reminded of me."

"Did you guys talk to each other in those days?"

Libby couldn't find the words to answer that one. A huge lump had settled in the back of her throat. Out of the corner of her eye she saw her father head for the barn. She let out her breath in a shaky sigh. For a moment she'd thought he was going to speak to her. That he was going to look her in the eye and acknowledge—silently, at least—that she was his daughter. She should have known better. He was too stubborn for that, and a part of her hated him then, for shutting her out and closing off his feelings so utterly and completely.

But a part of her couldn't hate him, because she remembered so clearly every detail of the bedroom he'd shared with her mother: the open book, the unmoved slippers, the unwashed pillowcase. And she couldn't hate him, because she felt too sorry for him.

THEY ARRIVED with a flurry of other guests. It seemed Allie had invited half her class, and since the party was so far from town, all the parents were encouraged to stay and join in the festivities. Libby felt a moment's anxiety as she parked her father's truck behind a string of vehicles. She hadn't thought about having to mingle with her neighbors; now she was certain she'd feel awkward and out of place. But Nicole was bouncing on the seat beside her, so there was nothing to do but take a deep breath and go.

It was the third day of June, sunny and warm. A

balloon arbor hung over the gate to the backyard, and a huge wooden sign saying Happy Birthday, Allie was propped up against the fence. Helium balloons were tied to many of the fence posts, providing a colorful frame for the patio table, which was adorned with tablecloth, napkins and paper plates all decorated with pretty pastel-colored ponies.

The real McCoy stood in the corral just beyond the party setup. Posh's and Sporty's manes had been braided with ribbons, and children were already forming lines for rides. Allie's grandfather was in charge: he lifted the girls up into the saddle and led the more nervous riders around in a tight circle.

As Nicole rushed to join the queue, Libby glanced around. People were everywhere, all talking to someone, all busy doing something, except her. She eyed the gift in her hand and thought that she could look for someplace to put it. After that, she could find herself a drink. Then maybe she'd watch the children on the ponies for a while.

It seemed like a safe plan. But then she felt a hand on her shoulder.

"Nice hair, Libby."

She recognized his touch before she heard his voice. Turning slowly, she saw the sun shining off his golden hair, his blue eyes fixed on her.

"You've been busy." She scanned the lavish decorations.

Gibson appeared sheepish. "Well, I'm finished seeding. I needed something to occupy my time. Allie's out of her mind with excitement. She's been waiting for Nicole to get here. See—they're lined up together for a pony ride.''

Libby drew in her breath at the sight of Allie in a beautiful cotton chintz dress, her blond hair curled in a mass of perfect ringlets. ''She looks like a doll, Gibson.''

''Doesn't she? Mom did her hair.'' He watched Allie for a few moments before he turned back to Libby. ''But you need a drink, and I can take care of this.'' He took the gift and gently guided her with a touch on her back toward the kitchen. Moira was doing bar duty, serving wine, soft drinks, beer and punch to the adult guests.

*He looks gorgeous,* Libby thought, shooting sideways glances at Gibson as they walked. His skin glowed with health; his body was muscular and strong beneath a pair of stiff black jeans and a crisp white shirt with black detailing. Rolled-up sleeves revealed the strong muscles of his forearm.

Suddenly the kiss they'd shared was all she could think about, and when he asked her what she'd like to drink, she found herself unable to tear her eyes from his lips, remembering how they'd felt brushing hers.

As if he could read her mind, he whispered, ''You'll have to stop looking at me like that Libby, or I'll be forced to kiss you. Again.'' He leaned in close to pass her a glass of punch. ''And that'll really get the neighbors talking.''

Nothing could have grounded her more quickly. She figured there was already enough gossip circulating about her in the close-knit community. No

need to give people something else to talk about.
While sipping her punch, she checked out the crowd.
More mothers had brought their children than fathers,
and on average they were probably five to ten years
older than she. As she surveyed the faces she realized, with great amusement, that many of these
women were former girlfriends of Chris's.

"What's so funny?" Gibson edged nearer.

Her host *was* eminently kissable, no doubt about
it. "So let them talk," she said softly. Saying the
words felt like a dare. Right away she knew she was
in trouble. Gibson never backed down from a challenge.

"All right, I will," he said. Then his eyes began
to close and she realized he was going to kiss her
despite the fact that people—his neighbors and
friends—were standing all around them. He was going to kiss her, and God help her, she was going to—

"Daddy! Daddy!"

Libby heard the words at the same moment as Allie pulled at Gibson's arm.

"Everyone's had a pony ride. Can we do the scav-
enger hunt now? Please, please, please?" With every
*please* she pulled harder on her father's wrist.

"Calm down, pumpkin. Of course we can." Gibson gave Libby a rueful glance before allowing his
daughter to tug him toward the group of children
standing expectantly beside the patio table.

Libby watched him go, not sure whether to feel
sorry or grateful.

"Gorgeous, isn't he?"

A trim woman with short dark hair, wearing nicely

fitted dark jeans and a beautifully embroidered denim shirt, stepped up beside her. She looked familiar, but Libby couldn't remember her name.

"Tobey Stedman," the woman said, eyeing her up and down. "I'm Ardis's aunt."

Libby spotted the little, dark-haired girl in the crowd. For once her long brown hair was not in braids but cascaded freely down her back, well past her bottom. "Yes. I know Ardis. She rides my bus."

"And you're Libby, of course. You look a lot like your brother."

"So I've been told." Libby gave a slight shrug. She remembered the woman now. Chris had brought her home for Sunday dinner once. Tobey had spent the entire meal pointing out the character flaws and beauty imperfections of the other girls around Chatsworth, and after Chris had taken her home, their father, who usually kept his opinions to himself, had said, "Do me a favor, Chris. Don't invite that one back." And amazingly, for once, Chris had complied with his father's request.

Tobey's eyes were back on Gibson, who was handing out lists to the girls.

"You can work in pairs," he told them. "Once you've collected every item report back to me for your prize."

Immediately Allie linked hands with Nicole, who was reading intently. "A handful of hay," Nicole said. "We need to go to the barn."

The two girls were about to run off, when Ardis came up beside Allie. "I want to be your partner."

Allie shrugged. "I'm partners with Nicole."

"But we were *always* partners before." Ardis crossed her arms and fixed Nicole with a stare. "Before *you* had to move here."

Libby was about to intervene, but she stopped herself when she realized Nicole had the situation under control.

"We could all three work together." After a bit of haggling and negotiating they finally agreed, with Allie walking in the middle between Nicole and Ardis.

Libby refocused on Tobey. She was oblivious to the girls' exchange; her attention was still on Gibson, who was now starting up the barbecue.

"I can't imagine why we didn't all go crazy over him when we were in school," she said, more to herself than to Libby.

"Because we were too busy chasing after Chris." Another woman came up from behind Tobey, and this one Libby recognized right away.

"Garnet!" Libby smiled at the redhead with the pretty face and animated expression. Chris had dated Garnet more than any other girl she could remember, and her parents had both hoped that he would eventually settle down with her. But at about the same time that Gibson had married, Garnet had announced her engagement to a successful farmer several miles closer to town.

"Hi, Libby! Great to see you back in Chatsworth. I know Violet's enjoying Nicole at school." Garnet tugged at the bottom of her short, bright-purple skirt, which she was wearing with an equally vivid turquoise-and-pink top.

"Violet is your daughter?" Libby scanned the farmyard, looking for a likely candidate.

Garnet pointed to a red-haired girl directing another girl who was attempting to climb an old poplar tree by the barn. "There she is. Violet's in grade three, but she usually hangs around with Allie and her friends."

"You may have been interested in Chris," Tobey said, ignoring the discussion about the young girls and returning to Garnet's opening line, "but I never was. At least not seriously."

"Really?" Garnet pursed her lips, and when she looked at Libby, devilment flashed in her emerald-colored eyes. "Then it's a pity you missed out on Gibson, as well."

"It's not too late. Why do you think I volunteered to take my niece to this party? Not that Gibson seems at all interested. Do you know he hasn't dated any women since his wife died?"

"Not true," Garnet said. "He went out with a lawyer from Yorkton for a while."

"Really? I hadn't heard about that. Is he still seeing her?"

"I don't think so. I don't think he's seeing anyone right now. Unless..." She raised an eyebrow at Libby, a gesture that Tobey didn't pick up on.

"He hasn't been at any of the town dances, or even at the bar, in ages. Doesn't he ever go out?"

"I haven't seen him around lately, although Mick and I used to socialize with him and Rita quite regularly." Garnet turned to Libby. "We curled together. I don't think Rita enjoyed the sport very

much, but she loved the social activities that went
with it. You know, the potluck dinners and the smok-
ers—not that very many people smoke anymore, but
somehow the name seems to stick.''

Libby wanted to hear more about Rita, but Tobey
commandeered the conversation again. ''So do you
and Mick still curl?''

''Sure. We've partnered up with Darren and
Christy.''

''Darren?'' Libby couldn't stop herself from asking. ''Darren O'Malley?''

''Yes. Do you remember him? He was a few years
older than you, wasn't he? He married a good friend
of mine from high school.''

''Do they live in Yorkton?'' Libby prayed the
other women couldn't see how her heart was pounding. She held her drink down so they wouldn't notice
her trembling fingers.

''No, they stayed on Darren's farm, just south of
Sledgewood. I suppose you remember what an athlete Darren was.''

Libby nodded, feeling a bitter taste fill her mouth.
She remembered, all right.

''Once they were married he kept bragging that he
was going to raise his son to be the next Eric Lindros.
So what happens?''

''Four girls,'' Tobey said, finally demonstrating a
sense of humor. ''Serves the guy right. Always was
a little too cocky if you ask me.''

''Oh, he's not that bad,'' Garnet said, defending
him. ''And he adores those girls.''

Tobey shrugged, then turned to Libby. ''So what

brought you back to Chatsworth? I gather you and Owen have split?"

Libby should have seen the question coming, but she didn't and had no response ready. Thankfully, Garnet came quickly to her rescue.

"And why shouldn't she come back? It's her home, isn't it? I'll bet her father is delighted."

"I don't know if I'd go so far as to say *delighted.*"

Not to be put off, Tobey angled in for another question. "Did you and Owen get married after you ran off like that?"

"Tobey!" Garnet exclaimed, but her disapproval didn't erase the expectant look on Tobey's face as she waited for Libby's answer.

"Well…" Libby cast her eyes about, desperately seeking a way out of this quagmire.

"Excuse me, ladies."

With perfect timing, Gibson stepped between her and Garnet and placed a hand lightly on her shoulder. His touch was casual, but there was something solid and reassuring about it that helped to work the tension out of her body.

Tobey's attention shifted from Libby to Gibson, as Libby was certain he'd expected it to. He gave them all an apologetically charming smile, letting go of Libby's shoulder to hold out his hand. "Sorry to interrupt, but I need help with the barbecue. Got a second, Tobey?"

"Of course I do." A pleased smile spread across her face as she held out her arm to him.

As they walked away Gibson turned back and gave Libby a quick wink, and she smiled in return, a private thank-you for a much-needed rescue. Except not that private, because Garnet had witnessed the entire exchange. She apologized for the other woman.

"Don't pay any attention to Tobey. You remember what she's like."

Libby sure did. Even though she'd hoped people would accept her and Nicole, no questions asked, she'd always known it would never be that simple. There was no concept of minding your own business in a small town, where folks felt their neighbors' affairs were their legitimate concerns.

The truth of the matter was that without Gibson's intervention she'd have been in hot water right now. Either she would have had to tell Tobey a direct lie, or would have had to admit that Owen wasn't Nicole's father. Both options were unacceptable. Yet it was only a matter of time before she'd be forced to make the choice.

Even more dangerous, of course, was the possibility that she would run into Darren one day. She'd hoped he'd moved from the area, but obviously that had been asking too much. Now that she knew he was married and settled in Sledgewood, the chance that their paths would one day cross seemed highly likely. And that she knew she couldn't handle.

Which made her wonder if coming back to Chatsworth was the biggest mistake of her life. And underscored how important it was for her and Nicole to leave as scheduled in the fall.

# CHAPTER EIGHT

TOBEY'S QUESTION about Owen played through Libby's mind over and over the next morning. She told herself not to worry. Even if people guessed Owen wasn't Nicole's father, no one would link her with Darren O'Malley. Garnet hadn't even realized they'd known each other.

After driving the kids to school on the bus, she stopped at the hardware store to pick up a couple of industrial-size pails of paint—pale yellow for the house, barn red for the outbuildings. At home, she changed into an old pair of Chris's work overalls and pulled her ponytail through the back of a baseball cap.

She planned to begin with the house, but it would require a good scraping first to prepare the surface for the new paint. The tools she needed were in the machine shed. She walked over to the shed and got the ladder, then lugged it to the front yard, anticipating the day's hard labor ahead of her.

It was a bright, glorious morning, signaling a day meant to be spent on outdoor pursuits. The sun was warm on her as she settled the ladder against the wall of the house. She thought about her garden, all the seeds tucked into the moistened earth. If the weather stayed this nice, they'd soon be sprouting, just as the crops in the field had begun to do. All the way to town this morning, she'd seen the light dusting of green that signaled successful germination. Soon the grain would be shooting skyward.

She wasn't sure what her father had planted this year. Probably canola in the field next to Gibson's. It would make a fine sight come mid-August when it bloomed brilliant yellow, especially in contrast to the lavender-blue flax Gibson had seeded next to it.

The sound of her scraper dragging along the old wooden boards soon filled her ears. When she paused she could hear the swallows and the robins bickering overhead, and beyond them nothing except the peaceful quiet of a country morning. How nice not to have the incessant drone of city traffic, the high-pitched squealing of air brakes, the inevitable loud music or sounds of arguments from next-door tenants.

*Did you and Owen get married...* The fragile peace of the morning evaporated as Tobey's phrase resurfaced in Libby's consciousness. If it hadn't been for Nicole, it would have been so tempting to blurt out the truth. *Owen and I didn't run off together. After Darren raped me, my father kicked me out of the house.* She would have liked to see the look on Tobey's face then.

But she'd never have that satisfaction, because it was too late for the truth. The proof of what had happened was long gone. The bruises had healed; the torn clothing had been burned.

A few mental scars remained, Libby acknowledged, but it didn't matter much as she'd never dated since. She'd had no time; she'd had no money for sitters. And the few men she'd met in Toronto who'd seemed interested had always left her cold. It didn't help that she knew nothing about them. Her mother hadn't gone to church with their mothers; they couldn't laugh about their funny grade six teacher or reminisce about learning to swim at the local pool.

Those small common interests were what Libby had missed most in the city. Everyone was separate and distinct, and glad to be so. Not her. As a school-girl, she'd liked knowing that she, as well as all her classmates, had been born at the Yorkton Union Hospital. It made her sad that Nicole hadn't been.

Nicole herself asked few questions about her father. She knew he was a boy Libby had once dated. Libby had described him but had never told Nicole his name. One day the whole truth would have to be revealed. But not yet. It had been hard enough for Libby to reconcile her daughter's existence with the brutal assault she'd suffered from Darren O'Malley. How could a seven-year-old child come to grips with such a thing? Nicole didn't even know what the word *rape* meant, for heaven's sake!

Flakes of faded yellow paint rained to the ground as Libby scraped hard and fast. The muscles in her fingers and forearm ached with the constant effort of pushing the metal scraper back and forth over the old wood. She switched hands and thought about the way Gibson had appeared at just the right moment to waylay Tobey's inquisition.

He must have overheard at least part of their conversation. And he must have been curious. After all, Tobey was essentially voicing the same questions he'd been asking ever since Libby had returned. Had he been tempted to remain quiet and listen to her answer? If so, she was glad he'd resisted the urge.

A glance at her watch had Libby panicking. It was well past the family's normal lunch hour. Soon her father would be coming inside for the sandwich she always left on the counter. She dropped the scraper on the ground and ran to the kitchen, where she hurriedly slapped slices of cheese and tomato inside whole-wheat rolls. She was just pouring a glass of water, when the back door opened.

She couldn't see him, but she felt her father's presence behind her. What would he do? Would he finally say something to her?

The moment stretched, and Libby's tension mounted. She stood with her hand poised over the cold-water faucet, the water running uninterrupted into the sink, the empty glass in her other hand. At the kitchen window a horsefly buzzed angrily, throwing his round black body into the clear glass, again and again and again.

Then she heard her father rub his work boots against the bristles of the mat by the door, followed by a series of heavy thuds as he walked past. When he stopped, just a foot or two from where she was standing, she finally turned to face him.

He'd been looking at her, all right, but now he pivoted and disappeared into the bathroom.

Coward! Libby could have screamed, although she

didn't. Would it kill him to speak to her? One little sentence, say, thanking her for the sandwich...

But no. Libby turned back to the sink, filled her glass, then shut off the water. Taking her sandwich with her, she went outside to eat on the steps of the veranda.

GIBSON DISMOUNTED from his horse and tied the reins to the wooden fence that penned in the cow barn and pasture. As he walked past the school bus parked by the side of the house, he saw a tall figure, lean but undeniably female, dressed in paint-splattered denim coveralls and standing on a ladder. Using a roller brush, Libby was applying yellow paint to the wooden siding in long, even strokes.

Damn, she looked good, even dressed like that, maybe especially dressed like that. Gibson had never cared for women dolled up in fancy clothes, primped with makeup and hair spray and smelling like a pull-out from a woman's fashion magazine.

He preferred them like Libby. Whether she had on her old jeans, her cutoff shorts or even these baggy overalls, she always looked perfect. He couldn't even imagine her in city clothes, working in an office, going out to dinner and the theater. Perhaps it was up to him to convince her where she really belonged.

She didn't hear him approach; the sound of the roller drowned out the faint rustle of his footsteps on the grass. His glance settled on the curly brown ponytail that fell from the back opening of her baseball cap. He grinned, thinking of days gone by. What the hell. He reached out one hand.

"Hey!" Libby swiveled on one foot. She almost fell when she saw Gibson right behind her, eyes lit with mischief.

"Couldn't resist," he said, tugging on her ponytail once more, a little harder this time.

"You're lucky I didn't fall," she grumbled, lowering the roller into the tray of paint that she'd balanced on the edge of the porch roof.

"I was kind of hoping you would."

She twisted around again, and found that he had climbed to the rung immediately below her, putting his face just a few inches lower than hers.

"I would have caught you, Libby. You know that, don't you?"

"Don't sound so sure." Lord, if her heart didn't stop pounding so madly, he was going to hear it. Or maybe it was *his* heart she heard—his eyes sparkled with emotions she knew were neither neighborly nor brotherly.

"You're too close," she said.

"Or not close enough?" He'd inched forward so his voice sounded in her ear and his body pressed into hers.

Much, much too close for comfort. She felt a newly familiar warmth steal up her legs and across her stomach to her breasts.

"Let me by, Gib. I'm out of paint."

His gaze remained locked with hers as he removed his arms and slowly backed down the ladder.

She felt the rush of spring air against her body, filling the void where he had once stood, and tried to ignore the cool chill it gave her. Carefully, she backed down the ladder, then felt his arm at her waist as she stepped to solid earth.

She pivoted, and noticed he was dressed in his typical work jeans and plaid shirt. She liked the look—solid and dependable. Libby thought of the game they'd played as kids. Trust. Stand with your back to someone and fall down. Gibson would catch her, every time.

"Did Nicole enjoy herself at the party?"

"She had a wonderful time. And so did I. Although there were moments when I felt I was attending a reunion of Chris's old girlfriends."

Gibson laughed. "Yeah, I guess he did date most of those women, didn't he?"

"What about you?" Libby fixed him with a challenging look. "I don't suppose you dated a few of them yourself."

"Not as many as Chris. Anyway, that was all long ago. I don't think about those days anymore, and I'm sure none of them do, either."

"I wouldn't be so sure about it." Nonchalantly, Libby poured more paint into her tray and started work on the lower portion of the house. Casting a glance over her shoulder, she threw out a name. "Tobey Stedman, for instance. She's still single, isn't she?"

"She's single," he agreed. "Went off to Regina to work for the government for about five years. Got engaged while she was there, but something happened and she moved back home. Now she's working at the library in Yorkton and living in the basement of her sister's house."

He picked up an extra tray, poured in some paint, then climbed the ladder and began to paint where she'd left off.

"She's quite attractive, isn't she?" Libby glided the roller along a wooden board near the ground.

"Mmm, hmm."

She guessed that was agreement. "And she certainly seemed interested in *you*," she added.

"Is this an attempt to pry into my love life?" Gibson looked down at her from his perch on the ladder.

"So you admit you do have a love life?"

"Hell. Think I'd confess if I didn't?"

Libby laughed, then dipped her roller into the tray of paint, ran it up and down the aluminum washboard until the excess liquid was squeezed out, then began to work again. The wet paint gleamed in the sunlight, smooth and colorful. The instant transformation gave her pleasure.

"Thanks for helping me out, Gib, when Tobey had me cornered."

"I guess I'm not the only one who's curious about what happened between you and Owen. Lately I've been wondering if you're keeping quiet to protect his reputation."

That was a laugh. By letting people assume Owen was Nicole's father, she was doing quite the opposite. "Owen and I never got married...." She began to tell him the truth but found she just couldn't finish. "What about you and that lawyer woman from Yorkton? I heard you were pretty serious for a while."

Gibson's laugh was as dry as the clothes she'd taken off the line that morning. "You *did* get around at the party yesterday, didn't you? My God, are they still talking about that? It's been over for almost a year now.''

His light tone didn't fool her. She could see by the tightness of his expression that this had mattered to him. ''What happened?''

Gibson shrugged. ''A lawyer and a farmer don't make much of a mix. At least, not when the lawyer has aspirations of running her own firm and the farmer is looking for someone to share his life, not just intersect it in a couple of places.''

There was a moment's silence, then he said, ''Oh, damn!''

Libby looked up, expecting to see spilled paint. Instead she saw Gibson, his expression accusatory.

''Why do I keep telling you all my darkest secrets?''

She considered. ''I guess because we feel comfortable around each other.''

''Oh, we do, do we?'' His gaze was probing. ''Is it just me, or am I the only one who's been doing the confiding in this relationship?''

Libby stared resolutely at her roller. ''I've told you what I could.''

He expelled his breath like a man who'd been hoping for more. ''You're a hard woman, Libby Bateson. But I guess you've had to be.''

Libby felt a shiver travel down her back at the accuracy of his last statement. It was almost as if he knew. But of course he didn't. She'd told him she'd had money problems, but he couldn't know that their situation had been close to desperate for most of the eight years she'd been gone. He had no idea of the hardships she'd faced, yet he spoke as if he did.

Being with this man was more dangerous than she'd thought.

ONCE SHE'D COMPLETED her afternoon bus route, Libby parked at the side of the house, noticing that Gibson had finished both the front and side walls of the second story. She found the sight nostalgic—it was the house from her childhood, reborn.

"Hey! You started painting!" Nicole said as she raced off the bus. "It looks so much better. Is this the same color it was when you were growing up?"

A gruff voice came from behind the bus. "The house has always been that color. My father and mother put on the first coat of paint the year they were married."

At this time of day her father was usually out in the field. Libby paused, wondering if he would say anything further, but he merely strode past her. She checked out her daughter. Her eyes were big and round, like the centers of a couple of brown-eyed Susans. Nicole's gaze remained riveted on her grandfather until he disappeared inside. Then she turned to her mother. She obviously didn't know what to make of this latest development. Neither did Libby.

They followed Henry Bateson into the house. Behind the closed bathroom door Libby heard the sound of running water. She put out an oat bran muffin and apple for Nicole's after-school snack.

"I'm going to paint until suppertime. I have a lasagna in the oven. After you finish eating you can play, if you want, or you can change into your oldest clothes and come help me.''

Nicole took a bite from the apple. ''My jeans with the holes in the knees?'' she asked around the piece of fruit in her mouth.

Libby ignored the infraction, too focused on the bathroom door. ''Yes. And the T-shirt with the large bleach stain in the middle.''

Nicole nodded. ''Okay.''

Libby ran up the stairs to get back into her overalls. Lord, her father had almost sounded like his old self when he'd made that comment about the paint. Of course, it didn't escape her attention that he'd spoken to Nicole, not to her.

Well, that was fine with her. She was a big girl; she hadn't expected a father-daughter reunion when she'd decided to move back here for a few months. All she'd asked for was a roof over her and Nicole's heads and food on the table.

Libby changed quickly, then slipped out the back to resume painting, leaving Nicole still eating and her father behind the closed bathroom door. She moved the ladder to the other side of the house, then pried open the pail of paint, filled her tray and unwrapped the rollers from the airtight plastic Gibson had placed over them. She was about to climb the ladder, when she heard footsteps from behind.

She turned to face her father for the second time that day. His gaze seemed dismissive as it swept past her to the tray of paint in her hands.

''I'll do the second story,'' he said. ''You paint down here.'' And before she knew it, he was on the ladder, making his way to the top. He moved spryly, belying his aged appearance.

Libby watched him for a moment. He really was a stubborn old coot. At his age, he ought to be the one working on the lower level. But she wasn't going to argue about it. She picked up the other roller and started painting where he'd told her to.

When Nicole joined them fifteen minutes later, Libby handed her a brush and demonstrated the appropriate technique for spreading the paint into the crevices between each of the boards. "See how you make out with that. Then, when you get tired, you can try rolling for a while."

"Okay."

At five o'clock Libby went into the house to check on the lasagna. When she came back outside she could see that Nicole was lagging.

"Why don't you take a break, sweetie."

"No, I want to keep helping." Determined, Nicole increased her pace. After a few minutes she said, with studied casualness, "Lots of the kids at school are going to take swimming lessons at the pool this summer."

Libby smiled, remembering. "I used to teach at that pool, Nicole. And lifeguard. We had a lot of fun." Her eyes narrowed on her paint-splattered daughter, who was suddenly working so diligently. "I suppose we should really enroll you in lessons, too. Would you like that?"

"Oh, yes!" Then, more slowly, Nicole added, "But are you sure we can afford it? I'll have to get a bathing suit...."

Libby slid her roller over the next board and watched the yellow spread. In her mind she was doing the calculations, hating herself for begrudging the money. She only had one more month of work before school would be out for the summer. Still, Nicole almost never asked for anything. And swimming lessons were practically a necessity.

"I'm sure we can." She smiled at the glee that infused her daughter's face. "The lasagna should be ready by now. Why don't you put down that brush and go clean up."

Libby wrapped her roller and Nicole's brush in plastic, then went around the corner to where her father was still laboring away on the top rung of the ladder. He must have known she was there, but he didn't acknowledge her in any way.

She turned to leave, then changed her mind. "Coming in for dinner, Dad?" Her heart hammered as she asked the question. If he said yes, everything would change.

But he just grunted and shook his head.

She should have known better.

LIBBY SAT on her lawn chair near the centerline with all the other parents. She was here to see Nicole play soccer, but she kept training her gaze on the coach, instead.

Gibson was such a natural athlete. He'd been a pleasure to watch on the ice as a teenager. But Libby thought he was even more arresting over a decade later on the soccer field. His legs were tanned and muscular; his blond hair kept flying in his eyes, thanks to the wind. Certain men were made for the outdoors and for activity, and Gibson definitely was. She observed as he shouted words of encouragement and advice to the girls, occasionally brushing his hair back with a casual gesture.

Lord, she hadn't had a crush like this since... Her mind shied at the remembrance and the comparison. Truth was, she'd barely known Darren; his reputation as an athlete and his popularity among her peers had lured her. Of course, her loneliness hadn't helped. She'd been used to a warm, loving family. Naively, she'd sought that same affection in a relationship with Darren. With tragic results.

At least now she had her daughter, so maybe her mother was right after all. Nicole was the silver lining that had made all Libby's troubles worth enduring. Libby placed her feet on the lid of the cooler she'd brought from home, resting elbows on knees and cupping her chin in her hands. She caught sight of a familiar pair of pigtails streaking past centerline.

"Go, Nicole!" she called along with the rest of the spectators as her daughter made yet another breakaway toward the opponents' goal. Confidently Nicole zigzagged her way to her third goal of the game.

The ball was no sooner past the goalie than the whistle blew. "Halftime!"

Libby removed the cooler lid and soon hands were flying as she passed out fresh fruit and cold drinks to the team members. Nicole waited until the end.

"Did you see my goals?" she asked proudly.

"I sure did, sweetie. Both of them."

"What...?"

"Just kidding." Libby smiled and pulled on one of Nicole's pigtails. "I saw the third one, too."

Nicole grinned and grabbed a crescent of cantaloupe. "I'm going to practice."

Libby shook her head in wonder. "Don't you ever need to rest?"

Nicole shook her head, already maneuvering the ball toward some of the other players. "Could you give us a drill to work on, Coach?"

Gibson had been walking toward Libby, looking as if he'd be glad of a break, but he didn't hesitate. "Sure, Nicole." He yelled to the rest of the players, "Anyone else interested in running through a few drills?"

Some of the other kids came forward; Allie joined unenthusiastically, at her father's urging. Gibson asked one girl to play goal; the others lined up for a turn to take a shot. The exercise had been going on for a few minutes, when Libby noticed that every time Allie finished she would butt in front of Nicole instead of queuing up at the end of the line. At first Nicole didn't object, but after it had happened several times, she began to urge Allie to the end of the line.

Soon the girls were tussling, with Nicole finally caving in, shrugging and letting Allie in front of her. Gibson, his back to Allie and Nicole as he concentrated on helping the players make their shot on net, didn't notice what was going on. Libby found it increasingly difficult to sit on the sideline without saying anything. At the same time, she didn't want to interfere. Nicole would probably be mortified if she tried.

"Not a big deal, Libby," she muttered. "Just forget it."

During the second half of the game Libby kept her attention on Allie, instead of her father. When Nicole scored her fourth goal, she saw Allie's shoulders sink. She also noted that whenever Allie got possession of the ball, she never passed to Nicole, even if Nicole was the only player open. Once it looked as though Allie was going to get a good shot at the goal, but just as she was swinging her leg back, an opponent sneaked in to steal the ball away. When Allie almost cried with frustration, Gibson walked up and patted her on the back.

Chatsworth ended up winning, five to two, and several of the parents made a point of congratulating Nicole on a game well played. Libby saw Allie's bottom lip become shakier and shakier with each compliment Nicole received. However, when Gibson suggested they stop at the café in town for an ice cream before heading home, Allie's pout turned to a smile.

They drove the few blocks to Main Street and settled into one of the brown-vinyl booths near the window.

"Let's sit on this side," Allie said, rushing ahead of the adults to claim her seat. "Come on, Nicole. What are you going to order? Let's each get something different, then share, so we can have more than one flavor."

Libby slid in across from the girls and Gibson sat

down after her. The small bench caused Gibson to sit so close that his shoulder touched hers, but Libby's attention was still focused on the girls. She was bemused by Allie's sudden change in attitude toward Nicole. The two girls were now laughing and talking like the best of friends she'd assumed them to be, the differences from the soccer field obviously forgotten.

Well, almost forgotten. Nicole had a wary expression, as if she, too, was wondering why the sudden switch in Allie's mood.

"Still like strawberry?"

"What?" Gibson was looking at her, his blond hair wind tousled, his cheeks still ruddy from exercise and fresh air. He was smiling, and there was a warmth in his eyes that set her stomach to fluttering.

"Still like strawberry ice cream?" he repeated. "I remember your mother trying to dig out all the pink from the neapolitan ice cream for you, and all the chocolate for Chris and me."

"I wonder why Mom didn't make it easier on herself and buy three kinds of ice cream. She and Dad always wanted vanilla."

The waitress, Donna Werner, who owned and operated the small-town café with her husband, stopped at their table. Donna was a tall, strong woman in her fifties, with blond-gray hair pulled into a bun and a stern demeanor.

"Heard you were back, Libby. This your little girl?" She nodded at Nicole.

"Yes. Nicole, say hello to Mrs. Werner."

Nicole smiled shyly.

"Same coloring, but prettier than your momma, aren't you?"

Nicole's face reddened.

"Suppose you're in here for ice cream," Donna said. "What'll it be, girls?"

"Bubble gum," said Allie.

"Chocolate, please" said Nicole, after consulting Allie with her eyes.

"I'll have chocolate, too," said Gibson, "And Libby will have..."

"Strawberry." She hated to confirm his guess. "In a dish rather than a cone, please."

After Donna had left, Gibson leaned closer to her and touched her cheek softly with one finger. "The things I know about you."

"And the things you don't," she retorted, too quickly.

"Isn't that the truth."

She shifted her gaze to the window, wondering why she'd had to remind him of all the secrets she was keeping from him and everyone else in Chatsworth. When Donna had made that comment about Nicole's appearance, her heart had almost stopped for fear that Donna would ask about Nicole's father. Thank God she hadn't.

Absentmindedly, Libby scratched off a blotch of red paint on her knuckle, which she'd missed when she'd done her washup. She'd been working on the barn this week, and with her father helping in the evenings and Gibson having stopped by a couple of afternoons, she was almost finished.

Gibson's assistance was definitely a mixed blessing. This attraction between them was mounting, and she knew that was dangerous. But she appreciated his generosity. What with the scraping and the need for at least two coats—three on some of the southern exposures—the job would have taken forever on her own.

"Don't you ever get tired keeping everything locked so tight inside yourself?" Gibson's voice was so low she could barely hear him. The girls, singing while playing a two-person clapping game, couldn't have been more oblivious.

He was so right. Keeping her worries to herself *was* a strain. She was constantly afraid of accidentally meeting Darren when she was in Yorkton stocking up on supplies, or at the gas station refueling the school bus. Was his resemblance to her daughter as obvious as she imagined? If it was, what would she do if he guessed the truth?

"I'm scared, Gib," she admitted.

"You don't have to be, Libby. I'm here. I can help."

"Not with this." No one could, and that was why there was no point in telling Gibson. He might not believe her anyway. Even Garnet seemed to think Darren was a good father and husband. Given his past history as the local hockey hero, who'd ever believe he'd raped Libby Bateson? Poor Libby, who'd never even finished high school but had gotten pregnant and had to leave town...

Gibson reached for her left hand. "Here, you missed some." Gently he worked his fingernail under a speck of the dried red paint, scaling it from her skin. His hands were rough from work, large and warm, yet his touch was soft. She remembered how those hands had felt on her face, running down her shoulders and the length of her back. She looked at his chest, broad and muscular, and remembered the strength she'd felt when he'd held her close.

But that kiss had happened weeks ago, and she couldn't risk a repeat experience.

She pulled away her hand. "Here comes Donna."

The waitress passed out their orders, then set a pitcher of ice water and glasses on the table before turning to some newcomers. Allie and Nicole asked for permission to eat their cones on the bench in front of the café, and both Gibson and Libby assented.

With the girls gone, so was her buffer zone. Libby decided it was time to draw the conversation away from herself. "I remember when you were a teen-ager, you were offered the chance to play junior hockey for the Melville Millionaires. Why did you turn it down? Most guys your age would have killed for that opportunity." Even Darren O'Malley hadn't been that good.

"I was happy living in Chatsworth and Dad needed me on the farm. Playing professional hockey was never a dream of mine."

"Chris felt guilty about your decision. As if he'd pressured you not to go."

"I would've missed his friendship, too," Gibson admitted. "I've always thought I was lucky to know what I wanted from life from such an early age. Not everyone would see it that way, I'm sure. Besides, I really don't think I could have gone the distance."

"Oh, I'm not so sure about that. I used to watch you guys, remember?" She'd gone along to most of her brother and Gibson's games, met her friends at the rink, bought herself a cocoa and hot dog at the concession stand. Those had been happy days.

"Your Nicole is quite a little athlete, too."

"It's so good to see her excel at something. I think it's giving her a confidence that she's never had before."

"Life hasn't been easy for her, has it?" Somehow he was holding her hands again. "Or for you, either."

That question again—how could he know how difficult their lives had been? Pride stiffened Libby's shoulders. She didn't want him, or anyone else, to know the role that welfare, food banks and thrift shops had played in her and Nicole's lives. Not that she was ashamed. But she didn't want him feeling sorry for her.

"Why won't you talk about those days, Libby? You were so open when you were a little girl. Sometimes it's hard to believe you're the same person."

His assessment was apt. Libby didn't feel like the same person who'd grown up in the comfort and security of her parents' home. So much had changed— was it any surprise that she had, too?

Gibson's hold on her hands tightened. "Did Owen hang around at all after Nicole was born?"

Finally. The question she'd dreaded. Libby stared down at the table as if suddenly captivated by the patterns in the flecked Formica. She tried to pull her hands away, but he held firm.

"You never did run off with Owen, did you? And Owen isn't Nicole's father, is he?"

# CHAPTER NINE

LIBBY WASN'T SURPRISED that Gibson had figured out the truth. But now she was trapped. Physically and otherwise. Her back to the wall, Gibson in front of her, holding her hands, pinning her down with his eyes as well as his words. She wanted to flee and hide so she wouldn't have to lie. But there was nowhere to go.

At last she had to look at him. "I never said I ran off with Owen," she pointed out. "That was just what everyone assumed. I let people believe what they wanted to."

"You don't buy that excuse any more than I do," he said bluntly.

She couldn't meet his gaze without admitting he was right. "I know. I should have set things straight from the beginning. But it was hard. The worst thing about coming back to Chatsworth was having to face people who would want explanations about where I had been, who Nicole's father was, all that. When you told me Owen's family had left town, it seemed like a heaven-sent opportunity."

"And of course the truth would never have done."

She hated the hard edge to his voice. He was judging her again, before he'd heard her side of the story.

# PLAY "LUCKY 7" AND GET
# THREE FREE GIFTS!

## HOW TO PLAY:

1. With a coin, carefully scratch off the silver box at the right. Then check the claim char
see what we have for you — **2 FREE BOOKS** and a gift — **ALL YOURS! ALL FREE!**

2. Send back this card and you'll receive two brand-new Harlequin Superromance® nov
These books have a cover price of $4.50 each in the U.S. and $5.25 each in Canada,
they are yours to keep absolutely free.

3. There's no catch. You're ur
no obligation to buy anything.
charge nothing — ZERO —
your first shipment. And you d
have to make any minimum num
of purchases — not even one!

4. The fact is thousands of readers enjoy receiving their books by mail from the Harleo
Reader Service®. They enjoy the convenience of home delivery...they like getting the r
new novels at discount prices, BEFORE they're available in stores...and they love their *H
to Heart* newsletter featuring author news, horoscopes, recipes, book reviews and much m

5. We hope that after receiving your free books you'll want to remain a subscriber.
the choice is yours — to continue or cancel, any time at all! So why not take us up on
invitation, with no risk of any kind. You'll be glad you did!

## YOURS FREE!

### PLAY LUCKY 7 FOR THIS EXCITING FREE GIFT!

*THIS SURPRISE*
*MYSTERY GIFT*
*COULD BE*
*YOURS FREE WHEN*
*YOU PLAY*

# LUCKY 7!

Visit us online at
www.eHarlequin.com

butter when she heard feet tearing down the stairs. A second later Nicole burst into the room.

"Mom! Thank you, thank you, thank you!" She held a bathing suit in each hand—one a flowery, frilly affair, the other sunshine yellow with a practical racer back for swimming.

Libby wiped her hands on a nearby tea towel and knelt to accept Nicole's ambush-style hug. "Wait a minute, sweetie."

But Nicole didn't seem to hear her. "And you registered me for the lessons—" she lifted a pink carbon copy of the form "—and bought me goggles and a new towel!"

"I did?" Libby held her daughter at arm's length. "What are you talking about?"

Nicole's smile slipped a notch. "I found everything on my bed, with my swimsuits."

"On the bed?"

Nicole nodded. "Why are you acting so funny? Are you just pretending to make it more of a surprise?"

It was unbelievable. Preposterous. But there was no other explanation. Libby remembered the conversation she'd had with Nicole. He *had* been on the other side of the house at the time, so conceivably he'd overheard Nicole's request.

"Nicole, I didn't register you in swimming, or buy those suits or the goggles or the towel."

"But then—"

Libby pressed a finger to her daughter's lips. "I think your grandfather must have."

"Grandpa? Really?"

"Yes. He must have overheard you asking me if you could take lessons."

"Wow!" Nicole's eyes rounded. "He must like me, at least a little, after all."

"Of course he likes you!" Libby's protective instincts came out full force. "I told you he was angry at *me,* not *you.* The problem is, he's never had a chance to get to know you. Maybe now he's ready."

Nicole mulled that over. "I'm going to sit by the gate and wait for him to come in from the field so I can thank him."

"I think he'd like that."

After Nicole ran outside, Libby turned back to the bowl in front of her; automatically she sifted the dried ingredients before adding them to the liquid mixture. Somehow she couldn't imagine her father actually going to the community center to pay for the lessons, then driving into Yorkton—there was no store in Chatsworth that would carry such a variety of swimming supplies—to go shopping.

If he'd just felt sorry for Nicole, if he'd acted out of obligation, he could have given her the money. To have planned it all out as a wonderful surprise— that implied a whole different set of emotions.

The lines on the recipe card blurred. Libby gripped the edge of the counter. Why did she feel this ridiculous certainty that he'd stood in front of the rack of children's bathing suits a long, long time, anxious to make just the right selections? She could almost hear the insecurity in his voice as he'd asked the sales-clerk for help with sizes.

Libby wiped her eyes with the back of her hand,

angry with herself for breaking down. Maybe this was the start of something really positive in Nicole's life. It would be good for Nicole to have a real relationship with her grandfather.

As for Libby's relationship with her father, she wasn't holding her breath. She had a feeling there would be no new goodies on *her* bed when she went upstairs.

After filling the watering can, she went to the living room to water the few new houseplants she'd started from slips Connie Browning had given her. From the vantage point of the front bow window Libby could see Nicole sitting high on the fence by the gate, waiting. Libby hoped that her daughter's efforts wouldn't be ignored or, even worse, spurned.

Quickly she went back to the kitchen to put together a shepherd's pie with some leftover roast beef, but she found herself continually drawn back to that front window, her anxiety growing as the time for her father to return from the fields drew near. After rinsing the lettuce, she picked up a rag and went into the living room yet again. She was dusting the top of the television set when she heard the distant rumble of the tractor. Moments later it came into view. She stood watching, dust rag in one hand, her other hand to her mouth.

Her father parked the tractor by the fuel tanks as always, then jumped out of the cab and headed for the gate. Nicole was standing on the second rung of the wooden fence. She waved as her grandfather walked closer. Libby half expected the man to look away or even turn in another direction.

But he didn't. He stopped right by Nicole. Rubbed his grimy face with one hand, then actually seemed to be answering her. When he held out one hand, Nicole took it, then jumped down from her perch to the solid ground below.

They remained like that for a few moments, hands locked, gray head bent low, small child looking up. Then her father brushed his hand over the top of Nicole's head and started for the barn to feed the cattle, Nicole trotting at his side.

NICOLE SWUNG HER ARMS in ever-widening circles, so excited she felt ready to burst. She took off down the soccer field as fast as she could, then veered at the goal post and ran in the opposite direction. The cleats on her new running shoes gave her so much traction—there would be no stopping her now!

The shoes were another gift from her grandpa—they'd gone into Yorkton together to pick them out. She'd asked him to come watch her play that night, and he said he would one day, but not yet. The time wasn't right, he'd said. Whatever that meant.

"Hey, Nicole! Maybe you should save some of that energy for the game!" Gibson called to her from the sideline. But he was smiling, so she knew he didn't really want her to stop. Allie was next to him, clutching his hand and trying to convince him that her stomach hurt too much for her to play tonight.

Nicole knew Allie's stomach didn't really hurt. She was just trying to get out of playing soccer. Nicole tore past the two of them, running full speed across the field. It felt so great to focus all her energy on the game ahead of them. Lately things had been awful at school. Thanks to Allie, who'd gone from best friend to worst enemy.

And Nicole still didn't know why. She'd tried to talk to Allie a couple of times, but each time Allie had ignored her, just the way her grandpa used to do.

Tonight, though, none of that mattered. When she was playing soccer there was no time to think of anything else. She reversed directions and jogged back to Gibson. Ignoring Allie, she asked, "Who do we play?"

"Sledgewood," he answered. "I hear they've got a good team this year. That must be them now." He pointed to the side street, where two minivans and a truck had just pulled up beside the field.

No sooner had the vehicles stopped than girls wearing matching orange T-shirts began spilling from the doors. Thirteen players, Nicole noted, as she checked them over carefully, trying to guess which ones were going to give her the most trouble. Last out were the grown-ups. Two mothers and a man, who was obviously the coach since he was wearing an orange T-shirt, too, and had a whistle tied around his neck.

The coach turned back to the van and out jumped one last girl. She was smaller than the rest, but obviously pumped about the game. She dashed out on the field with a confident stride and was soon jostling a teammate for possession of the ball.

Meanwhile, the coach grabbed his team's goal

posts from the back of the van and strolled toward Nicole and Gibson.

"Nice night to play soccer, isn't it?" he said.

"Sure is," Gibson replied.

Nicole turned away impatiently. As far as she was concerned, every night was a great night to play soccer. Seeing a stray ball, she raced for it and gave it a good whack. When would the game start? She was more than ready.

LIBBY WATCHED in shock as Darren O'Malley walked toward the soccer field. Eight years hadn't changed him much. His sandy hair had receded slightly and he had thickened a bit around the middle, but what she really noticed were certain attributes that reminded her of Nicole—the shape of his face, his pointed chin.

He would be twenty-eight now, she calculated, and if he had a child on the team, he must have gotten married and had children shortly after she'd left town.

Libby searched out Nicole, and for a moment felt as if her heart had stopped when she saw her little girl standing still on the field, staring at Darren with mild interest in her expression. Libby felt a sudden fear—that somehow the two of them would look at each other and immediately know what she had tried so hard to keep hidden. But the next second Nicole turned away and began playing with a couple of the girls on her team. Libby let out a long, shaky breath.

It had been bound to happen, and Libby had tried to steel herself for the eventuality, but the soccer field was the last place she'd expected to run into him. It shouldn't have been. After all, Darren had always loved sports and excelled at playing them.

He was talking to Gibson, a clipboard in one hand and a pen in the other. She noted he was left-handed. So was Nicole.

Even as Libby made an effort to focus on the field where the girls were playing, in her mind she saw him as he'd been eight years ago. She could remember every last detail of the hockey jacket he'd always worn. It had been a great source of pride to him, especially the red letter C embroidered on the back of it, which identified him as team captain.

Her friends had been so envious. Darren's image had completely deceived them, but Libby couldn't fault them for that, because no one had been more deceived than she.

Hoping her sunglasses would be a shield, she turned her back on him, wondering if he would remember her and what had happened that night. He'd been so drunk. She'd had to wait until he'd passed out before she could slip on her torn clothes and walk home. Thank goodness there wasn't much traffic on the country roads at four in the morning. She would have made quite a sight.

"Libby Bateson?" Although she was standing some distance away, his voice carried easily. She hunched her shoulders against the sound.

"Is it really you, Libby?"

Guarding her expression, she faced him and smiled frostily, hoping he would get the hint and leave her be. He didn't.

"When did you come back to town?"

Gibson was watching, slightly curious. He'd been polite since their conversation in the café last week. But distant, too.

"I moved in with my father in May." She avoided eye contact by fiddling with the hem of her shirt. "I'm driving the school bus and my daughter, Nicole, is going to school here in Chatsworth." Her voice barely tripped over the name of her daughter and she was glad the sunglasses hid her eyes from his gaze.

"I didn't recognize you at first. You used to wear your hair short, right?" He moved in on her, his expression one of concentration as he struggled with old memories, trying to pinpoint the way things had left off between them.

So Darren *didn't* remember. That was a relief. She hoped he never would. Nothing could be done to right the wrong between them. All she wanted now was to live in peace.

Still, she was unprepared for the emotion she felt at seeing him again. She hated to look at him, hated the sound of his voice. The temptation was to run away, but she knew that would only raise questions. In his mind and in the minds of those around them. Like Gibson.

No, she had to act normally. And pray the sight of her wouldn't bring back memories of that night for him. She couldn't bear his knowing he was Nicole's father, any more than she wanted anyone else to know.

Darren addressed Gibson. "It's always nice when

the pretty ones move back. It doesn't usually work that way, does it, old boy?'' He clapped Gibson on the shoulder, seemingly not noticing that the other man wasn't sharing in the fun.

Darren glanced out on the field. ''Which one is your daughter? What did you say her name was— Nicole?''

After a moment's pause, Gibson answered. ''The one carrying the ball.'' His voice was low and steady, but Libby heard the hint of a question behind it. She ducked her head, not wanting him to see her. Even with her sunglasses on, she was afraid he would read too much from her face.

''She's good,'' Darren said, watching Nicole work her way past two girls before landing a solid kick past the goalie.

''Thanks. What about you? Do you have any kids?'' Libby needed the conversation diverted from Nicole. Fast.

''Yeah. That little one out there is my Ivy. She's younger than the other girls, but we put her in this division because she plays so good.'' The open pride in his voice was almost laughable. Libby wasn't in any mood to be amused, though.

Ivy *was* tiny relative to the other girls on the field; however, it only took a few moments of observation for Libby to realize Darren wasn't exaggerating her abilities. The sprightly girl knew just how to move the ball down the field, and Libby held her breath as Nicole stepped forward to challenge her.

The confrontation was quick, and Nicole emerged with the ball.

"Sh—" Darren choked off a curse as Ivy whirled around and came at Nicole from behind.

Libby couldn't stop herself from doing a quick comparison between the two girls, and was thankful that their differences in coloring made any other similarity too vague to be noticeable.

"I've got three other girls at home," Darren said proudly. "A three-year-old and one-year-old twins. Imagine I'll be doing the soccer circuit for a good many years to come." He didn't look as though he minded one bit. "Well, I'd better get the team organized. Start the game in about five?"

Gibson nodded. "Sounds fine." Once Darren had gone he lowered his voice and turned to Libby. "I didn't realize you knew Darren. He was a few years ahead of you in school, wasn't he?"

Libby swallowed, staring resolutely in the direction of the soccer field, hoping Gibson would think she was concentrating on Nicole. "My friends and I used to watch him play hockey. I think I may have seen him at some of the after-game parties."

"That's it?"

She nodded.

"Like hell it is."

A few seconds ticked by with neither saying a word. Finally, Gibson blasted the whistle right next to her ear.

"Let's play soccer!"

## CHAPTER TEN

AT HALFTIME the Chatsworth team was ahead four goals to three and Nicole had scored all but one of her team's points.

"These new cleats are fabulous, Mom!" she said, dancing excitedly from side to side.

"You look great out there, sweetie. Your grandfather is spoiling you."

Nicole's smile vanished. "Do you really think so?"

"No. Of course not." Libby put a reassuring arm around her daughter. "I was just teasing. It's wonderful that he's taking an interest. Lately he hasn't seemed such a bear—have you noticed?"

The growing relationship with her grandfather was good for Nicole, too. Of course their home situation would be even better if Libby and her dad were now speaking to each other, but unfortunately her father's turnaround had not extended quite that far.

"I like Grandpa," Nicole asserted. "I wish he would eat with us in the kitchen...." Her voice faded as her gaze fell on the other team, who were gathered round their coach. "Why does that man keep staring at me?"

Dread pressed in against Libby's chest. She didn't

have to ask to know who Nicole was speaking about. "He's probably impressed with how well you play the game." She felt a cold breeze down the back of her neck. "I think I'll get my sweater out of the truck. Would you like your jacket?"

"Are you kidding? I'm *sweating!*" Nicole rubbed the moisture from her brow as proof and Libby laughed.

"So you are." Leaving Nicole to dig into another orange slice, she went to Gibson's truck, knowing it wouldn't be locked. Just as she was throwing her blue cardigan over her shoulders, she heard footsteps behind her. Of course they belonged to Darren.

"Libby." Darren rested one hand on the cab of the truck and leaned in close just as she stepped back. "Hey, I didn't mean to scare you. I just want to talk."

"We don't have anything to talk about." She kept her voice quiet and low, wishing she could tell him to get lost but not wanting to attract any attention.

"I guess I can't blame you for that. I recall that we went out a few times. My memory's not really clear on the details...I dated a lot of girls and did a fair amount of drinking in those days, as you probably know. Anyway, it sort of occurred to me, based on the way you were acting, that I may have been out of line that last time..."

"Out of line," Libby repeated bitterly. People went to jail for what he had done to her, but if he honestly didn't remember what had happened, they would all be better off. "I guess you could say that."

She started to head back to the field, but he grabbed her arm.

"Wait a minute, Libby. I just wanted to apologize to you, that's all."

She shook herself free, hating the way his fingers gripped her flesh. "Don't touch me, okay?"

"Come on, Libby. We had some fun together, right? Maybe things went a little too far one night. Maybe I pushed a little harder than I should have...."

He scrutinized her face. Libby knew he was searching for a clue to which it had been. God help her, she wasn't going to let her face reveal a thing.

"...but you can't tell me that you didn't—"

Libby stepped onto his foot. Hard. She put her mouth close to his ear and said through clenched teeth, "I hope you weren't planning on telling me that I *enjoyed* it, O'Malley. And for the record, there was nothing between us that I could have enjoyed. Got it?"

She saw confusion mingle with surprise on his face and felt a lash of satisfaction. Without meaning to, she'd given him the impression that he had somehow failed to perform.

"I had my pick of girls, you know? And not one of them has ever complained...."

"That's just great, Darren. I'm so pleased for you." She was about to walk away, when he grabbed anew. This time her shoulder.

"Wait, Libby. I don't want to leave hard feelings between us. I know I'm not from Chatsworth, but this is a tight community. We're bound to run into each other again. Whatever happened between us is in the past. Can't we let bygones be bygones?''

Uncertainty edged his words. Obviously he was frustrated that he couldn't remember exactly what *had* happened.

She steadied her voice. ''I told you not to touch me and I'm not interested in making friends. All I ask is that you leave me alone, okay? No pretending we're long-lost buddies or anything like that. Just leave me alone.''

''But you don't understand—''

Libby tried to twist away from his grasp, but he was holding tight.

''I think Libby asked to be left alone.'' Gibson's voice, laden with suppressed anger, came from behind her. He moved in close until she could feel his shoulder, solid and dependable, at her side. Then he pushed Darren's hands off her.

''Come on, Gibson. I wasn't doing any harm.'' But Darren backed away nonetheless and returned to the playing field, where his daughter was looking for him.

Libby found herself tucked underneath Gibson's arm. It was so tempting to accept the support he offered. Yet she didn't dare. She let out a long, trembling sigh and prayed she wasn't going to do anything ridiculous, like cry.

''You didn't have to intercede,'' she said.

''He was bothering you, wasn't he?''

Libby stepped out from his protection. ''Yes,'' she admitted, pretending to focus on the buttons of her sweater. ''But I had the situation under control.'' She looked up, to find his eyes steady on hers. "The last thing I was after was creating a scene."

She felt bad the minute she spoke the words. He'd come to her aid; he'd been trying to help. And all she could do was criticize. Now she saw the way he seemed to have shut down.

"Wouldn't want to have people talking about you, would you, Libby?"

"Give it a rest, okay? You may not care about gossip, but I've got Nicole to think about." As soon as the words were out, she knew she'd made a mistake.

Gibson zeroed in quickly. "He's her father, isn't he?"

Libby yearned to deny it. But how could she lie when his face was just inches from hers, his eyes so close she could see the flecks of pale gray hiding in the midst of all that blue. Instead, she shut her eyes, wishing that she'd stayed home this game.

"We have to talk about this," Gibson said, his body pressing ever closer. She felt her temperature rise, making her sweater superfluous.

"But not now," he added. "The game is going to start any second. Meet me tonight. At the old tree house."

On the border between their properties, Chris and Gibson had built it out of scrap lumber when they were thirteen. She'd been five, and her feelings were sorely hurt when they insisted that no girls would ever be allowed inside.

"I don't know...."

"You remember where it is, don't you?"

"Well, sure I do." Once the boys had grown older and forgotten about their hideout, she'd claimed it as her own, taking her pets out for picnics and inventing all sorts of adventures and subterfuges for them.

"I'll be waiting. At midnight."

God, the witching hour. "I can't." Libby said, but he'd already turned and didn't hear her.

LIBBY EDGED OUT the kitchen door, into a night that someone used to living in a city could never comprehend. She stood still for a moment, waiting for her eyes to adjust, reluctant to use the flashlight she held in her left hand. The heavens above her sparkled in the clear air. A half moon sliced through the blackness, brighter than all the stars.

She could smell the evening-scented stock that she'd planted by the kitchen window, a sweet, seductive fragrance full of promise. Cautiously Libby stepped forward and headed for the field she would have to cross to reach the tree house. When she got to the fence she stopped and turned back.

The house was dark; she'd turned off the yard light before venturing out. Nicole had fallen asleep shortly before nine. Her father had shut off the television and gone to bed about an hour later. Now it was midnight, and they would both have been asleep for hours.

Hours filled with possibilities.

Libby grasped the rough wood railing in her hands, pressing her palms deep against the weathered spruce. She stared out across fields that were slowly becoming visible under the glow of the moon and stars.

She didn't have to come. She'd hadn't made any promises. For all she knew, he wouldn't even show up.

*Oh, yes, he would.* Funny how sure she was about that.

Around her the vast space of the prairie seemed to mirror the emptiness that she felt deep in her heart and soul. She'd been alone for so long now she yearned for someone. Arms to hold her tight. A face to turn to in the night. Comforts she'd never really had, never even allowed herself to dream of having.

Maybe one day she would find love, but it couldn't be here in Chatsworth. These feelings she had for Gibson, these tantalizing, contradictory, confusing feelings, could only lead her astray. After seeing Darren tonight, the need for her and Nicole to leave had never been stronger.

Yet when she looked into Gibson's eyes, the compulsion to stay seemed almost as strong.

Off in the distance she heard the eerie noise of a coyote yip-yipping his secret messages across the prairie. Seconds later came an answering call. The sounds didn't frighten her; they were as familiar as the tractor starting on a cold winter morning, or the cows complaining as they were led in from far pastures to the milking barn.

She threw a jeans-clad leg over the fence. The other followed. Then she jumped to the ground, the thud resonating in the clear night air. Instinct propelled her forward; she wasn't moving of her own free will anymore. Because only a fool would consciously decide to do what she was about to.

Gibson had said he wanted to talk, but she already knew there wasn't anything more she could tell him. And so there was no point to this meeting.

Yet she couldn't turn back.

She'd tried to convince herself otherwise during the long ride home from the game, then later, when she was sitting at the kitchen table, attempting to concentrate on math questions.

If two people were moving toward each other, at the same speed and at the same time, headed for the same place... If one was a man and the other a woman...

She was in front of the tree house before she knew it. And there he was, sitting above her, his feet hanging off the wooden platform. His fair hair gleamed in the moonlight; the rest of him was revealed in varying shades of gray shadow.

"Need help up?" His voice was husky, as raw as the rope she felt in her hands.

"No." She planted her grip above one of the evenly spaced knots, then jumped, her feet finding purchase against a lower knot. Slowly she worked her way upward, enjoying the exertion and the sensation of swaying in the night air.

He was there when she reached the top; pulled her up; helped her find her balance. It seemed only natural to rest her hands on his chest—like solid bedrock, it was there for her to lean on. Moments passed with neither speaking. Libby was glad for the comforting cloak of darkness.

When he finally dropped his hands from her shoulders, she brushed her own against her jeans and began to pace the length of the old structure. Half the fort was covered with a makeshift wooden roof. The other half, where they were standing now, was open to the sky. She tilted her head and searched out the familiar Big Dipper. The northern lights were dull tonight—just a vague glow against the far horizon.

"I was right in what I said, wasn't I?" Gibson asked. "Darren is Nicole's father."

"And if he is? Why do you care? It has nothing to do with you."

"No. But it has something to do with *you*. Libby, my God, you must realize how I feel...." He put his hands on either side of her face, twining his fingers through her hair.

Libby forgot about the stars and focused on the man. She was already halfway to falling in love with him.

"I dream about you every night. I've been alone since Rita died, never thought it would be any different. But then you came back and now...now, I just want to know you. To understand you."

"You watched me grow up. You know me, Gibson." The way no other man ever could. His connection to her family, to her past, only made her want him all the more.

"I *knew* you. But you've changed. Tell me, Libby. What happened to make you so afraid?"

The description was disconcertingly accurate. But she couldn't confess to Gibson about that night with Darren. If he didn't believe her, it would kill her.

And if he did— He'd want to beat the man to a pulp. Soon the truth would be out, and Nicole could never live under a shadow like that. And what about Darren's wife and kids?

As far as she could tell, Darren had turned out respectably enough. A good father, a contributing member of the community. Maybe she wished he'd suffered, at least a little, for the pain he'd caused her. But she didn't bear the same grudge against his family. And they would be the real ones to suffer if his past was exposed.

"You know Darren is Nicole's father. Can't that be enough?"

He lowered his head and angled it to one side. "It'll have to be. Because I can't wait any longer to kiss you."

Yes! She closed her eyes, expecting the same sweet pressure she'd felt the first time. Instead, his mouth came down hard and demanding. Her first instinct was to pull back.

"I'm sorry, sweetheart. Was I too rough?" Gibson was immediately contrite. He lulled her back into his arms with a warm hug, followed by light touches from his lips on the top of her head.

Libby could tell right away that she'd overreacted. Gibson wasn't Darren. He wasn't headed anywhere she didn't want to go. Slowly, she tilted her head back, letting him know that his touch was okay.

His mouth came down softer, and this time she sought to deepen their kisses, opening her mouth wide, teasing his tongue with hers. She tasted a hint of coffee and sweet brandy as he inched open the valve on his passion.

Then his mouth left hers, seeking the hollow at her collarbone. She tilted her head back and the weight of her hair fell behind her. She felt him grab a handful of the curls in one hand, as his other hand kept her secure.

"Gibson, don't…"

He stiffened as he had before. "What?"

"Don't stop." Something fierce and wild was taking hold in her. That frisson of fear was gone now. She was more than ready to experience love, this time the way it was meant to happen between a man and a woman. She had no fear, no reluctance, despite her lack of experience and the unknown future before them. In fact, she'd never felt more alive or strong, whole in body and mind.

He pulled her in tighter, so she could hardly breathe, then covered her mouth once more with his. The burn from his unshaven cheeks and chin was the perfect contrast to his sweet kisses.

"If I could, I'd crawl right into your skin." Gibson was rubbing his cheek to her neck as he worked his hands under the hem of her sweatshirt.

She knew exactly what he meant. It was impossible for her to get near enough to feed the craving she had for him.

"This has to go," he murmured, drawing the fabric of her top up from her back. She agreed, lifting her arms to the air as he removed the garment in one smooth motion, leaving her with nothing but a skin-tight white tank top.

"Libby." Gibson ran his hands from her waist, up the sides of her breasts.

She wore no bra, and as he paused, she caught her breath wishing he would explore further, before she burst with need for his touch.

Down his hands traveled again, this time to the hem of her small tank. In a second he'd disposed of it, and she was naked from the waist up.

"You are beautiful...."

His eyes were so full of admiration she really did feel beautiful. Funny how natural it was to be without clothing. The night air was cool on her breasts and she wanted nothing so much as his hands, his mouth, on her skin.

"Can I make love to you, Libby?"

The fact that he'd asked, when she was so obviously ready to give, made her realize how right this was.

"I really think that would be a good idea." She was filled with the euphoria of her newly found power. At the same time, the weakness in her knees made her close to collapse.

She swayed, and he caught her, one hand at her waist, the other just below her breast. "Steady..." Gently he pulled her to the floor of the tree house and cushioned her body with his.

This time his kisses focused on her breasts, then trailed a line of fire down her navel.

"This spot," he breathed, his fingers dancing along the skin just above the waistband of her jeans, "has been driving me crazy for far too long."

"You're kidding." She sat up, sliding her thumbs

under the denim, working them toward the metal snap. "This spot right here?"

He kissed her below her belly button. "Right *here*." He kissed her again, as his fingers worked open the front clasp of her jeans, then tugged down the zipper.

Desire surged in her. "I see what you mean."

In slipped his hand, under the soft cotton of her panties, his fingers searching for the hot moisture that awaited. Pleasure came in a succession of bright explosions.

"You are so ready. Aren't you, sweetheart?"

As was he. Her hand skimmed the length of his erection through the denim barrier. She wanted to remove his jeans the way he'd done for her, but his touch made concentrating on the task difficult. Her breath caught and held as the waves of pleasure grew stronger and stronger.

"Gib, I really think you'd better stop touching me there."

"Why would I want to?" He pressed his mouth to hers, then very lightly touched the tip of her breast with one finger.

"Oh!" Just like that, the waves crested into the most exquisite pleasure. She was embarrassed at how quickly it happened, how desperately she ground her pelvis into his hand at the end, but Gibson seemed pleased as could be.

"That's my sweetheart. I want tonight to be perfect for you."

She trailed her hands down his chest, more interested than ever in removing his jeans. Already she could feel the desire building in her again. Was that normal? She decided she didn't care.

"We aren't finished, are we?"

"No!" He shifted his weight as she pulled down on the faded denim. "But we're definitely off to a good start...."

TO EYES ACCUSTOMED TO the light from the heavens, the night revealed as much as was necessary. As Gibson walked naked to retrieve the bottle of brandy he'd brought from home, Libby marveled once more at how powerful he was. Long legged, broad chested, tough, raw strength built from a lifetime of work in the fields and participation in sports.

The air was sweet in her lungs. A rare feeling of contentment made her happy to just lie there. True, the tree house floor was hard, despite the sweatshirt Gibson had placed under her head. And her body ached a little. But this ache was pleasant. Nothing like...

"No glasses," Gibson said, passing her the open bottle. "You'll have to rough it."

"I think I already have." She tipped the heavy glass container in his direction before lifting it to her lips. The wash of warmth relaxed her further. She handed the bottle back, then invited Gibson with her arms to join her.

He settled next to her, cocooning her head against his chest. "I wasn't sure you would meet me."

"Were you waiting long?"

He thought for a moment. "Ever since that first morning at the school."

Had he really wanted her right from the start? She wondered when her own feelings for him had crystallized into the desire of a woman for a man, and wasn't sure she could pinpoint the exact moment.

"The last time I was here was to share a dozen beers with your brother."

"Really? How old were you?"

"Not old enough. Were we ever sick!" He shook his head and smiled.

Libby felt that old familiar yearning for a life that was long over. The days when getting drunk and sick were the most dangerous things you could imagine.

"Libby?"

Soothed by the way Gibson was stroking her hair, she found it hard to respond. "Yes?"

"I didn't mean to jump at you about Darren. It was a bit of a shock, but I've been thinking it over. I guess what puzzles me most is that he never acknowledged Nicole as his daughter. He's such a devoted dad to his other children."

Strange how quickly contentment could steal away from you. Libby blinked and raised her head. As Gibson's arm fell back she was suddenly conscious of her nakedness. She reached for her clothes.

Gibson propped himself up on his elbows and watched as she got dressed. "Darren knows he's Nicole's father. Right?"

"Once, just once, couldn't you give it a rest?" She pulled the zipper on her jeans closed.

Gibson grabbed for his clothes, not answering her question.

Libby raked her fingers through the tangles of her

hair. Real fear made her tremble now. "Gibson, you can't tell—"

"I swear to God, Libby—"

"I'm serious, Gib. You can't tell Darren he's Nicole's father."

He zipped his jeans, then crossed his arms over his chest. "Don't you think a man has a right to know when he's fathered a child?"

Darren had forfeited all rights that night in his truck. Only Nicole and her rights concerned Libby. "You have to promise."

Gibson's expression was full of contempt, but after a long moment he nodded. "Don't worry. I'll keep your secret. But that doesn't mean I think it's right. Damn." He bent to pick up his shirt, "I didn't even know that you were once Darren's girlfriend."

Libby took a deep breath. "I wasn't really. We only dated a couple of times."

She angled her body away from him, not wanting to see how he reacted to that comment. Attitudes had changed in small towns, but the concept of the nice girl still remained. Oh, nowadays the nice girl didn't have to stay a virgin until she was married. But she did have to be in a serious relationship to justify making love.

Not that what had happened between her and Darren could be called "making love."

"Do you think you've been fair to Darren?" he asked.

Libby felt a bitter sob at the back of her throat and forced herself to swallow it down. As usual, Gibson was quick to judge. He still felt she was to blame for having left her father. Now he thought she'd behaved sexually irresponsibly, then blown Darren off without giving him a chance.

Of course, it wasn't his fault he kept drawing the wrong conclusions, when she wouldn't tell him the truth. But once, just once, it would be nice if he could think the best of her, instead of the worst.

## CHAPTER ELEVEN

GIBSON SPEARED a bale of hay with his pitchfork, then dropped it into the horses' trough and broke the rough twine with one of the steel prongs. Twisting to get another bale, he found himself trying to remember if his other relationships with women had been as emotionally volatile as this one with Libby was turning out to be.

As far as he could recall, his courtship of Rita had run pretty smoothly. Same with the months he'd spent dating his lawyer friend. There'd been none of these depressing lows when he felt hopeless. But no highs like the one he'd had last night after they'd made love, either.

He was falling for Libby bad. God, he'd felt a physical pain when she'd left him to return to her father's farm. He'd wanted so much to be with her all night and wake with her at his side.

They'd left on bad terms again, and all because of his blasted inquisition. Why did he keep making the same mistakes with her? Posing questions about her past, when he knew they were guaranteed to push her away.

Yet he was so damn frustrated! Last night, there'd been vulnerability, even a touch of naiveté, behind

her passion. Which made it hard for him to believe
she'd been sexually active at seventeen with a boy
she'd dated only a few times.

That she *had* been—Nicole being the proof—just
felt so wrong, so incompatible with his understanding
of the girl Libby Bateson had been and the woman
she'd become. Sure, teenage sexual curiosity was a
strong force to reckon with. But Libby's heart was
too big, too tender, for her to give it recklessly. He
was sure she'd done that very thing, either with Darren or Owen or maybe with both. What else could
explain the hurt and disillusionment he sometimes
glimpsed in her unguarded moments?

He swung his fork into another bale, enjoying the
pull on his shoulder and back muscles. It galled him
to think Libby had ever cared enough about Darren
to sleep with him. Darren had been with just about
every pretty girl within driving range of Sledgewood.

Still, when he'd gotten one pregnant—his current
wife—he'd openly admitted it and married her. Why
hadn't Libby given him the same chance with her?
Had she been so in love with him she'd been scared
he'd say no? Or so desperate to leave the farm she'd
been scared he'd say yes?

Whatever the reason, falling for this woman now
was the biggest gamble Gibson had taken in years.
Sort of like seeding a field when grain prices were
so low it seemed impossible to turn a profit. Gibson
had known years like that. Sitting at the kitchen table, doing his calculations, he'd added the cost of
seed, fuel and spray and realized planting would ex-
ceed the potential payoff. Yet come spring, he'd been

out there, driven by the need to work his land, hoping that prices would miraculously recover by the time harvest rolled around.

What would harvest hold for him and Libby? By September, she planned to be gone, just when he'd be swathing, combining and hauling grain full-time. Was it unrealistic to think that one day she could be a part of that life?

"Daddy!"

Gibson hung his pitchfork on a nail on the barn wall. His daughter's voice brought a smile to his face, a lightening of the tension he felt between his shoulders.

Lord, but she was a sweetheart, her blond hair streaming behind her as she ran. She'd dropped her lunch bag on the ground when she spotted him. Now he opened up his arms for her to barrel into.

"Pumpkin." He squeezed her tight, thinking nothing could ever be hopeless as long as she was happy and healthy. "I missed you last night. How was the sleepover at Grandma's?"

"It was great. But I missed you, too." She laid her head on his shoulder for a few seconds, and he remembered hours of holding her like this when she was a toddler and groggy after a nap. She was too old now, though, to be content in his arms for long. Within seconds she was squirming to the ground.

"Did the bunnies miss me?"

"I'm sure they did. Why don't you say hello. And give them a little something to eat while you're at it."

"Okay." She trotted to the wooden bin and scooped up some pellets.

He took a pail of water and filled the small water dispenser at the same time. For a moment he had a vision of Nicole out here with them, and Libby on the other side of the lane, working in his mother's old garden. The mental picture filled him with hope and a sense of rightness.

"Seems like we haven't had Nicole over for at least a week." He paused while Allie dropped pellets into the bunnies' feeding dish.

"I was thinking maybe you'd like to invite her for supper and a sleepover tonight," he continued when she was done. The idea had just popped into his head. He could invite Libby, too. Not for a sleepover, of course, at least not yet...

"No. I don't think so. Ardis wanted me to go to her place tonight. I was supposed to ask as soon as I got home."

"What if you invited both Ardis and Nicole?" A double sleepover would be irresistible.

He was shocked when his daughter shook her head.

"I'd rather it was just Ardis and me."

Gibson looked at Allie suspiciously. Something was definitely going on. But he wasn't going to press the issue. "Okay, fine. Why don't you go back to the house and give Ardis a call. Tell her mom I'll drive you over after I finish chores."

"Thanks, Daddy!"

As he watched her run for the house, he was perplexed as hell. He'd thought she and Nicole had be-

come such close friends. Was something going on
between those two that he didn't know about?

"PLEASE DON'T SQUIRM."

"But you're *hurting* me!"

Libby cast her eyes to the ceiling. *Give me patience.* "I'm trying to be as gentle as I can, Nicole.
I *did* ask you to use conditioner." Libby divided out
a small section of her daughter's hair and slowly began to comb.

Nicole hunched her shoulders. She'd been quiet—
even quieter than normal—ever since Libby had
picked her up from school. She'd also been uncharacteristically crabby. Complaining about the vegetables at dinner. Refusing to do her homework. Then,
in the bath, ignoring her mother's request to use the
shampoo with the built-in conditioner.

Libby was making an effort to cut her some slack.
Nicole had sat by herself on the school bus again.
Whatever the problems between her and Allie, they
were definitely not getting better. And Nicole, as
usual, was not sharing these problems with her
mother. Not that Libby had any answers to give. But
just to talk might make Nicole feel better.

"Anything interesting happen in school today?"

"Not really."

Libby parted Nicole's hair down the back and began braiding. "What did you do at recess?"

"Nothing."

"Just hang out with your friends?" Libby knew a
group of girls around Nicole's age always sat at the

far end of the softball field, under a grove of poplar trees.

"No."

She twisted a fuzzy elastic around one braid, then swiveled her daughter's shoulders so she could work on the second one. "I notice Allie isn't being very friendly to you on the bus ride home."

"I—I don't want to talk about it, Mom."

After twisting on the last elastic, Libby faced her daughter. Nicole avoided her eyes, her bottom lip trembling, her eyes suspiciously watery.

"Are the other girls at school ignoring you like Allie?"

Bull's-eye. Nicole pressed her lips together and cast her eyes down. A tear dropped onto her pink flannel nightgown. "I thought they were my friends. I thought they liked me."

"Did you and Allie have an argument?"

"No." Nicole's cheeks burned red as she tried hard to suppress her tears. "I don't know what I did to make her hate me so much."

"I'm sure she doesn't hate you."

"Oh?" Nicole stiffened. "That shows what you know! You should see the way she talks about me to the other girls. They laugh and pass notes back and forth during class, making fun of—"

Nicole didn't finish her sentence, but Libby could fill in the blanks. Somehow Allie knew exactly which buttons to press. *Allie.* Libby was beginning to rue the day they'd met the manipulative little girl. Allie was Gibson's daughter and Libby wanted to like her, but the way she behaved made it impossible.

Perhaps Libby should talk to Gibson…. He was so protective, though. He'd be sure to think the problems were all Nicole's fault. Just as she was so certain Allie was to blame.

"Maybe jealousy is making Allie act so unkindly."

"Jealousy? Are you crazy? Why would Allie be jealous of me? She's better than me at just about everything. Reading and math and making friendship bracelets." Nicole counted out each item on her fingers. "Besides, she's the prettiest girl in the class and has the nicest clothes and the most toys. Plus ponies and bunnies!"

"I don't know if she's the prettiest girl…." Libby stroked Nicole's cheek, fighting back her own, unreasonable resentment. "Yes, Allie owns a lot of nice things, but did you ever stop to think Allie might wish she could play soccer as well as you can?"

"That's nuts." Nicole sat upright. "Allie doesn't care about soccer. She doesn't even like to play."

"Is that what she told you?"

Nicole nodded.

Libby wondered if Gibson knew about that. Then she wondered if it was even true. With Allie, you never knew what to believe. "Is there another little girl you could be friends with? Someone who doesn't care what Allie thinks or does."

"*Everybody* does what Allie says," Nicole said morosely.

"Surely not *everybody*."

"Well, not the boys," Nicole conceded. "But you can't expect me to play with the boys."

"Why not?"

"Because—" she paused "—because they always play softball at recess." She pondered that for a moment. "Do you think they'd let me join the game?"

"Only one way to find out." Libby smiled encouragingly. "Now, do you want some cocoa before bed?"

LIBBY SAT at the kitchen table and stared despondently at the essay topic at the top of the page. She couldn't think of one reason she should care how Mark Twain had used irony effectively in *Huckleberry Finn* to show the inhumanity of slavery. Well, maybe one reason: because she wanted to pass her grade twelve. But that was the only one.

She wrote a heading on a blank page, deciding she should start with an outline. But that was difficult when she didn't have any idea what to say. She fought the urge to leave the table and get a snack. She'd already taken one break to go to the bathroom and another to make herself a cup of tea. It was time to buckle down and do some work.

But she simply couldn't concentrate.

Libby sipped the cooling tea, then forced herself to pick up the novel and flip through some of the sections she'd marked when reading. A few ideas occurred to her and she jotted down some phrases in the margin of her paper.

A tapping at the kitchen window drew her attention.

Absentmindedly she looked up. And saw Gibson's face pressed against the glass. She jumped out of her chair, stifling her scream but sending her chair crashing backward.

"What?" her father called from the front room, where he'd been watching television. He'd been startled, too.

"It's okay, Dad. I just knocked over my chair."

She held her breath, waiting to see if he would say anything else. He didn't. As his relationship with Nicole developed, his stilted avoidance of Libby had come to feel more and more absurd. What magic could ever ease the tension between them? She'd made several subtle overtures, but he'd ignored each one. No way could she pretend his repeated rejection didn't hurt.

She opened the door to Gibson, who waited patiently.

"Surprise," he said.

"I'll say." He smelled of soap; his hair was damp, his clothes clean and freshly pressed.

"Where's Allie?" she asked

"At a sleepover. With Ardis."

His hands were in his pockets, but his eyes were all over her, reminding her of the situation they'd found themselves in less than twenty-four hours ago. Making love. The memory was one she'd always cherish, but not the argument they'd had after. She wrapped her arms in front of her chest and nodded toward the living room.

"Dad's in there. Did you want to say hello?"

"Maybe later." Gibson took a step closer. For a second she thought he was going to touch her, then he changed direction and picked up the chair that had fallen and sat down. He surveyed the papers strewn over the table. "What's this?"

Libby swooped them into a pile, suddenly self-conscious and embarrassed. "Just a report I have to do for one of my correspondence courses." She plugged in the kettle. "I was having some tea. Would you like a cup?"

He nodded.

She got down a clean mug and a fresh tea bag. The kettle whistled almost instantly, the water having boiled just a few minutes ago. He took the mug from her, brushing his fingers unnecessarily against hers. "How's Nicole?"

Libby sat on the edge of the counter—about as far from Gibson as she could manage. She didn't dare think about what those fingers of his had been doing to her body not that long ago. "She's sleeping."

"Right. After ten, isn't it?" He looked at the kitchen clock for confirmation. "She's sort of the reason I came over."

"Oh?"

"Yeah. I wondered if there was some problem between the girls."

Was there ever! "They haven't been sitting together on the bus lately."

"Really? I figured something was up when Allie turned down my offer to have both Ardis and Nicole for a sleepover at our place."

"Did Allie tell you what the problem was?"

"No-o-o." He angled his head, eyes narrowing. "Did Nicole tell *you?*"

Libby watched the pattern on her sock as she

swung her leg, sorely tempted to vent her feelings, to complain that *his* daughter was a self-centered egotist, who was making *her* daughter's life miserable. However, she had enough sense to know that an accusation like that would be nothing short of destructive.

Gibson thought the world revolved around Allie. He'd never believe a word against her. Besides, Libby was honest enough to admit that there were usually two sides to a story. She'd heard Nicole's. Perhaps Allie had some legitimate grievances of her own.

"Maybe, if we give them a little space, they'll sort this out themselves."

"You're probably right. But it's hard standing on the sideline, isn't it?" He stared into his cup. "I still expect I should solve all her problems for her. I don't know why, when I can't even solve my own."

"You have problems?" The very idea intrigued her. He seemed so in control, so self-assured.

"One in particular. And she's looking right at me."

"So now I'm a problem, am I?"

"You always have been, come to think of it. As a kid you could be quite a pest. Did I ever tell you that?"

"No." Even as a boy, Gibson had always been kind.

"Well, actually, you *were* kind of cute."

"*Were?*"

"Still are." He stood and in an instant was in front of her, pressed up to the counter so that her legs straddled his hips. He brought his lips within inches of hers. "What am I going to do with you, Libby Bateson?"

*What would you like to do with me?* Libby bit back the flirtatious comment. Nothing tempted her more, but she was not going to kiss Gibson Browning in her kitchen, with her father in the next room. So she put her hands on his shoulders and pushed him back a few inches.

"As I recall, you were pretty angry with me last night."

"Last night I was a fool. What happened between us was fantastic. I was an idiot to spoil it with an argument. You know, ever since the first day you came back, you're all I can think about."

Her heart swelled at Gibson's being preoccupied with *her*. If he had any idea how much time she spent dreaming of him... "Maybe coming home was a mistake...."

"No, the mistake was—"

She prepared herself for his usual recriminations, but he surprised her by asking a question.

"How about going to dinner with me Saturday night?"

"What?" Panic had her pulling out the first excuse that came to mind. "I don't have a baby-sitter."

"What about your dad?"

"We're still not, um, speaking."

"We'll take the girls, then."

Libby considered. As long as Allie and Nicole were present, Gibson wouldn't be able to bring up the subject of Darren. And getting together might give the girls an opportunity to overcome their differences. "I guess that would be okay."

"Such enthusiasm." He cupped her face, his eyes searching. When his gaze focused on her lips, she caught her breath, half expecting he would try to kiss her again. Instead, he issued another invitation, lowering his voice a notch. "We could go for a little walk to the tree house. Right now, if you wanted."

Libby swallowed. The idea that she could be in his arms again in a few short minutes sparked instant heat throughout her body. One more time... It would be so heavenly....

"I can't." She pushed at his chest, then slid from the counter. "I have work to do." She picked up her pen and jabbed it against the notepad on the table.

He moved behind her. "Right. I forgot."

Libby stared at the blank page, thinking how aptly it mirrored her thoughts at this moment. All of a sudden she felt Gibson's hands on her shoulders. Gently he began to massage, working across the muscles that still ached from all that painting.

"Tight," he observed.

"Mmm." She closed her eyes.

"You go ahead and get started," he said. "Don't worry about me."

The words in the novel swam in wavy lines. Huckleberry Finn, Tom Sawyer and Jim all jumped on a raft and floated completely out of her mind.

"Working on an essay?" Gibson's lips brushed the outer tip of her ear.

"Yes. On *Huckleberry Finn.*" She jerked her

thoughts to the topic she'd chosen. Or attempted to. "Can you give me an example of irony?"

He bent lower, his whisper now a breath against her neck. "Having made love to you last night but not being able to kiss you today."

Seconds ticked by on the kitchen clock before she could reply. "Not that sort of example. One from *Huckleberry Finn*."

"Well, why didn't you say so?"

Libby twisted out from under his hands. "I think you better leave, Gibson. I'm not going to get anything done while you're here."

"It's been a lot of years since a girl asked me to go home so she could do her schoolwork."

Was he making fun of her? She didn't think so, but she felt sensitive about not having finished high school. She tried not to let it show. "It's been a long time for me, too. Believe me, it's not easy to take the time to pore over books and assignments when you've got enough real work to keep you busy."

His expression became more solemn. "I know. And it's great that you're doing it."

"Just get out of here, okay? Unless you feel the urge to write an analysis of *Huckleberry Finn*."

"No. I haven't had one of those urges since I provided Chris a summary of the top three Playmates of the Year when we were thirteen." He dashed for the door then, as if sensing that he'd finally crossed the line.

Libby threw a tea towel at him, but she was too late. It hit the closed door and slid to the floor, a puddle of blue checks against the cream-colored linoleum. He was gone. She'd gotten what she'd asked for—peace and quiet.

Funny. Looking down at the papers on the table, she realized that his leaving wasn't what she'd wanted after all.

How ironic.

# CHAPTER TWELVE

LIBBY WAS REACHING into the freezer bin at the local grocery store for a package of ground beef when she felt a tapping on her shoulder.

"There are some really nice hams on sale today, Libby. Over in the corner." Gibson's mother pointed. "And here's a coupon for an extra dollar off."

"Thanks." Libby took the coupon and thought how much she'd miss simple moments like this once she and Nicole were gone. In Toronto she'd never once seen anyone at the grocery store whom she'd known.

"Do you have time to stop for a cup of coffee before you go home? I put on the pot just before I went out.

"We're only a couple of blocks from here," Connie added persuasively. Unnecessarily, too, since just about everything and everybody in Chatsworth were within blocks of the store.

Libby hesitated only a second. She had lots of work waiting at home, but Gibson's mother had always taken time for her when she was a little girl. "Sure. I could use a break."

Ten minutes later Connie was setting out cups and

saucers. "It's nice to have a visitor from the old days. I meet several women in town regularly, but I still miss your mother's company. Living out in the sticks the way we did, we were pretty dependent upon each other for our sanity." She put out a plate of home-baked butter tarts. "I'll never forget her cinnamon buns, either."

Mom's cinnamon buns. Libby hadn't thought about them in years. Coming home from school to find the house warm and smelling sweet was a Friday tradition....

"You haven't happened across that recipe by any chance, have you?" Connie asked, pouring coffee. "She was such a tease and would never tell me how she made them."

"No, I haven't. I don't remember Mom even using recipes. She had them all stored in her head."

"I figured as much. Ah, well. Now, tell me, how *is* that father of yours doing?" Connie asked frankly. Her blue eyes, so like her son's, gazed at Libby.

"Well, he's not himself yet. But I think he's improving. You should have seen the house when I got home." Libby shook her head. The filth and neglect were too much to describe.

"I'd heard it was bad." Connie nodded, her eyes suddenly brighter. "I tried to give him a hand cleaning a few times. But he told me where to go, with no mincing of words. Wouldn't even let me in the door."

Libby could well imagine. "At least he's keeping himself clean, and eating properly now. And he seems to have taken to Nicole...." Libby didn't mention that he still avoided *her* like the plague. That topic was just too painful to broach.

Connie was sympathetic. "He was devoted to your mother. And for all that he and Chris used to go at it, he thought the world of his son."

Libby nodded. There was no sense pointing out that he still had a daughter. She'd obviously proven a poor consolation prize.

"Unfortunately, your father's antagonized a lot of his old friends. He's even launched a lawsuit against the Tylers. And it isn't his first one."

"I've heard. It's so strange. As though he's turned into a completely different person."

"You say he gets along with Nicole?"

"He's starting to." Libby told her about the swimming lessons and the new soccer cleats and the way Nicole followed him around while he did the chores. "So maybe there's hope yet."

"Oh, there's hope. I just wish I could say the same for my granddaughter."

"Allie." Libby shifted in her seat. She should have guessed where this was heading.

Connie took Libby's hand and cupped it between both of hers. "I want to apologize for the way Allie behaves on the soccer field. I know Gibson would do something about it if he realized what was going on. But Allie's always had a talent for presenting a good front to her father...."

"He has twelve other children to keep an eye on," Libby pointed out in his favor, wondering why she should argue on his behalf.

"I wish I could talk to him about Allie, but I feel

it wouldn't be right. He'd take it as criticism of his parenting skills. And it would probably remind him of all the negative things I said about Rita.''

Connie ran her fingertip over the lip of her coffee mug, pensive. ''How I wish I'd kept my mouth shut about that marriage. Now, when my interference might do some good, my hands are tied. I've tried talking with Allie about good sportsmanship, but I don't think I've had much impact. And I feel so badly for your Nicole. She's such a sweet little thing.''

Libby nodded, her throat suddenly constricted. Connie didn't know the half of it; Allie's rude behavior on the soccer field was just the tip of the iceberg. But there was no sense in getting poor Connie even more upset than she already was. And there were, as Libby had to keep reminding herself, two sides to every story.

''I'm sure the girls will sort themselves out eventually.'' She'd said the same thing to Gibson last night. Was it just her, or were those words starting to sound a little too pat?

NICOLE WOULDN'T MEET Libby's eyes when she got on the bus after school that afternoon. She sat in a middle seat, immediately pulled a book out of her backpack and started reading. Libby assumed from the studied indifference on Nicole's face that the day had not gone well. The details came out later, in the kitchen, while Libby was rolling the dough for cinnamon buns.

She'd found her mother's recipe in an old Purity

cookbook at the bottom of the tea towel drawer. Pen scratches cluttered the cookbook's pages—adaptations to the original recipes, as well as comments on the various dishes. The unexpected legacy was better than a treasure of gold. Libby had spent half the afternoon reading.

Now she stuck a knife into a pound of soft butter, then slathered a generous helping over the freshly rolled dough. That was when Nicole finally emerged from her bedroom, eyes red and puffy, lips pale and swollen.

"Want to help me make cinnamon buns? I'm using Grandma's secret recipe."

"Secret?"

"Yes. She made the *best* cinnamon buns. But she wouldn't tell anyone how she did it. I found her recipe book in the bottom of one of the drawers. See this?" Libby pointed to a container of corn syrup. "Her secret ingredient."

Nicole walked closer. "How do you get the cinnamon and sugar all rolled up inside?"

"Come here and I'll show you." Libby gave her a spoon and let her sprinkle the sweet spicy mixture over the butter. Then she helped her roll the dough into a cylinder and slice out perfectly shaped pinwheels.

"Neat!" Nicole dropped them onto cake pans, already lined with a mixture of sweetened chopped pecans.

"The buns need to rise first, for about twenty-five minutes." Libby set the timer, then they washed their hands in the sink together. "I take it the boys didn't let you play softball with them today?"

Nicole swung her head, so that her pigtails flopped across her face. "They laughed at me. Allie and all the other girls heard. Allie said...well, she said a lot of mean stuff about me wishing I were a boy because I wasn't any good at girl stuff."

"Girl stuff being?"

Nicole shrugged, her face suddenly red. "Oh, nothing." She headed for the kitchen door.

"Don't forget to come back for the cinnamon—" *Bang!* "—buns." Libby stared at the closed door. Poor Nicole. How mortified she must have felt when the boys spurned her. Perhaps it was time she made an appointment to talk to the teacher. Or would that only make matters worse?

Once again, Libby thought how wonderful it would be to have a husband to discuss these dilemmas with. Not surprisingly, Gibson came to mind. He was such a caring father, if slightly blind where Allie's behavior was concerned. Maybe together the two of them...

Lord, what was she doing? She couldn't harbor dreams like those; it would only make leaving harder. Libby turned on the taps to wash dishes, then began peeling potatoes. The ham was already in the oven, and after the buns had risen, she popped them in, too. She planned to serve them for dessert. Maybe she'd open a tin of peaches to go with them.

The canned goods were at the back of the tallest cupboard, so she got a chair in order to reach. Her head was almost lost among the beans and tuna when she heard the door open. Libby hoped Nicole was ready to talk this time.

"Hi. Any minute now and the buzzer—" Libby cut off her sentence when she saw her father standing there, hat in his hand, eyes dazed.

The confusion in his expression was frightening. He didn't seem to notice her, but instead was focused on the empty space by the oven, as if he were seeing a ghost. Had it finally happened? Had her father lost his mind? She slipped off the chair, wondering if it would be better to say something or to remain silent.

"Virginia?"

Hearing the combination of longing and uncertainty in her father's voice as he called her mother's name, Libby put a hand to her throat. He didn't really think...did he?

She took one step forward, and her father's gaze shifted. The moment he saw her, reality gained the upper hand. The hopefulness seeped out of his eyes like tears and soon he was the same defeated, tired man she'd come to know too well.

"I thought..." he said. "That is, I smelled..." He glanced back toward the oven, his confusion less evident now. In a way Libby was sorry. The hope, however fleeting, had brought him briefly back to life. Now he was gone again.

He exited the kitchen, leaving Libby with her mouth open, but no words to say.

GIBSON TOOK HIS attention from the road for a second and pondered his daughter in the passenger seat beside him, her lips set in a mutinous line, hands crossed over her chest. He couldn't, for the life of him, figure out what was going on between her and Nicole. When he'd told Allie they were driving to the Batesons' for a quick visit she'd been strangely reluctant to come along.

He'd spoken with Moira about the problem.

"Any idea why Allie and Nicole haven't played together recently?"

Moira shrugged. "Allie has other friends, you know. No reason she should drop all of them just because of Nicole. And it's not like Libby and Nicole are here to stay, anyway.

"I hear she just came back to finish her grade twelve. Imagine running off before graduation. And she didn't even manage to keep him."

"Him being—"

"Why, Owen Holst, of course. Though heaven knows how long he's been out of the picture. That's what happens when girls throw away their future for some young man who catches their fancy. I've always warned my own children, and I must say I'm pretty proud of how…"

She'd droned on and Gibson had tuned out. He wondered if others in Chatsworth were judging Libby as harshly as Moira. Of course some were, and he was one of them. No wonder Libby wanted to live somewhere else. Damn, but he was such a fool.

Henry Bateson was in front of the machine shed, working on his tractor, when they drove up. The sound of his whistling traveled through the early-evening air. Whistling. Now, that was interesting.

Abandoning his goal of the house for a moment, Gibson wandered over to the older man.

"Troubles?" he asked. He was shocked when Henry answered with something other than a grunt.

"Not really. Just cleaning out the fuel line." Henry stopped to wipe his greasy hands on a rag by his feet. "Your flax seems to be off to a good start."

Gibson nodded at the compliment and returned it. "Same with your canola."

"Planning to spray this year?"

"Probably, in a few weeks or so." Years had gone by since he'd had such a long conversation with his neighbor. Gibson could hardly keep his tone matter-of-fact, the way Henry would expect.

The old man bent over his tractor again. "Well, I expect you came to see Libby. She's in the house baking cinnamon buns."

"Cinnamon buns?" A distant memory twigged. "Are they the ones—"

"The very same. She must have found Mother's recipe. Now, make sure you get one straight from the oven. Nothing on earth can beat 'em."

Nodding his thanks, Gibson headed for the house. Imagine that. Henry Bateson was talking again. Having Libby and Nicole around had to have made the difference. But what would happen when they left? Determination quickened his stride. He couldn't let that happen.

"Come on, Allie. Let's go see Libby."

"I don't want to go in that house."

Her obstinacy puzzled him. "Allie?"

"Can't I just wait outside?"

"I guess." He left her standing by the truck. The aroma of sweet cinnamon and yeast rose out from the house to greet him as he passed by the open kitchen window. He tapped on the glass and peered inside.

Libby bent her head to look at him and pushed against his nose with the tip of her finger. "This isn't a drive-through. Come in if you want something."

He smiled and went around to the back, then stopped for a moment in the entryway. Seeing her reminded him of things he wanted a whole lot more than cinnamon buns, even if they were hot from the oven. She was in those worn jeans of hers, and the smudge of cinnamon on the chest of her white T-shirt was exactly the color of...

"Well, don't just stand there gawking." She passed him a plate and an empty cup. "Those buns are still warm. And the coffee's fresh. Dad and I just had a cup."

"Does that mean the two of you are talking?"

Her expression softened. "Sort of. Not really. He came in the kitchen about an hour ago when the first batch wasn't quite ready. And I think it shocked him—the smell of the cinnamon buns, which you know, were Mom's specialty."

Gibson nodded as he put a bun on his plate, then poured the coffee. "I know." The smell of fresh paint did it to him. Rita had spent so much time and energy fixing up his home—*their* home. He hadn't realized at first that he associated the smell with her, until he'd walked into the hardware store a couple of months after the accident and they were mixing paint for a customer. The smell had almost made him sick.

"Where's Allie?"

"Out by the truck."

"She didn't want to come in?"

He nodded, hating to admit it, hating even more the coolness that suddenly washed over Libby.

"I think our dinner on Saturday is going to be pretty awkward, Gibson."

"Dinner on Saturday is going to be just fine," he promised. Probably Allie and Nicole would be over this spat by then. If not, he wasn't sure what he would do. But he'd think of something.

"I don't know...."

"Trust me, Libby." He reached for her hand and was gratified when she didn't pull away. It wasn't the right time or place, but he so wanted to kiss her. That vulnerable look was back in her eyes, and he hated to think that somehow he'd put it there.

He pulled her closer, and felt her trembling. "Libby, sweetheart, are you okay?"

"Of course I am." Her chin tilted in a familiar gesture of self-reliance. Did she know it also made her lips more available to him? He lowered his head, determined to seize the moment. But his lips had barely brushed hers when a creak from the stairs startled them both.

"Nicole's up there," Libby said. "Doing her homework."

The reminder of her daughter brought back the coolness from before. She stepped away from him and picked up the dishrag to gather crumbs from the table.

"Did the smell of my baking travel all the way to your house, or did you have some other reason for stopping by?"

His reason had been to see her, but he had an excuse prepared, as well. "Only two more weeks of soccer and then softball season starts. I wondered if you wanted me to sign up Nicole."

"Yes. I know she's dying to play. And this time," she added, opening one of the kitchen drawers and pulling out a checkbook, "you're going to let me pay for my own entry fee."

Damn. "How did you know?"

"Nicole brought the softball form from school. I figure if they charge for softball, they must charge for soccer. I want to reimburse you for that, too, by the way."

Libby started to write out the check. "How much was soccer?"

"You don't have to pay me." He didn't want to take any money from her. Her mouth straightened into a firm line. He recognized the look.

"I appreciate the loan, Gibson. I was a little strapped for cash at the time. But I've got a job now."

She waited expectantly.

"Oh, hell. It was twenty-five dollars. But Libby—"

She filled in the amount and tore out the check. "No buts, Gibson. Here's your money."

He accepted the check. He didn't want to, but he respected Libby's pride.

"I guess I should head home."

Libby nodded, her brown eyes wary beneath her expressive eyebrows. He admired the strong line of her jaw and cheekbones, the generous curve of her lips, the straight line of her nose. Despite the vulnerability he often sensed beneath her surface, there was nothing weak about Libby Bateson.

"I'm looking forward to Saturday, Libby."

"It'll be interesting."

# CHAPTER THIRTEEN

BY SATURDAY, the situation between the two girls had not improved, and Gibson was a desperate man.

"You used to have so much fun with Nicole," he said to Allie as he combed her hair. "What changed? Did you have an argument?"

Allie swung her feet, remaining mute. She was wearing the new skirt and top she'd received from her grandma for her birthday, and to him she looked absolutely adorable. Even with a fat pout on her lips.

"Pumpkin, I want this to be fun. For all of us."

"Then let me stay at Grandma's or go to Ardis's."

Gibson checked an impatient reply. Libby had no baby-sitter, or he'd be delighted to comply with Allie's request. What he really wanted was time alone with Libby. But the realities of being single parents dictated otherwise.

"Please try to have a good time, pumpkin. Okay?"

Libby and Nicole were waiting on the porch when he drove up in the truck, a silent Allie by his side. Two brown-eyed, curly-haired beauties. As usual, Libby didn't have to do much in terms of makeup or glitzy clothes to look fantastic. His heart skipped, along with his feet, as he hurried out to meet them.

"Sorry I'm a little late." Allie had made a fuss about which shoes to wear. He couldn't have cared less but had been forced to wait as she changed her mind not once but a total of three times.

Now his adrenaline soared as the evening he'd been so anticipating was finally about to begin. Knowing he was grinning like a brainless fool, but unable to stop himself, he opened the front passenger door for Libby.

"Why don't you move to the back with Nicole, pumpkin."

"Can't I sit up here with you?"

His daughter's refusal caught him by surprise. He glanced over at Libby, expecting her to back him up, but instead she demurred. "That's okay, Gibson. I'll sit with Nicole in the back."

What the hell… Gibson wasn't sure what to do. Finally, he just gave in and got into the driver's seat. On the drive he tried to joke with Nicole and tease a smile from her mother, but it was no use. Allie's sullen presence set the mood. It didn't improve at the movie theater when Libby snapped at Allie about the refreshments.

That was the last thing he would've expected from her. He paid for the tickets, so she insisted on buying the snacks. While he and the girls reserved seats, she went through the lineup to get popcorn and drinks for all of them. When she came back, Allie changed her mind and decided she'd rather have a chocolate bar than popcorn.

True, it was annoying, but it wasn't a big deal. He

was amazed at the way Libby plunked down in her seat.

"I'm sorry, Allie, but you did say popcorn."

"I'll buy one for you, pumpkin," he offered. "I don't mind missing the first couple of minutes of the movie," he explained. However, Libby, who was closer to the aisle, was already rising again.

"If you want her to have the bar, I'll get it," she said tersely.

"I don't mind—" He tried to stop her, but she was already halfway up the aisle. Throughout the film they sat with Allie between them, and when the show was over Libby was clearly still cross. She barely spoke on the way to the pizza parlor. And that was when he knew his wonderful family outing was a total bust.

LIBBY WISHED THAT Gibson didn't look so handsome in his pale-blue denim shirt and tan cotton slacks. She wished she didn't long for him to smile at her, to reach across the table for her hand. She also wished that his obvious disappointment with the evening didn't tug at her heart the way it did.

He'd been so excited when he'd jumped from his truck. His joy had been contagious—for one wild moment, anticipation had sizzled through her. Until Allie had refused to move to the back seat. Poor Nicole had been mortified at the undeniable insult.

Allie's sullen silence on the drive, her spoiled demands at the theater followed by her rude ignoring of both Nicole and Libby during supper, had ruined everything. Now she and Nicole were playing at separate video terminals. And Libby had had enough.

"I told you this would be a mistake."

"I'm sorry." Gibson was putting his coffee spoon through a series of headstands and somersaults on the vinyl place mat in front of him. "I know the evening hasn't turned out the way I promised. Allie's been temperamental...."

"Temperamental?" She'd vowed never to broach the subject of Allie with him, but she was past her breaking point. "That's not the word I would use to describe your daughter's behavior."

"No? What word *would* you use?" Gibson's tone suggested she be careful what she said. But Libby had never felt less like being careful.

"How about selfish? Or spoiled? Or completely self-centered?"

Gibson recoiled, obviously hurt, as well as angered. After several agonizing seconds he shook his head. "I don't think you mean that."

"Oh, yes, I do."

His broad chest expanded, straining the buttons of his shirt. "Okay, so Allie's been difficult. But she's just a kid. She probably senses something going on between us. We've got to give her time to adjust."

"Gibson, this isn't about you and me. Allie's always been like this. Even your—" She stopped abruptly, putting a hand to her mouth. No way could she divulge Connie's confidences. No matter how mad she became.

"I can't believe you could be so judgmental about a motherless seven-year-old."

"She may not have a mother, but she has a father." Libby pointed her finger at him, stopping inches from his chest. "Stop making excuses, Gibson. The truth is she's out of control and you're not doing anything to stop her."

Anger had the upper hand now, as Gibson's face flushed and his mouth hardened. "I'm warning you, Libby. Don't say another word against my daughter."

"I'm not blaming Allie. She's just a child, Gib. Don't you see how you're—"

"I said, enough."

He was deadly serious. Libby had never seen him like this. But now that she'd started, she wasn't going to back down.

"I have the right to protect my own daughter. Why don't you try asking Allie what she's been saying about Nicole at school? The answers might surprise you."

Gibson blinked. A muscle twitched at the side of his mouth. "What are you talking about?"

With incredibly bad timing, their server suddenly appeared at Libby's elbow. "A refill for your coffee?"

"No, thanks." Libby couldn't lift her gaze from the table. She was afraid Gibson might explode. And that she might burst into tears. "I think we're ready for the check."

Gibson whipped out his wallet. "I'm paying."

She didn't dare argue.

"Can we go now?" Allie came out of nowhere, a quiet Nicole standing well behind her. "I'm *bored*."

"Watch your manners, Allie."

Allie flinched at her father's rebuke.

"That's okay," Libby said quickly. "I think maybe we should leave. It's getting close to the girls' bedtime."

"Not mine." Gibson looked as though he could have strangled his daughter when she spoke up again in an insolent voice. "I get to stay up as late as I want on the weekends."

"Really?" She didn't care if Gibson heard the reproach in her tone.

"Now, that's a bit of an exaggeration," he said. "Let's go, then."

Libby put an arm over Nicole's shoulders as they walked out. Undoubtedly, the children were aware of the tension between the adults, and she regretted having brought the subject up when they were around.

But she wasn't sorry about the things she'd said. Now even Gibson would see how impossible a relationship between the two of them was. She climbed into the back seat with Nicole, not surprised when Allie began wailing because her father hadn't bought her a bubblegum on the way out.

"But Daddy!" she cried. "You always buy me gum after pizza."

"Not always, Allie." His voice was calm, but there was steel behind it. He leaned over to check her seat belt before starting the ignition. As he drove, Allie cried with little sobs that made her entire body tremble.

Libby suspected she wasn't reacting to the bubblegum so much as her father's inexplicably hard behavior. She felt a genuine sympathy for the both of them. They had so much to work out. After ten, fifteen miles Allie finally fell asleep.

Libby caught Gibson's glance in the rearview mirror.

*Happy?* he seemed to be saying as he lifted his eyebrows. She turned her head to watch out the side window. The drive home from Yorkton had never felt longer.

Nicole shot off for the house after a polite, if insincere, thanks to Gibson for the movie and the pizza. Libby hung around a few seconds longer. "I think it's better that we don't see each other for a while," she suggested.

"No bloody kidding. Don't tell me you didn't have a good time."

She didn't say anything.

He curled his hands into fists, as he stared past her, to the place where his property met her father's, across and down the road about a quarter mile.

After a long moment, his anger shifted. From the glow of the outdoor yard light, Libby saw true regret soften the line of his mouth. "For a while I thought we might have something special...."

He didn't finish the sentence and she was glad. This was hurting so much more than she'd expected. She'd known from the start they had no future. To be disappointed was illogical.

"It wasn't supposed to turn out this way," he said. She knew exactly what he meant.

"We have to consider the kids," she said. "This is only going to hurt them."

"Maybe we *should* have tried going out just the two of us."

"That wouldn't have solved anything. Gib, you probably think I'm being callous, but somebody has to be realistic about this. A definite break now will be easier for all of us in the long run."

"So that's what this is? A definite break?"

God help her, he sounded as bleak as she felt. Was it possible she was wrong...?

She only had to remember Darren to know that she wasn't. "Yes," she said.

Amazingly, her voice was steady and true. Still, she had to turn and run for the house so he wouldn't see her tears.

IN ONE NIGHT, Gibson felt he'd lost everything. Libby and his hopes for their future. Allie and his delusions that the two of them were getting along okay on their own.

His number-one goal since Rita's death had been to do right by his daughter, yet somehow he'd failed. He'd tried to be mother and father and ended up being neither. Angry as he was at Libby for speaking out the way she had, he knew she was right.

He *was* spoiling his daughter. Why hadn't anyone said anything sooner? He thought of several subtle comments made by his mother and realized she'd tried.

Sleep was impossible in his tormented state. Gibson didn't even try to settle beneath his sheets. Instead, he paced the circumference of the farmyard, around the house and gardens, the barn and pasture.

He passed the coils of hay, stacked from last winter, and several granaries, empty in anticipation of harvest.

Stars were still visible in the sky when the first birds began to sing. Their chorus was nonstop by the time the eastern horizon turned a pale turquoise. He watched as a band of watermelon pink stretched out against the green of his new crop. Then he went inside and made a pot of coffee.

By six, daylight was well established and he was on the last cup.

His anger toward Libby had abated, although his resentment had not. True, his control over Allie was not what it should be. Maybe he gave in to her demands a little too often. Maybe he wasn't firm enough in applying consequences when she was out of line.

And maybe sometimes he'd used material possessions in an attempt to compensate for the loss of her mother. He was willing to concede on that one, too.

But Libby didn't understand how hard it was, raising a child without a mother. Sure Allie had him. Little girls needed their mamas, though. You'd think Libby, who'd had a close relationship with her own mother, would understand that.

When Allie woke up the chores were done and he had waffles and sausages ready. Allie's favorite.

"I used to think Libby was really pretty," Allie announced out of the blue, her mouth full of waffle. "But I don't anymore."

"Oh?"

"I think blond hair is much nicer than brown,

don't you, Daddy? Mommy had blond hair just like mine, didn't she?"

"Yes." He reached across and rubbed the top of her head, wishing he could as easily erase whatever insecurities were driving her to make these comments.

"You're beautiful, Allie, just like your mom. But brown hair can also be nice." Especially when it had a wild curl to it that made it seem as if the woman had just gotten out of bed.

He chased the last drops of syrup on his plate with a final square from his waffle. One comment of Libby's last night had been particularly bitter. Now he cleared his throat. "Allie, have you been saying mean things about Nicole at school?"

When his daughter shifted her eyes down to her plate, he felt a dull ache in his chest. "Why, Allie?"

"I don't know," she whispered.

Tears pooled and dropped. Her distress broke his heart. But he couldn't leave this alone; the consequences were too high. He knew that in Allie's circle of friends, her opinion held a lot of sway. It was possible she'd turned poor Nicole into a virtual outcast.

"I'm afraid we have to ground you for two weeks, Allie. No sleepovers, no playing after school. I want you to think about Nicole and what it would feel like if someone said nasty things about you at school."

Allie squirmed. "Please, Daddy, you already said Ardis could come over today. I promise I'll be nicer to Nicole on Monday at school."

He was surprised to feel something harden inside

him at this plea. "No, Allie. We're going to have to cancel those plans with Ardis. It might be a good idea if you helped me with a few jobs this morning. Then maybe this afternoon we can kick the soccer ball around for a while."

Allie's shoulders seemed to slump further. "I'll never be as good as Nicole."

"That's not a good attitude. You certainly won't be if you never practice. Help me with these dishes, then we'll go outside." Gibson swallowed the last of the old, bitter coffee. Now he was sounding like a parent. Wasn't he?

*I SHOULD CALL Gibson and apologize,* Libby thought for the hundredth time as she ran the power lawn mower across the grass in front of the house after supper on Sunday. The neatly mowed strips were in complete contrast with her frazzled state of mind.

Since last night, she'd agonized over every word she'd said— Lord, she'd exploded like an overheated radiator. Not that talking to Gibson about Allie hadn't been overdue. But she should've waited until she was calm and rational.

If Gibson had sat in the driver's seat of the school bus every day, though, he'd have understood the pressure she was under. Having to watch while Allie and Ardis excluded Nicole day after day. Of course, if he was there, Allie wouldn't dare behave the way she did. As Connie had said, the little girl had radar where her father was concerned.

Libby paused to wipe the sweat off her hands, running them down the denim material on her hips. An apology was in order. But what if Gibson took it to mean she'd changed her mind about ending their relationship? Which of course she hadn't.

Yet the possibility that she might be able to patch things up between them, at least temporarily, was temping. She hated how much she longed to do exactly that. Why had there been such magic between them if they weren't meant to be? Going on alone would have been easier if she hadn't had a taste of what love and passion were all about.

Now she knew how the sight of one special man could lift a woman's spirits higher than a bright summer day. Now she knew how beautiful making love could feel, and how comforting a broad shoulder was in the middle of the night. Problems shared were halved; pleasures shared were multiplied.

With Gibson, she'd glimpsed the kind of life she hadn't dreamed about since she was a child. But that life was a mirage, because in about two months she and Nicole would leave Chatsworth, although it wouldn't be easy. Despite the problems with Allie at school, she knew Nicole was happy here, and so was she.

This place was in her blood. Her father and her mother, each in their own way, had been as rooted to their section of prairie land as the invasive grasses and weeds that grew naturally along the sides of the roads, down in the ditches, to the border of the tilled soil.

In fact, this very tie to the land had probably saved her father in the midst of his grief. The need to go out every spring and cultivate and seed; the desire to nurture the crop, to guide it through to fruition; then the hard work and joy of harvesting. Her father would have been controlled by the same instinct that takes birds south in the winter, Libby was sure; by a force stronger than the overpowering pain of his loss.

And the prairie was doing the same for her, healing the wounds of the past years more quickly than she would have thought possible. If only she could stay.

Libby turned the mower around the corner of the yard and headed back toward the house. How unfortunate Darren O'Malley hadn't been one of the many young people lured away to the city by the prospect of an easier life. Then staying wouldn't be such an impossible choice.

A large stick ahead caused Libby to pause and clear the mower's path. She picked up the twisted lilac branch and hurled it into the hedge. At that moment the mower's motor cut out. Probably out of gas.

But no. She turned to see Gibson, his hand on the lever that switched the machine off. "You look like you could use a break. I brought a beer from home." He tossed a cold can toward her.

Despite the slick of condensation on the can, she snared it. Once she popped back the tab, she took a long swallow, hoping to give her heart a chance to stop pounding.

He couldn't have caught her more off guard. Although she'd been thinking of him and their situation practically nonstop since he'd dropped her off last night, she still had no idea what she wanted to say to him. The words of the apology she'd been considering earlier stuck like dust in her throat.

When she'd brought the can down from her lips she noticed someone standing behind Gibson's legs.

"Hello, Allie."

Cautiously the young girl stepped forward. "I want to say sorry for being rude the other day." She looked up at her father, and he gave her an encouraging nod. She swallowed, then held out an envelope. "I wrote you this note, too."

"Thank you." Libby took the envelope, softening toward the girl despite her earlier anger.

"I have one for Nicole," Allie continued, staring at the ground.

"I think she's in the barn. That fat old tabby had a batch of new kittens this morning."

"Oh." Allie's interest perked a little, but she checked with her father before running off to the barn.

Leaving Libby with Gibson—and she didn't like the way that made her feel. Giddy, awkward, excited. She had in mind that this would be a good time for her own apology, but Gibson's expression was not encouraging.

"I've grounded Allie," he said tersely. "For two weeks." He cleared his throat, then added. "You were right, Libby. I need to take a firmer hand."

Here was her chance. "You did the right thing, Gibson. But I'm sorry I spoke out the way I did."

He brushed off her apology. "Yeah, well, I guess I've crossed those boundaries with you a few times myself."

It was the truth, and she was glad he knew it. Not that it helped the current situation. She reminded herself of the calendar. Of the fact that soon she and Nicole would be leaving. It seemed Gibson was reading her mind.

"In just a little over two months you and Nicole will be free of us." This time a touch of bitterness edged his words.

"You know that isn't why we're planning to leave."

"Like hell I do. I wish you'd tell me. And I hope you tell your father, too. Because he's going to be devastated when you're gone. Probably revert to the same cantankerous pain in the butt as before."

"Don't try to make me feel guilty."

He gave a short laugh. "You just don't get it, do you? I wasn't counting on guilt being the reason you would stay."

God help her when he looked at her the way he was doing right now. Her determination softened the way the soil did after the rain. If only there were a way... Just admitting her love would be such a relief.

"Oh, God, Libby..."

He was reaching for her when Allie's voice came from behind. Libby turned to see the girls approaching. They walked several feet apart, the coolness between them evident.

"Can we go home now, Daddy?" Allie put her arms around his waist. "I did what you told me."

He reached down to stroke her hair. "Did you apologize to Nicole, too?"

"Yes."

Nicole confirmed this with a small nod. In her hand she clutched an envelope identical to the one that Libby held.

"Fine, then. Let's go." Before turning around to leave, however, he had a parting message for Nicole. "Don't forget we have our last game on Thursday. We'll need our star player in top shape!"

He glanced at Libby. "There's a little ceremony after the game where we give all the kids medals for participating. You might want to bring your camera."

Libby nodded, while Nicole whooped with excitement. "Who are we playing, Coach?"

"Sledgewood." He gave Libby a sardonic look, then followed Allie into the truck and drove away.

# CHAPTER FOURTEEN

THE FEELING that her stomach was full of molten lava lessened as Nicole watched Allie get off the bus. Allie had been even meaner than usual at school today. She'd told everybody it was Nicole's fault that she got grounded. Then she organized the other girls to make fun of Nicole's clothes and how slow she was at coming up with the answers in math.

Worst was when Allie had mocked Libby's dirty hands and the way she always kissed Nicole before and after school.

"Mommy's girl," Allie and her friends had called out during recess.

The problem was, Allie had lived in Chatsworth all her life. She had so many friends and everybody listened to her. Nicole didn't know what to do about it. At recess she'd watched the boys playing softball, but she hadn't dared ask again if she could join in. Their last rejection was still fresh in her mind. And maybe it was just as well. She'd never played the game before; she'd probably have made a fool of herself if they'd said yes.

Nicole saw her mother watching her in the rearview mirror, and she scrunched lower in her seat. Out the window she could see the fields were now a lush green, and most of the crops were about knee high. At least her grandpa's were.

Living on a farm was just as great as she'd always thought it would be when she'd listened to her mother's stories in Toronto. She didn't even mind the problems at school so much, knowing she had her mother and grandpa to come home to, the new kittens and calves, even those pesky chickens. Her mom was happier, too. She rarely had that sad look anymore, although she was wearing it right now as she turned in her seat after parking the bus at the side of the house.

"Do you want a snack?" her mother asked.

"I'm not hungry, but can I take some milk out to the kittens?"

"Okay, but change your clothes first."

"I will," Nicole said as she rushed off the bus. In the kitchen she grabbed an apple, then raced up the stairs to her room. Heading for her dresser, she noticed something on the bedspread: a softball and a real leather glove.

She slid her backpack off her shoulders to the floor and exchanged the apple for the glove. It felt stiff and awkward on her hand, and when she placed the ball in the pocket, it took effort to close the leather around it.

"It'll soften with wear." Her grandfather's voice came from behind her; although she hadn't known he was there, he didn't startle her.

"Wow, grandpa! This is just the neatest thing...." She threw the ball gently into the mitt. Again and again. She couldn't believe it was really hers. And the mitt was genuine leather, not cheap plastic. She could tell by the smell.

She looked at her grandfather and saw that he was smiling. She ran over to him and gave him a big hug.

"How about we play some catch?" he said.

Then she noticed that he had a mitt on his hand, too.

"I used to play with my son, Chris."

The folded skin around her grandpa's eyes seemed to hang lower. She squeezed his hand. "The one who was killed in the car accident? With Grandma?"

He nodded. His mouth turned down, but the pressure he applied to her hand told her he would be okay.

"The front yard is the best place to play," he said.

They went outside, going through the kitchen, but her mother wasn't there. She was in the garden—weeding or something. As they passed the side of the house, Nicole could see the occasional white flash of her shirt in between branches of the lilac hedge.

"We'll start out nice and slow," her grandpa said. "When you feel the ball hit your mitt, bring up your other hand to make sure it doesn't fall out." He demonstrated.

She nodded and waited for him to throw. The first toss came in a nice gentle arc. She eyed it and positioned herself at the bottom of its trajectory. It landed neatly in her glove, and she quickly closed over it with her other hand.

"Well done. You're a natural."

Her grandfather was smiling again, the way he had

in her room. Nicole grinned and tossed the ball back to him. He was a neat guy, her grandpa.

She only wished that he were as nice to her mother as he was to her. She couldn't imagine what the two of them had fought about. Her mother hardly ever got angry and she rarely raised her voice. So what could have made her so mad? As for Grandpa, well, he was so much fun. Nicole thought grown-ups were very strange sometimes.

THURSDAY CAME all too quickly. At least from Libby's point of view. She watched as Nicole counted the days, then the hours, with anticipation, and yearned to share the excitement. But all she felt was a nervous dread at the prospect of seeing Darren again. As Libby rinsed early leaf lettuce at the kitchen sink, she listened to the happy sounds of Nicole and her grandpa playing catch in the side yard, and tried to convince herself she was worrying about nothing.

After all, Darren didn't remember they'd had sex together, let alone that he'd forced her to. And even if he did, he wasn't likely to make any trouble for her now. It had been so many years ago; so much had happened since. He now had a wife and children he adored. He probably hadn't given Libby a second thought since the last time she'd seen him—while he was a constant, unwanted disturbance to her peace of mind.

"Will you come to the game tonight, Grandpa?"

Libby's attention swung back to the present as the

sound of Nicole's voice floated through the open kitchen window.

"It's the last one," Nicole added. "Do you think the time is right yet?"

Libby watched her father toss the ball back. Nicole caught it with a satisfying *snap*. He was slow to reply. "Yeah...maybe it is, Nicky. Do you think your mother would mind?"

Obviously he didn't know she was at the window and could hear every word. Libby stepped back, guilty at having eavesdropped, however unintentionally. Her father's words reverberated in her brain, making her feel peculiar, almost a little dizzy.

Why did he think she might object?

More important, why did he care?

Libby rubbed at the muscles behind her neck. She was sore from having spent hours in the garden. Her hands felt rough and strong on the smooth skin of her back. Despite the apparently growing relationship between her father and Nicole her relationship with him hadn't progressed at all.

It was still almost as though she didn't exist.

And yet he'd said, *Do you think your mother would mind?*

Libby finished preparing the salad. The table was set; everything else was ready. She went out the front door to where the two of them were still playing catch. Nicole saw her first and her arm froze, the softball still in it.

"Dinnertime, Mom?"

Libby nodded. She half turned to go back into the

house, then hesitated. She forced her gaze to her father. "Coming, Dad?"

The moment stretched, like a pull of taffy, and then suddenly it snapped as Nicole threw the ball toward her grandfather.

*Pop!* It landed center mitt. Henry Bateson put his hand over the glove to hold the ball tight. Then he looked back at Libby. "Be right there."

And that was that. They ate together for the first time since Libby had returned to the farm. Meat loaf, mashed potatoes and fresh garden salad. There was no awkwardness, because Nicole was so excited she talked the whole time. And then they were in a big rush because the game was scheduled to start in thirty minutes. Libby was surprised to see her father stand up to rinse the dishes.

"Why don't you call Gibson," he said, "and tell him you don't need a ride."

Libby nodded, her eyes not quite raising to meet her father's. There was something surreal about having him speak to her so matter-of-factly. As if the eight years between them had never happened. As if he'd never told her not to come home. As if he'd never told her to leave in the first place.

Reluctantly, Libby went to the phone. Her fingers trembled as she dialed. She prayed for Allie to pick up. But of course Allie's father answered.

"Hi, Gibson." She felt self-conscious even saying his name. "I wanted to let you know we won't need a ride to the game. Dad's coming and we're taking his truck."

"Your dad's going to the game?"

He sounded incredulous, and Libby couldn't blame him. "Yes. Nicole wanted him to."

"Well, that's great."

Libby wished she could see his face so she could better judge his words. Undoubtedly, he was glad that her father was getting out, reverting to a more normal lifestyle. But was he sorry they wouldn't be driving up with him? Or relieved?

"So I guess we'll see you there...." Oddly, she now felt loath to disconnect the call. Even the sound of his breath coming gently over the wire was something worth hearing.

"Right." The single word came out clipped, emotionless. He hung up, leaving her no time to reply. Well, he was probably busy getting ready to go. As was she.

Libby made sure Nicole had her shin pads and T-shirt, then she went upstairs to brush her hair and put on lipstick. For a moment she paused at the dresser, musing on the changes since she'd come back home, which she saw reflected in the mirror. She appeared healthier; she could say that much for herself. The tan helped, and so did getting more sleep. Yet she still had that anxious look in her eyes, and she acknowledged it would never disappear as long as she had Darren O'Malley to worry about.

Darren's van, already parked and unloaded, was the first thing she noticed when they drove up to the soccer field.

She peered over Nicole's head at her father who had driven into town without saying a word. She'd never told him who was responsible for her pregnancy. For all she knew he, like the rest of the towns-people, thought Owen Holst was responsible. She was glad of that now. Relieved not to have to fret about any reaction between the two men giving her and Nicole away.

The moment the truck stopped, Nicole bounded over Libby's lap and ran out to the field. Libby took a deep breath, gathering her courage. She could see Gibson and Darren conversing near the center of the field, girls darting around them like so many fish in a tank. It was strange to see the two men together. One she detested more than anyone else on earth; the other...well, the other...

She couldn't stop the floating feeling she got when Gibson raised his hand in greeting to her. She waved back, ignoring the man beside him, then made a pro-duction of setting up her folding lawn chair, in order to give herself a chance to calm down.

Across the field, her father positioned himself apart from the other spectators, reminding her of her-self that first time she'd watched one of Nicole's soc-cer games. She'd been the outsider then, and now it was her dad, who had lived in this community all his life. Even knowing he'd brought his isolation on himself, she felt sorry for him.

Libby said hello to some of the other parents and spectators, including Connie and Stan, before settling into her chair for the start of the game. Nicole played well in the first half, and while she didn't score a goal, she set the ball up for two of her teammates and even made a good pass to Allie.

Libby thought it was pretty decent of Nicole, considering the way Allie had been treating her lately, and she wished she could be as generous in spirit as her daughter. Allie's apology on Sunday had seemed a good sign, but nothing had changed in her treatment of Nicole at school and on the bus. Allie was still doing her best to make Nicole's life miserable, and Libby was getting darned tired of it.

She'd talked to Mrs. English this week and the teacher had admitted Nicole was becoming increasingly withdrawn during class. Unfortunately, neither of them could see any obvious solution to the problem.

Perhaps blaming it all on Allie wasn't fair. She certainly didn't look very happy out on the soccer field. Libby's sympathy died a sudden death, however, when she saw Allie elbow Nicole in the chest. "Pass a little sooner next time, why don't you." Allie's words floated across the field to Libby's tuned ears. She saw her father shake his head in disapproval; so he'd noticed, too. But this time they weren't the only ones.

Gibson blew his whistle, calling the game to a halt. He stalked up the field to his daughter and took her arm none too gently. With a few words about inexcusably rough play he told her she would sit out until halftime.

"Good!" Allie cried, yanking her arm away. "I hate this game anyway!" She marched off the field, head held high, and went to sit in the front seat of Gibson's truck.

Libby's heart went out to Gibson. He started up the game again and continued to follow the play as closely as ever, calling out the same words of encouragement and direction as always. But the spring was gone from his movements and his voice was untypically flat.

At halftime Gibson went to talk to his daughter. Nicole kicked a ball over to where one of the mothers was handing out cookies and chunks of apple. Too late, Libby realized she'd left herself exposed. Darren was heading her way.

"Hey, Libby. Tie game. Think we're going to beat you this time."

"Maybe so." As if it mattered. She would have given him the provincial championship right that minute in exchange for a promise to leave her alone.

"That girl of yours sure can play soccer." Darren's eyes slid insolently over her as he spoke. He still had the cocky air of a man who expected to be admired by all women and envied by all men.

Libby shuddered at the idea of Darren coming into contact with Nicole on the soccer field. Her every instinct warned her to keep the two of them as far apart as possible. She felt trapped, and angry for being trapped. It was his fault, all of it, and she had paid the price, she and Nicole, and yes, even her father, while Darren was untouched, to the extent that he had actually *forgotten*. How did you ruin someone's life and not even remember?

"Has she played a lot?" he asked.

"What?" Libby blinked, refocusing her thoughts. "Oh, Nicole. N-no, this is her first year." Libby's tongue tripped over the words. She didn't want to discuss her daughter with this man. "Your daughter's obviously very good, as well."

"Yeah, Ivy's a chip off the old block." He stuck out his chest proudly.

Libby found his posture ridiculous. She'd watched him with his daughter and knew that they shared a genuine bond. Part of Libby grieved for everything that Nicole had missed. Was one parent enough? She knew Gibson suffered from the same insecurity. But they'd both had no choice.

Most people in Chatsworth figured Darren had turned into a respectable citizen, a good father and husband. But she would never see him that way. That night in his truck she'd pleaded with him to stop, and he'd laughed at her. He'd torn her clothes, hit her, forcefully parted her legs and violently thrust himself on her.

Maybe worst of all had been his vile, stale-beer breath on her face while he was doing it; his panting, the wild look in his eyes. For a long time afterward, she'd hated herself and hated the body that had attracted such behavior. It had taken her years to transfer that hatred to the person who rightfully deserved it.

Could any woman forgive such a violation?

Suddenly short of breath, she knew she had to escape. She picked out Gibson's truck from the line of vehicles on the side of the road. He was still inside with Allie, talking. She wondered what they were saying. Darren's gaze followed hers.

"So what was that Browning kid up to? Why'd her old man kick her out of the game?"

"I couldn't see from here…" Libby lied without any sense of guilt. "I think I'll go check if Allie would like some cookies. Excuse me."

"Wait a minute." Darren held out his arm. He was going to grab her, but he must have remembered what happened the last time he tried, because when she moved away, he allowed his arm to fall back to his side.

"Later, Darren," she said, moving quickly now that her escape route was clear. She stopped to pick up a couple of cookies, then headed for the truck. Now that she was close, she slowed her pace. She didn't want to interrupt the conversation between Gibson and his daughter.

She waited until the truck door opened. Gibson emerged, then Allie, red-eyed but not crying anymore.

"Hi, Allie. I saved a couple of cookies for you. They were going fast."

"Thanks, Libby." Allie took the cookies. "Can I go sit with Grandma for a while, Dad?"

"Sure, pumpkin." Resignedly, Gibson watched her sprint ahead of him.

"Is she okay?"

He scratched the top of his head. "I suppose. I did talk to her on the weekend, Libby. I'd hoped she'd changed her attitude toward Nicole…."

Libby admired the fact that he didn't try to make excuses for his daughter. "Unfortunately, the situation was even worse this week."

The worry lines on his forehead deepened. "I'm so sorry. I blame myself for not noticing earlier."

"You were busy...."

"That's no excuse." He let out a long, tired breath. "What I can't understand is why. I know Allie isn't perfect, but I never thought she had a mean streak in her."

Libby considered that for a minute. "Did you ever wonder about those body checks Chris used to give you sometimes during hockey practice? A little stronger than necessary, I used to think. Especially when you were on a scoring streak." Chris always said Gibson came down easier when he had a swollen head on him. Libby, though, had realized what it was really about.

"You think Allie is jealous of Nicole because she's such a natural at soccer?"

"It's possible."

"Yeah." Gibson kicked at a few pebbles as they headed back to the soccer field. "No wonder you gave me such a piece of your mind the other night. I've been a lousy father."

His misery was almost more than she could bear. "Maybe you've made some mistakes, but you *are* a good father. You love Allie and you listen to her and you always make time for her. Those aren't small things, Gib."

"And you?" He caught at one of her wrists and laced his fingers with hers. "Libby, I'm not so sure I can do what you asked—stop seeing you. It hasn't even been a week and it's killing me."

This separation was destroying her, too, because she was twenty-five and had only met one man she could imagine sharing her life with. Were she and

Nicole destined to always be alone? She foresaw no alternative. She had to leave Chatsworth and there was nowhere else in the world where Gibson could be happy.

"Let's just concentrate on the kids for now. Okay?"

"No. It's not okay. Libby, I don't want to be without you."

She couldn't tell him she felt the same way. It wouldn't be fair. A whistle on the field signaled the end of halftime. Gibson grimaced. "Time to start the second half."

Libby watched as Gibson called out positions to the players. "All right, now. We've got a tie to break! Everyone ready?"

"Yeah!" The girls called back enthusiastically.

"How 'bout you, Allie?" His daughter was still standing with her grandmother. "Want to finish off the season?"

She didn't look as though she was going to say yes, but Libby saw Connie whisper something and give her a gentle push on the back. After a few hesitant steps, Allie ran to join her teammates.

Ten minutes later, Nicole broke the tie with a goal. Libby grinned when she noticed her father hollering and cheering louder than anyone. The game was almost over when Nicole got her second chance to score. This time she was almost at the goal when Ivy came out of nowhere to wrest the ball away.

It dribbled to the side, and suddenly Allie was there with no time to think. She ran forward and kicked, and miraculously it went in. For a few minutes she stood rooted to the spot, her mouth hanging open in shock. When she turned to face her father, her expression was one of incredulity.

"Did I do it, Daddy? Did I really score a goal?"

"You sure did, Allie!" Gibson gave her a high-five, then swooped her up on his shoulders. Allie's confused look turned to a grin broad enough to touch the hardest heart. The other girls joined in a circle around Allie and Gibson. Since Sledgewood was two goals behind and there were only minutes left to play anyway, they conceded the game.

As the coaches tried to organize the teams to shake hands and get their medals, Libby noticed Nicole maneuver into line behind Allie.

"Good goal, Allie," she said.

"Thanks to your pass," Allie answered softly.

"Way to go, girls," Libby murmured, watching from the sideline.

## CHAPTER FIFTEEN

NICOLE DIDN'T SIT with Allie or Ardis on the bus the next day, but for the first time in weeks it was her choice. Instead, she sat in the front by her mom so she could tell her the good news.

"One of the boys asked me to play ball at recess." Nicole perched on the edge of her seat, up closer to her mother. "Ryan Newsome. He's a really cool pitcher. He let me play catcher and I hardly missed a throw. I stopped one of the best hitters from making a home run, and I caught a fly ball that was so high it looked like a tiny dot in the sky at first."

"Wow! That sounds impressive."

"The boys said I could play again tomorrow if I wanted. Anytime I like."

"And the girls?"

"Oh, they teased me about playing with the boys, but you know what, Mom? I don't care what they think. I'd way rather play sports with the boys than sit around with the girls. All they want to do is talk, talk, talk. So boring."

"Good for you."

"There's one other girl who wants to play softball. Her name is Marisa. She came up to me after the bell and asked if I could get the boys to let her play on Monday.''

''And?''

''I think I can. It would be so cool to have another girl on the team. Marisa's signing up for softball this summer, so maybe we'll get to play together then, too.''

''Most definitely.''

Nicole proceeded to give her mom a play-by-play of the game. A few times she noticed Allie and Ardis from the corner of her eye, giggling and talking as usual, but she was concentrating so much on her story that she didn't even try to hear what they were saying. At first it had really hurt when Allie had stopped being her friend and had started saying all those mean things about her. But now it seemed so unimportant.

Who cared what a bunch of silly girls said, when there were fun things to do like soccer and softball? And not everyone was interested in what Allie thought. Both Marisa and Ryan had said she was nothing but a big sissy.

Once the bus passed Ardis's stop, Allie usually buried her nose in a book, as if she were too important to bother with any of the remaining passengers. Today, however, she walked up to the front and sat in the seat across from Nicole.

''Hi,'' she said to Nicole.

''Hi.'' Nicole frowned at the interruption. She was just getting to the good part—when she'd hit a solid grounder past the shortstop her second time at bat and had made it all the way to second base.

"I'd like to have seen that!" her mother said. After a brief pause, she added, "Do you like to play softball, Allie?"

Allie grimaced. "I hate it even more than soccer."

Nicole shook her head in disgust and turned back to her mother. She was in the process of explaining the lingo for the players' batting order, when Allie interrupted her again.

"Maybe we could be partners for the new science project we started today."

"I've already said I'd be Marisa's partner."

"Oh."

"What's the new project?" her mom asked.

"It's about dinosaurs," Nicole said. "Learning about fossils."

"Yeah. Our teacher says that some of the most interesting fossils have been found in Alberta and Saskatchewan—right here where we live!"

They were now at the Brownings' farm. As the bus stopped, Allie picked up her backpack. "Maybe we could play today."

Nicole hesitated. Allie had been so mean.

"I'd love to see your new kittens again. They're cute!"

"Aren't they..." Nicole thought for a moment, then nodded. "Mom, is it okay if Allie comes to our place?"

Strangely, her mother didn't appear pleased. "I'm not sure." She waited several moments before saying reluctantly, "You could ask your father, Allie. If he says yes..."

Allie whooped and ran out the open door. A moment later she was back with Moira. The house-keeper came up to the door and peered at Libby. "Allie says she's invited to play."

"If that's okay," her mom said.

"Gibson's working out by the shop," Moira said. "I'm sure he wouldn't mind if Allie went over, though. We'll pick her up in an hour or so."

"Fine."

Her mom didn't sound too pleased with Moira's decision. Almost as if she didn't want them playing together. But why not?

"HI, MOIRA." Gibson came in the kitchen door, his hands and clothes dirty from changing the hydraulic fluid in the John Deere. He poked at a pile of bills and a copy of the *Western Producer* on the kitchen table. Moira was just sticking a casserole into the oven.

"Is Allie in the barn?" It was unusual for his daughter not to run to greet him when he came home.

"No." Moira shut the oven door and set the timer on the stove clock. "She's gone to play with Nicole."

Gibson froze in the process of opening his gas bill. "But she was grounded for two weeks."

Moira put the oven mitts away in a drawer. "Oh, that's right. How could I have forgotten?"

The older woman had her back to him as she took her jacket and purse from the hall closet. When she finally faced him, she avoided his eyes, and he knew she was lying. She hadn't forgotten. She'd given Allie permission to play at the Batesons', deliberately violating his edict.

"You know, Moira, I can't discipline Allie properly without your help."

She fussed with a button on her jacket, as a guilty flush spread across her brown cheeks. "I understand that. It just slipped my mind. Besides, the poor thing gets lonely being by herself all the time."

"I guess if she gets lonely enough, next time she might think twice before she behaves like a spoiled three-year-old."

Moira took a deep breath, then finally met his gaze. "Do you want me to go bring her back home?"

He shook his head. "No. I'll get her."

Moira hesitated. She was probably thinking it would be easier for Allie if *she* got her. And she was right. With a frustrated sigh, he followed Moira out the door and climbed back into his pickup. It was a blazing hot day, and he flipped the air-conditioning on as he started on his way.

His annoyance was fast becoming anger. He would have to have a serious talk with Moira. But she wasn't the only one to blame. Allie knew she'd been grounded. So did Libby, come to think of it. He distinctly remembered telling her about it when he'd brought Allie over to apologize.

She had her nerve. Blaming him for his lack of discipline, then ignoring the limits he finally set. After all the things Libby had said about Allie, he was surprised she even allowed his daughter onto the Bateson farm.

Poor Allie. It wasn't her fault he had done such a miserable job of raising her.

At the Batesons' he paused halfway up the driveway. Libby was in the garden, hoeing for all she was worth. While he watched, a butterscotch-colored tabby brushed by her legs, seeking attention. Libby set down her hoe, picked up the cat, and stroked the fur.

The sight brought back memories of Libby as a young girl. In those days you never saw her without an animal, whether it was a new kitten from the barn, a runt calf, even the occasional snake or frog.

He sucked in a bellyful of air and thought how right she looked standing there, the tabby in her arms, the garden sprouting around her. She'd worked miracles in the weeks she'd been home, restoring her house to its former gentle beauty. The garden alone had been an enormous task.

And the thing was, he was sure that she'd loved every minute of the work. Didn't that tell her anything? It sure as hell spoke volumes to him.

Libby belonged here. She was happy here. Why wouldn't she admit the truth of that?

The sound of an approaching engine roused him from his thoughts. Henry was a few hundred yards behind him, bringing in the tractor for the evening. Gibson put the pickup back into drive, then pulled up alongside the yellow school bus. Libby had noticed him by then. She set down the cat and strode toward him, her heavy suede work gloves in her hands.

How could a woman look so grubby and so beautiful at the same time? Her hair was in a mess of a ponytail, and her jeans and sleeveless gray T-shirt were streaked with dirt. Half-moon sweat stains darkened the gray cotton under her breasts. He watched those breasts sway gently as she moved, then raised his eyes to see the carefully controlled expression on her face.

"Moira said Allie was here."

Libby dampened her sun-dry lips with her tongue. "They were in the barn playing with the kittens. Then I think they went into the house for a snack."

He pressed his fingers to his forehead, started toward the back door, then stopped. "You knew she was grounded, Libby. Why did you let her come over?"

"Oh, no." She dropped her hands to her sides. "I forgot, Gib. I'm sorry."

Unlike Moira, Libby seemed genuinely remorseful. Still, her lapse didn't ease his anger any. "I'm surprised you'd have her over, given what you think of her."

Libby dropped her eyes. "I'm sorry if I was too hard on her, on both of you. She's just a kid. If Nicole can forgive her, why shouldn't I?"

"Well, I'm glad the two of them are getting along again." He'd been so encouraged by Allie's behavior after the talking-to at yesterday's soccer game. Maybe he was finally getting through to her.

"Yeah, I'd say they're doing better than their parents."

"And whose fault is that?" He didn't know why he said it. They'd agreed not to see each other anymore. But he longed to know if their being apart was tearing her into little pieces the way it was him.

"Don't make this harder, Gib..."

As far as he was concerned, nothing could make it harder. "I love you, Libby. I want to be with you."

There. He'd laid all his feelings on the line. But if he thought telling Libby how he felt might change the way she looked at her future, he was mistaken.

She turned away. "Oh, Gib. I'm so sorry."

Gibson grounded his hands in the pockets of his work pants. He wasn't interested in her pity. "Hell, I guess a city girl like you can only take so much of this quiet, rural living."

She ignored his sarcasm. "That's right. I can't wait to get back to a little civilization for a change."

"Right." She was lying, and that was for sure. "Look in the mirror when you say that, Libby. Then you'll know why I can't believe you. These past months I've tried to imagine you in the city, shopping at the big department stores, going to plays and restaurants or whatever it is that people think is so damned great to do in those metropolises. But I can never get a clear picture in my head, because it just isn't you."

"Maybe you don't know me as well as you think."

For a second he doubted, but his answer came from the heart, and he was certain he was right. "I know you almost as well as I know myself. And I think there's another reason you won't stay in Chatsworth." He was almost too scared to ask, but the possibility had to be faced. "Is it Darren? Do you still love him?"

She made a choking sound. "I *never* loved Darren."

Relief gave him hope. It wasn't what he feared; she didn't still care for the father of her child.

"Could you ever come to love me?"

"Oh, Gibson!" Her voice was so full of hopelessness that he finally realized nothing he said or did would make her pull down the wall between them.

LIBBY FELT EXHAUSTED, at the very limit of her endurance. The hours in the hot sun, the hard physical labor and now this. She couldn't stand up to Gibson anymore. She had to get away before she broke down and confessed the whole sorry story of her life.

"Let me go and get Allie for you."

Gibson squared his shoulders and nodded, avoiding her eyes. The hurt in his face made her want to comfort him, but what could she say to make him happy?

*You're right. I do love you, and I love living on the farm.* It was true, all of it. But why tell him, when she still couldn't stay? It wouldn't make things any easier for either of them. And she'd never want to put him in a position where he might feel obliged to leave his farm for her. Separating Gibson from his land would be the cruelest thing she could do.

"I'll just be a minute."

She ran to the house, stumbling occasionally on the uneven ground, her heart pounding in her ears, her eyesight blurred from unshed tears. The strongest, most dependable and loving man she'd ever known had just told her he loved her. And she'd had to turn him away.

He would hate her now, and she wouldn't blame him. She almost hated herself. If she'd had the courage to stand up to Darren years ago, she wouldn't be in this mess. She should have gone to the police. Why had she been such a coward?

Libby paused at the doorway to the house to catch her breath. She felt dizzy and her stomach lurched with nausea. She should have been wearing a hat in the hot June sun.

At last she went inside. The screen door banged behind her, the sound reverberating through the suspiciously quiet house. "Nicole? Allie?"

She walked past the empty kitchen to the stairs. "Your father's here, Allie," she called as she ran up to the second story. No answer. She checked the three bedrooms. She even checked the storage areas. No sign of two little girls. Maybe they were hiding, knowing Gibson would be angry because Allie was supposed to be grounded.

"This is no time for silly games," she warned as she went back downstairs to investigate the living and dining rooms and her father's bedroom. Finally, she went out the front, half expecting to find them hiding on the porch, but they weren't there, either.

Perhaps they'd gone outside, maybe back to the barn. She paused on her way to the outbuildings to ask her father, who was at the fuel tanks, filling the tractor for the next day. "Have you seen Nicole and Allie, Dad?"

He took off his cap and ran an arm over his forehead. "Nope. Nicole usually comes by to help me with the chores about now." He scanned the farmyard, then looked back at his daughter. "Allie's here, you say?"

"Yes. They made up today. It's a long story..." She shook her head to show that it was all beyond her. "I'll try the barn."

"I'll look in the machine shed when I'm finished."

"Never mind." Gibson's voice, low and firm, startled them both as he came up from the other side of the tractor. He was frowning, and as he stretched a long, tanned arm to rest on the large back tire, he tapped his fingers impatiently. "I've already tried both places." His gaze flickered back to Libby, then away. "I take it they weren't in the house?"

"No." She twisted one finger around a piece of her hair. "I didn't see them leave, but they must have."

"You wouldn't necessarily see them from behind the lilac bush."

"No, but Nicole usually tells me if she's going for a walk."

"Usually," he echoed.

Libby fought the instinct to defend herself. Gibson wasn't in any mood to listen. And the truth was the children had been in her care. If they had sneaked off somewhere, the responsibility was ultimately hers. But she didn't believe she'd been negligent.

Nicole often amused herself for stretches of time without checking in with her mother. As Libby had, too, at her age. She trusted her daughter. But she didn't know if she should have trusted Allie.

"They've got to be around here someplace," her father said. "Probably hiding and having a good laugh." He released the trigger on the gas hose and hung the hose back up on the side of the cylinder-shaped tank. "I'll look in the pasture. Maybe they went out to see the cows."

"I'll go check the house again and make sure they aren't hiding there," Libby said, "or back behind the gardens."

Gibson looked from one to the other uncertainly, then nodded. "I'll drive along the road allowance to see if they went for a walk. Let's all meet back here in fifteen minutes."

"Right." This time Libby ran to the house. The raw pain from her conversation with Gibson was quickly taking a back seat to her growing sense of unease about the girls. Where could they be? Land stretched for miles on every side of them. If they'd left the farmyard they could be anywhere. Finding them might take hours.

*Don't get paranoid*, Libby cautioned herself. What could happen to a couple of kids on a farm? It wasn't like the city, where you had to worry about your children every second of the day. There were no busy streets or potentially threatening strangers.

But there were dangers on a farm. Powerful, complicated machinery, like the auger, the combine or bailer. Animals. Cows were usually pretty meek, but there was the bull to consider. And the dry well back of the garden. Libby's heart constricted at the thought, and for the moment she bypassed the house and ran to inspect the old, stone-covered, hole.

"Nicole! Allie!" she called as she scrambled to the old well. But it was covered, with no trace of any fresh footprints around. She ran on a bit farther, still calling their names, then after about ten minutes turned back to the house.

This time she went through the rooms more thoroughly—peeking into all sorts of odd hiding places in case they were playing some ill-conceived game. She even opened the trapdoor to the cellar and went down into the musty dark, to no avail. The fifteen minutes were more than past when she finally returned to the fuel tanks to check in with the others. She could see instantly, from their faces, that neither of them had found the girls.

It had started to get dark, but not because of the setting sun; it was too early for that. Gray clouds were gathering from the west, and Libby suspected they were in for one of the late-afternoon thundershowers so common on hot summer afternoons.

"It's going to rain," she said breathlessly as she ran toward the men. "We've got to find them."

Gibson looked at her sharply, as if biting back an acrimonious remark. He was losing it, Libby could tell. Behind the cold anger and the grim determination was the hint of an emotion she was beginning to feel, as well.

Panic. His worst nightmare was coming true. His

daughter was potentially in danger, and he couldn't help her.

Libby gave her head a mental shake. The odds were that the children were absolutely safe. They'd just strayed a bit farther from home than usual. Surely they'd noticed a storm was on its way and any second they would come running over the hill in the far pasture. It sounded so reasonable that Libby turned to look. But there was no trace of either Nicole or Allie.

"Maybe I'm overreacting," Gibson said, "but I think we'd better call on some neighbors to help us broaden our search. Better safe than sorry. And that storm is moving in pretty quickly."

It was true. Clouds completely blocked the sun now, and the air had a peculiar stillness to it that made the hairs on the back of Libby's neck bristle. The three of them turned their heads upward to examine the quickly mounting gray thunderheads.

"My guess is we'll be seeing some pretty terrific lightning," Henry Bateson said, pulling out a handkerchief and rubbing dirt from his face.

Libby wasn't fooled by his casual tone or casual gesture. The saying that lightning never strikes the same place twice was absolutely wrong, and their farm had been a target more than once. She remembered the time a cow standing next to a grove of poplars on a hill had been hit and killed instantly.

High hills. Trees. Those were the spots to avoid.

And then a really scary thought occurred to her.

"The tree house," she said to Gibson. "Do you think they might have gone there?"

## CHAPTER SIXTEEN

"DOES NICOLE know about the tree house?" Gibson asked.

"Of course." The story of how Chris and Gibson had put up a No Girls Allowed sign—which Libby finally removed five years later—had been one of her daughter's favorites when she was little. "We had a picnic there just last weekend."

"I'll go check, then." He was already striding toward the west pasture. "In any case, I still think you should make those calls."

"I will."

Ten minutes later there were five sets of searchers on the way. Even the Tylers had said they'd be right over.

"Well, the rascals aren't up there." Her father came down from the second story, brushing dust from his hands. He must have searched the storage rooms, too.

"Oh, Lord..."

"Now, don't fret. I'm going to try the slough by the Tylers' property line. I remember telling Nicole about a pair of trumpet swans nesting there. She may have taken it in her head to hunt them out."

"Okay." Libby clutched the back of a chair, anxiety buzzing through her veins, making it hard to focus.

She no longer felt that Gibson had been overreacting. Something really bad could have happened to the girls. Maybe one of them had been hurt. Libby pictured Nicole climbing a tree, then falling and breaking her leg. Or what if she and Allie had wandered beyond familiar landmarks and become lost? They could be out in the fields for hours. With thunder and lightning on its way, the best the girls would get was the scare of their life.

And the worst—

"Dad, I never told Nicole what to do in an electrical storm. In the city there was never any need. Do you think Allie knows enough to stay away from trees and the crests of hills?"

"It won't come down to that," he said.

Yes. He was right.

"When the neighbors get here, you tell them where to search. Make sure we cover the whole property. I should be back in about half an hour."

Half an hour. Surely the girls would be found by then.

"Okay, D-Dad." Libby bit her lip and struggled to push her tears to the pit of her stomach.

"It'll be okay." Her father squeezed her shoulder, then left. Five minutes later the first neighbor pulled into the lane.

Ardis's father and Tobey were in the cab of the pickup. "Dad's gone to the far slough at the north end of the property and Gibson's checking to the west, up to the tree house." Libby showed them a map she'd drawn hastily on the back of a manila envelope. "How about heading east for about a mile along the road?"

"Sure thing, Libby," Tobey said from the open window. They didn't waste time getting out of their vehicle.

No sooner were they gone than the next vehicle arrived, with Garnet York and her husband, Mick. A steady stream of friends and neighbors followed and about half an hour later searchers were covering every square inch of the property. A couple of the older women were in the kitchen preparing coffee and soup.

Libby paced outside as she waited, scanning the horizon constantly for signs of the girls.

It wasn't long before she saw a man—with a child on his shoulders—coming from the west. Uttering a soft cry, she ran toward him.

"You found them!" she yelled, running faster as she recognized Nicole's brown curls. Relief mixed with new fear. Why was he carrying Nicole? Had she been hurt after all? Then came a second, more terrifying, realization.

"Where's Allie?"

Gibson was now within speaking range. She could see the grim lines around his mouth, the full-fledged panic in his eyes. "I didn't find her. The girls separated." He set Nicole down gently. "I'm going to check a little farther back of the tree house. The rest of the searchers get here?"

"Yes." Libby circled her daughter with her arms, while continuing to watch Gibson. "I've parceled them out in groups. It won't be long until we locate her.''

Gibson didn't appear convinced. ''I'd better get back out there.''

''I want to help.'' Libby rose, Nicole's arms still gripping her waist.

Gibson paused only a second, his glance sliding to the small girl beside her. ''You're needed here, Libby.'' Then he turned and began loping across the field in the direction he'd just come from.

''Oh, sweetie.'' Libby rested her face against Nicole's soft brown curls. They were damp from the rain, and her small body felt chilled, but she was home and safe.

If only Allie were, too.

''What happened, sweetie? I thought you and Allie were playing in the house.''

Nicole had been crying. Her eyes were red, her face streaked with tears. ''We went out to look for dinosaur bones.''

*Dinosaur bones.* Libby remembered the girls' conversation in the bus and kicked herself for not making the connection earlier. A faded childhood memory tugged at the corner of her mind, but Nicole was talking, and she bent lower to listen.

''I wanted to tell you,'' Nicole was saying, ''but Allie said we wouldn't go far. We ended up at the old tree house, Mom, but then I saw the storm coming and I said I wanted to come back. Allie wouldn't listen, so I just left on my own. Only, I got lost. When I couldn't see the house, or the barn, or even the pasture. I didn't know which way to turn.''

"Oh, Nicole." Libby squeezed her tighter, then pulled away to examine her face more closely. "Did you hurt yourself anywhere?"

"No." Nicole shook her head sadly. "I hope Gibson finds Allie, though."

"Me, too, sweetie. Me, too."

Libby led her daughter inside. One of the women dished out warm soup while another took Nicole into the bathroom to wash her up. Unable to concentrate on any one job for more than a second, Libby paced the kitchen floor. If something happened to Allie, Gibson would go crazy. As for herself, she could never live with the guilt, knowing she was responsible.

The storm hit with a vengeance. The house actually trembled as an ear-shattering crack followed a sky-splitting bolt of ice-white lightning. Nicole shrieked with fear, jumping up from her chair and spilling her soup.

"Stay away from the window," Libby warned as one of the women put her arms around Nicole. She wanted to comfort her daughter, too, but the memory that had baited her earlier had suddenly returned, as if jolted by the surge of electrical energy.

There was a place past the far pasture that her grandfather had used as a burial ground for old animals. She'd discovered it as a child and come running home, certain she'd found the ruins of an ancient civilization. Not that Allie could have possibly known about this place. But if she'd accidentally stumbled upon it she might have thought she'd found dinosaur fossils.

The worst thing was, it was on a hill, next to a grove of tall old poplars. Garnet and Mick were looking in that direction, but they didn't know the area the way she did.

Libby acknowledged that she couldn't stand waiting any longer. She pulled on a rain slicker of her father's. "If anybody's wondering where I am, tell them I've gone to the burying grounds beyond the far pasture."

The older women nodded, while Nicole's fear made perfect circles of her bright eyes. Libby wished she had the time to reassure her daughter, but every moment was precious now. The storm was moving closer by the minute. The danger from the lightning was very real. Not just to the little lost girl, but to the searchers, also. There was no way she could expect them to face the danger while she stayed in the relative comfort and safety of her home.

She ran out past the barns, toward the pasture. Forked lightning flashed in front of her, illuminating her way through the storm-darkened day, and she covered her ears against the terrifying clap of thunder that followed only one or two seconds later. Wind blasted the rain against her body, pelting her face and hands as she tried to shield her eyes to see ahead.

She thought of Allie in her jeans and T-shirt. No jacket or even a sweater for protection. The child had to be freezing. And frightened. Libby ran with everything she had in her, holding on to the image of the lost girl. Eventually her lungs began to burn; she couldn't suck the oxygen in fast enough. She had to slow to a jog, but still she kept moving.

"Allie!" she called. "Allie!" There was no chance her voice would carry in this storm, but she needed to say the little girl's name. It was like a prayer, and maybe if she said it often enough, Allie might somehow materialize.

Soon Libby reached the fence on the far side of the pasture, and she knew her destination was close at hand. Ahead was the rise where the grove of poplars stood. No sign of Allie from here, but she tried not to let that discourage her.

After parting the strands of barbed wire, Libby passed through the fence, then continued to run. The rain had turned to ice pellets that stung on contact. *Please don't get any bigger,* she pleaded. Not out of concern for the crops—which were still young enough to recover from the hail—but out of a fear for Allie. If the ice chunks became too big, that would only entice Allie to search for the cover of the trees—the worst place she could go during the electrical storm.

*Please be here, Allie,* Libby prayed as she crested the hill. A haphazard pile of rocks and stones defined the burial ground. To the north stood the poplars. But nowhere did she spot a little girl.

"Allie! Allie!" Libby's hope turned to despair. She'd known finding the child here was a long shot. Turning a full 360 degrees, she held her hands up to the sky, as if bargaining with the gods while she scoured the vicinity for the smallest sign.

It came during the brightest flash of lightning yet. For a brief second the blue-white light illumined the area, casting trees into long black shadows, rocks into menacing shapes and the earth itself into complex patterns of light and dark. Libby saw a movement within the grove of trees. She ran forward. Allie was grabbing on to the trunk of a tree, sobbing her heart out.

"Allie!" The keening wind smothered her cries. Libby ran faster. "Get away from those trees!" she reached the girl in seconds, although it felt like minutes. "Allie!"

The little face turned toward her at last. Terror instantly became relief. "Libby! I'm so scared!"

"I know, sweetie," Libby wrapped her arms around the shivering child. "But we have to get away from these trees." Once she'd gathered Allie in her arms, Libby headed down the hill, just as another bolt of lightning connected sky and earth in a blazing trail of fire.

This time the lightning struck close enough that she felt the heat, smelled the acrid stench of something burning.

"Libby!" Allie's shriek pierced her ears, as well as her heart. Libby stumbled, but kept moving until they were on lower ground. Then she collapsed at last.

"Take me home," Allie pleaded, her mouth against Libby's ear. "I'm so scared." She was still shivering. Her meager clothes were sopping, her hair plastered to her face.

"Soon, sweetheart," Libby promised, working her way out of her slicker, then throwing it over the freezing child. "We should wait for the storm to move on a little first. Stay low to the ground, like this.'' She helped Allie assume a curled position on the earth, then place herself above as a shield from the cold and the wind.

They stayed like that for long minutes as several more bolts of lightning jolted the prairie sky. With each boom of thunder Allie trembled beneath her, and Libby squeezed her reassuringly. ''We're safe here, Allie. The storm will pass soon.''

At some point she started crooning a lullaby she'd sung when Nicole was a baby.

Libby couldn't remember ever feeling so cold. Her clothing was soaked, too. The hail had stayed small, thank goodness, but the little ice particles made her feel as if a swarm of biting insects were attacking her.

Beneath her, Allie lay still except for her constant shivering and the rhythmic spasms that were the aftermath of her tears.

''Hush, hush,'' Libby said, pressing her lips against Allie's ear. ''It's going to be fine. I promise.''

Allie let out a long, trembling breath, then said, ''I found some dinosaur bones. I really did.''

''Good for you.'' There would be time enough later to explain that she'd really discovered nothing but skeletal remains from old and diseased cattle that had died decades, rather than millions of years, ago.

A few more minutes went by. Libby anxiously counted the seconds between lightning flashes. Slowly the intervals increased, signaling that the storm was finally moving on. Libby delayed until there was a good five-second interval before she stood up.

"We can go back now. Do you think you can walk, because I'm not strong enough to carry you the whole way."

"I can walk," Allie said bravely. She reached out a cold, damp hand to Libby. "Thanks for the coat. Do you want it back? You're really wet."

"So are you, sweetie." Libby smiled at the sight of Allie in the enormous old coat that hung almost to her ankles, the hood obscuring her fine blond hair and most of her face, except for two large, anxious eyes, a small pale mouth and a button of a nose. Intense relief and gratitude swept over her and she bent down to hug the little girl. "I'm so glad you're all right."

Allie smiled back tentatively. "I liked that song you were singing. It made me feel safe."

"That was Nicole's favorite when she was little."

"Do you think my mom sang to me, too, when I was a baby?"

Libby had to swallow before she could answer. "I'm sure she did. Maybe your daddy, also."

Allie shook her head. "Daddy says he has a voice like a frog. But he likes to whistle sometimes. Are you going to marry him?"

"Marry?" Libby stumbled around a dried old cow patty.

"Nicole saw you kissing. I saw you holding hands. Dad's always staring at you, and he wants me and Nicole to be friends so bad. Hey, if you two got married, she'd be my sister, wouldn't she?"

"Yes. But your dad and I haven't talked about getting married." And they never would. Lightning might strike the same spot twice, but Gibson would never again ask her to marry him, because he could never forgive her for what had almost happened to Allie.

"I think Daddy would like to have Nicole as a daughter. They're both crazy about sports. Grandpa tells me stories about all the tournaments Daddy won when he was a kid."

They trudged on, footsteps squishing in the rain-soaked grass. "I'm not much good at sports, you know," Allie added.

Libby squeezed her hand. "Me, either. And I wasn't even great at school, the way you are."

"There's nothing special about being good at school. Teachers act like it matters, but nobody else cares how you do in your math test, or what level of books you can read."

Libby thought about the cheers that went up every time Nicole scored a goal in soccer. "I know what you mean, Allie. But believe me, it matters how you do in school. It really does. If I had done well and finished my grade twelve when I was young, life would have been much easier for me and Nicole."

"Really? How?"

Libby never got a chance to answer, because they were close enough to the house now that they were spotted. The sound of people shouting to them was slowly becoming audible.

Libby made wide, waving motions with her free hand. "She's fine!" she yelled as she and Allie picked up their pace.

"Allie?" Gibson was unmistakable in the

crowd—a tall, imposing man, whose fair coloring was already discernible.

Allie couldn't see his features from this distance, but hearing her name was all the little girl needed to propel her forward.

"Daddy?" she called, scanning the crowd. Then, "Daddy!" She dropped Libby's hand and ran with all her might, yellow slicker flapping around her young, strong legs, her arms flailing, wet hair streaming behind her.

Gibson engulfed his daughter in his arms, taking care that she not see the worry and relief he knew were still etched on his face.

"Hush, hush, it's okay," he whispered over the little girl's sobs, unable to raise his voice for fear of it cracking. He took a deep breath, then another. *She was okay; she really was.*

Lifting his head, he spotted Libby standing several yards back. He could see her limbs shaking. It wasn't just from the cold, he knew. In the distance were the smoldering remains of a tall poplar tree. How close had the lightning been?

"Take me home, Daddy!" Allie was crying, and he tightened his hold on her.

He gave Libby one last look. A storm of emotion swept over him. He wanted to crush her in his arms as he'd done Allie. But he had no right; Libby had made that perfectly clear. She stood alone, as always, vulnerable, yet strong. Beautiful and wild, and utterly beyond his reach for reasons he might never have a chance to understand.

He wanted to damn her for her pride and for her

independence, even though they were partly why he loved her so much.

She'd saved his daughter, and he wanted to thank her. That much at least he was allowed. But already the crowd behind him was surging forward with blankets and words of encouragement. Someone handed him one for Allie, and he wrapped the warm wool around her, then carried her back to the house.

People had been busy inside the small farm kitchen and he could smell the coffee and chicken soup before the door was opened to admit him. Once inside he changed Allie out of her drenched clothing into a warm sweatsuit that Nicole offered. Her small face was concerned and, as usual, she was quiet.

"Thanks, Nicole." He forced himself to smile. "Don't look so worried. Everyone's fine. Your mom will be here any minute."

"Someone said the lightning hit a tree up behind the pasture," Nicole said.

"It was so close to us you wouldn't believe it," Allie said, suddenly drawn out of her tears. "I was standing in the trees when Libby found me. She carried me down the hill and we curled up like little hedgehogs."

"She was right," Gibson said, shivering at the picture of Allie in the midst of those old poplars. That image would haunt his dreams for a long time to come.

Once Allie was dressed they went back downstairs. She had some soup, while he drank a much needed coffee. In the dining room Henry was offering shots from his whiskey bottle, and Gibson went there next.

When he asked Henry where Libby was he was told she was in the tub.

"She was so cold. It seemed the best way to get her warm," Henry said.

"Well, I'd like to stay and thank her, but Allie's eager to get home."

"I can see that." Henry's old gray eyes focused gently on the little girl, who had come in from the kitchen and was clutching her father's waist. "You can drop by later if you want to give your thanks in person."

Gibson nodded. Maybe he would. Once everything had calmed down.

## CHAPTER SEVENTEEN

LIBBY SAGGED into the wooden kitchen chair, watching as her father reheated the chicken soup. Nicole was upstairs sleeping; the last neighbor had just left. The drama was finally over and everyone was safe, yet despite a long, hot bath Libby couldn't stop shivering. She drew up her legs, tucking them under the long hem of Chris's old sweatshirt, and pulled the heavy woolen blanket around her knees. It didn't seem to matter how much external warmth she applied; nothing could reach the cold chill.

Her father filled a bowl and set it in front of her.

"That oughta warm you."

"Thanks, Dad." Even through the most difficult periods in Toronto, Libby couldn't remember ever feeling quite as demoralized as she did right now. Putting a hand to her damp hair, she tucked one of the winding curls back behind her ear.

She'd been so quick to criticize Gibson's parenting skills, but it was while the girls were under *her* care that they'd almost come to serious harm. She'd never forget the ravaged look on Gibson's face when he'd brought Nicole home safely but still had no idea where his own daughter was.

When her father put the saucepan back on the

stove, a drop of the soup fell onto the element, hissing loudly in the quiet of the room. The pungent scent reminded Libby of the moment the lightning had struck. The crack, the sizzle, how the ground itself had trembled.

What if Allie had been standing under those trees and Libby had arrived just five minutes later?

Her father poured himself the last of the coffee and settled in the chair that had been his for as long as she remembered.

Libby ate her soup quietly, the ticking of the kitchen clock and the knocking of china against wood the only impositions on the thick cloak of evening silence. True quiet, she mused, could only be experienced in the country, during that brief period when it was too late for the croaking of the frogs and the grasshoppers but too early for the dawn serenade of the morning birds.

*Mother. Chris.* She felt their absence in a way she hadn't since she'd come back home. With regret and sorrow, rather than stabbing pain and resentment. Libby cupped the warm bowl in one hand and wondered if her father felt the same way.

He'd changed so much since they'd arrived. Had somehow become human again, gotten out of the dark empty space he'd locked himself into the day of the accident. She hoped that meant he'd finally come to grips with her mother's death, but she had no way of knowing for sure if that was it. Her father was not, never had been, an easy man to read.

Now she caught him staring at his mug of coffee. She was surprised to see he hadn't touched it.

"Dad?"

He tapped his sun-darkened, work-roughened fingers against the side of the large white mug. Black lettering pronouncing World's Best Dad had faded to pale gray, or disappeared in places.

"I'm thinking about how I felt when I saw you coming down from the pasture with that girl," he said.

He'd been the first to reach her—the other rescuers had focused on Allie and Gibson. He'd wrapped a blanket over her shoulders, along with his arm. And even though he wasn't as big as he used to be, he'd still been a solid, comforting presence at her side.

"I don't know what I'd have done if you hadn't been okay, Libby…." His voice wobbled, trailed off, until he was left shaking his head wordlessly.

Libby thought of the showdown she'd dreamed of for so many years. In her mind it had been a decisive confrontation, with her father finally admitting he'd been wrong to kick her off the farm. She'd nursed her pain and fear, imagining herself turning him away, telling him that she would never forgive him.

But life rarely played out with such high drama. Real apologies were actions, not words. And forgiveness could sneak up on you.

She and Nicole had suffered, but they had survived. There was nothing to be gained in holding grudges. Looking at her father now, she acknowledged that it was the last thing she wanted. If they had suffered, well, so had he. There was no way to figure out where the balance lay; all she knew was that it was time for the discord to end. For all of them. She reached across the table to cover the hand that was so old and worn, yet still strong and dear.

"It's okay, Dad."

He captured her hand and gave it a big squeeze. "I want you to know that the farm is yours, Libby. Yours and Nicole's. Giving it to you won't come close to making everything up to you, but I've had the lawyers working on the papers."

"Dad? What are you saying?"

"I don't want you to have to worry about money anymore. Or a place to stay. If you want, I'll move out. You can rent the land. To Gibson, maybe."

Libby reached out with her other hand. This was her father's atonement, the gesture that spoke the words he still couldn't utter. "I don't want you to move off the farm. You belong here."

He paused for a long time, before finally shaking his head in acceptance of that. "Are you still planning to leave?"

Libby examined the dregs of her soup, remembering Gibson's taunting words. What *would* happen to her dad once she and Nicole were gone? Damn him for being right about this. She didn't want to go, but she had no choice. That was what Gibson had never understood. Would her father?

"Yes," she said softly. "But it won't be like before. We can visit. We'll call...."

Her dad nodded and she could tell he hadn't heard anything beyond the fact that they were going to leave.

"You have to do what's right for you and Nicky," he said.

Yes. Nicole was the priority. Even though the thought of leaving made Libby feel dead inside.

But she had no choice. Darren's presence would be a constant worry and threat to her peace of mind. She couldn't live with a cloud like that hanging over her. And she couldn't keep blaming herself for the mistakes of the past.

She shouldn't have been alone in that car with Darren. They shouldn't have been drinking, especially not with Darren driving. But she'd been young; she hadn't had the experience to know the danger she was courting. Without her mother's love and influence, she'd been adrift.

Then later, after he'd raped her, she should have reported the incident to the police, one of her teachers, someone. Darren should have paid the price for what he'd done to her. But she'd been scared and alone. Her father had been off in his own dark world, her mother dead.

She had to forgive herself for that, too. Absolution, though, could not come at the cost of Nicole's happiness. Never had Libby been more certain that she was doing the right thing by protecting her daughter from the facts surrounding her conception.

She felt a hand at her shoulder. A soft touch against the top of her head. ''Don't worry, Libby. It'll work out, somehow.''

''I know. It's just—'' She sighed, wanting things to be different but not being able to make them so.

''When you go, take the money that was in your mother's savings account. She put a good bit away.

It should be enough to buy you and Nicky a nice little house.''

"That's your money, Dad.''

"You're wrong. It belongs to us, our family. And I know Mother would have wanted you to have it. Same as the money in the cookie jar. I saw you borrow a few dollars when you first came. I only wish I'd had the courage to tell you not to bother paying it back.''

But she had. With her first paycheck.

"That's very generous of you, Dad.''

"It's only money, Libby. I wish I'd been generous in the ways that really count." He rose awkwardly to leave the room.

"I love you, Dad.''

He froze. Even in the old days, these words had never been said, only implied. Libby saw his shoulders lift, then fall, on a long uncertain breath. When he turned, his expression was both sad and tender, and the wetness of tears glistened around his eyes.

"I love you, too, Elizabeth. My precious daughter.''

After he had gone to bed, Libby rested her head on the table and closed her eyes. She was too exhausted to cry, nevertheless the tears flowed. This evidence of emotion when she felt so wiped out internally was somehow comforting.

Finally she gathered the strength to stand. For a second she paused, imagining her mother and Chris in the kitchen, as if they had been there the whole time.

Would this room ever again know the happiness and laughter of those years they'd had together?

"HEAD UP. Yes, like that." Snip, snip. The hair stylist—tall, blond, as skinny as a boy but definitely not one—took a step back and eyed Libby's hairline critically. Frowning, she stepped forward and made another couple of minute cuts.

"Good," she muttered as she picked up yet another can of hair product and began to spray it at Libby's head. Libby closed her eyes and endured. Yolanda in Yorkton had come recommended. "A little pricey, but worth it," Garnet had told her.

In the end, Libby had decided against the short cut she'd favored when she was younger. She'd grown used to this longer look, so she'd asked the hairdresser to cut only a few inches and do some layering. Yolanda had added wispy bangs that gave new prominence to Libby's eyes and smile.

"There!" Yolanda held a mirror behind Libby's head so she could see the way the layers added fullness and style to her stubborn curls.

"This is more like it." Libby swung around in the chair to face Nicole. "What do you think?"

Nicole was still running her hands through her own hair, as if she couldn't get over the fact that most of it was now gone. She'd decided long hair simply wasn't practical for the summer or for softball, and Libby had to admit that her daughter's hair was really cute in the ultrashort cut she'd chosen.

"You look different," Nicole said slowly. "But pretty."

"Thank you. You, too. Now, how about we treat ourselves to an ice-cream sundae?"

The whole day had taken on the flavor of an ice-cream sundae—rich, decadent and totally indulgent. They'd begun with a mini shopping spree. Libby had bought them both shorts and T-shirts for the summer, a new pair of running shoes for Nicole to play softball in and a pair of sandals for herself. Then they'd gone to lunch before heading to the hair salon. Now, as they walked across the street to the Dairy Queen, Libby reflected that the dent to her savings account had definitely been profitable.

The frivolous day was just what they needed to put yesterday's misadventure in the hailstorm behind them. Nicole had awoken at three in the morning, crying from a nightmare—something she hadn't done in years. In the morning she and Libby had written thank-you notes to all the neighbors and had a long conversation about exactly what was on limits and off as far as roaming the farm was concerned.

They hadn't heard from Gibson or Allie, and finally Libby had called Connie.

"How's Allie?"

Connie had sounded troubled. "She had a restless night and got up with a cold and fever. We're going out to see her this afternoon. I think Gibson could use a break."

After the call, Libby'd felt even more racked with guilt than ever. What if Allie's cold turned into pneumonia? What if she never got over the trauma of her experience?

The worries Allie had confided after the storm

were also troubling Libby. The little girl's vulnerability about her father and her longing for a mother had been touching. For the first time Libby had seen her, not as a manipulator, but simply a child who had lost her way. Not that Allie didn't require a firm hand. But she also needed a lot of reassurance, as well.

"Wait till the kids at school see me," Nicole said, her spoon poised above her hot fudge sundae. She twisted her head so she could see her reflection in the big picture window overlooking Broadway Avenue.

"They'll wonder who the new kid is."

Nicole giggled. Libby was relieved to see her so happy. Monday was the last day of school. The children only went for half a day, to get their report cards.

"I can hardly wait for softball to start. And swimming. Do you think it'll take me long to catch up to the other kids?"

"Not if you work hard," Libby predicted. She thought of her own summers—those long lazy days on the farm had been among her happiest. She was glad Nicole would be able to share the experience, if only for this one year.

Of course, with the holidays came the end of Libby's job and finals for her correspondence courses. Libby figured they would stay the summer, so she could harvest her vegetable crop and Nicole could play softball. Come fall, however, it would be time to make their move. Nicole would begin the year at a new school.

She hadn't talked over these plans with Nicole recently. It had always been understood that their stay on the farm was only temporary. Still, Libby knew it would be hard for Nicole to leave Chatsworth just when she was beginning to fit in and to make her own friends.

Explaining why they had to go would be especially difficult now that Libby's relationship with her father was mended. But there was no alternative and Nicole would just have to accept that.

By coming home, Libby had accomplished all she'd set out to do. She'd soon have her high school diploma, and thanks to her father, she and Nicole would have even more financial security than she could have dreamed of.

Driving the school bus had been a good experience. It was something new to put on her résumé, and it wouldn't be such a bad job to get into once they moved to the city. Maybe now that Nicole was a little older, she'd have time for more correspondence courses.

Concentrate on the positive; that was what she had to do. Her relationship with her father was something to be glad about. And the changes in Nicole… Living in Chatsworth had been good for her.

As for Gibson, how could she have guessed she'd fall in love? She'd taken so much for granted during the past couple of months. The flash of his grin, the way he always seemed to show up whenever she needed help, the strength of his arms when he held her tight…

Yesterday, as she'd watched him caress and soothe

Allie, she'd longed for just one soft word, maybe a touch on the cheek or one of his special smiles. But Gibson had given her little more than a nod before turning back to the house with Allie in his arms. Her father had come then, to wrap a blanket, and his arm, around her.

Reminding her she wasn't alone. She may not have Gibson, but she had a father who loved her and a daughter who needed her. That was more than she'd had before, and it was going to have to be enough to face the future with.

LATER THAT NIGHT, after finishing her last math assignment, Libby went out to the veranda with a small glass of brandy. She'd re-covered the seats on both the rocking chairs with some dark-green corduroy from her mother's sewing supplies. She'd also polished the old wood frames until they were clean and shining and oiled the joints so the chairs glided once more. She sank into one gratefully, picking up her feet and leaning her head back.

She was exhausted, but too keyed up to sleep. Her head was swimming with algebraic formulas; little $x$s and $y$s floated around in her brain. And there was still Gibson. She tried hard not to think about him but he was now constantly in her dreams and always at the back of her every conscious thought and action—

The sound of a truck approaching cut into her musings. She listened as the engine was shut off. She heard the truck door open and close and footsteps crunch on gravel and dirt.

Slowly she moved to the screen door and pushed against it. A man was approaching in the glow of the yard light, but she knew right away it wasn't Gibson. Not quite tall enough. Not enough girth across the shoulders. And Gibson never wore his cap set back on his head like that. She wasn't afraid until the man emerged from the shadows into the glow of the front porch light.

Darren O'Malley.

# CHAPTER EIGHTEEN

When Darren put his foot on the first porch step, Libby let the screen door fall shut in his face.

"You've got the wrong address." She was determined not to show her fear.

Darren grabbed the door. "I don't think so."

"Think again, O'Malley." She reached for the doorknob. No sooner had she grabbed it than she heard him step onto the porch.

Before she could get inside the house he was there, grabbing her shoulder with one hand, quietly but firmly closing the door with the other.

"Let go of me!" She spoke as loudly as she dared. At this point she wasn't willing to risk the consequences of awakening Nicole or her father. She wasn't seventeen anymore. She could take care of this weasel on her own. To break his grip, she raised her arms, then brought them down hard.

"Libby! Would you be reasonable? I don't want to hurt you, I just want to talk to you."

"We have nothing to talk about."

"Says you, but I don't buy that, Libby Bateson. I've been doing a lot of thinking these past few weeks, about that last night we had together."

"I thought you said you didn't remember. You were so drunk you passed out."

"So I did. Was that why you left? That must have been quite a walk. We were miles from your farm."

He was fishing for information. He still didn't remember. Libby clung to that hope and tried to ignore the way his eyes fell to the front of her T-shirt, then lowered to her denim shorts and down her legs.

Just the touch of his eyes made her feel sick. She pressed her back against the smooth wood of the front door. He was standing way too close. The sight of his face only inches from hers, the faint scent of his breath behind the more obvious smell of stale beer brought back sordid memories.

He'd been drinking. Not so much that he couldn't drive, or walk straight, but enough. Again she fought for control, not wanting him to see the fear that pounded in her ears and dampened her palms.

"Get away from me, Darren."

"Now, that's not what I remember you sayin'." He leaned an arm to her left, against the side of the house, then moved in so near she had to turn her head to avoid his lips touching her skin.

"You have a pretty poor memory. I said that and a whole lot more. Not that you paid any attention." She tried to slip away to the right, but he put his other arm up to trap her.

"We did make love that night, didn't we? When you left Chatsworth, I have to admit I never thought twice about the story that went around—that you had run off with Owen Holst. I never dreamed you could have been pregnant. With my child."

"Don't call her that! You're not her father." The lie came automatically to Libby's lips. She'd never developed a plan for this moment, never suspecting in her worst dreams that it would ever come to this. She was supposed to have been gone, long gone, before the possibility even occurred to him.

Clearly, he didn't believe her. "Why didn't you tell me, Libby?"

"Because there was nothing to tell."

"Are you saying Nicole inherited her athletic ability from Owen?" Darren managed to make this seem completely ludicrous. "And what about the shape of her face? My mother's, if I've ever seen it."

"That proves nothing."

"Maybe a blood test will."

She would not panic. "Where does your wife think you are right now? Have you told her your theory? And how about your children?"

His thin mouth hardened. "You are vicious, aren't you? No, I haven't told her, but I will if I have to."

"There's no reason to tell anyone," Libby said quickly. "As long as you leave now and never bother me again."

He shook his head. "I just don't understand. Why didn't you tell me? When it happened, I mean. I had a right to know."

Libby looked at him with total disbelief. "You raped me, Darren. Why the hell would I tell you anything?"

"I *raped* you?"

Libby heard the forced incredulity in his tone. So he had known all along. Or at least suspected. For a moment she let the hatred flow freely through her, glaring at him with all the vitriol she had stored over the years. "You tore my clothes. Bruised my body. Ignored me when I begged you to stop. I was only a kid. A kid who'd just lost her mother and brother..."

He took a step back, holding out his hand. "It wasn't like that. You wanted it, Libby. You can't say you didn't. You were *crazy* about me."

"I was crazy, all right. Crazy to have given you the time of day. But then I paid the price for my mistake, didn't I?" She'd thought she was past the pain of that night, but now she felt as though she could cry forever, she was so bitter and angry.

Darren kept at her. "So I *am* her father."

"You must be hard of hearing, O'Malley. I distinctly heard the lady say you weren't."

Gibson. But it took a moment for Libby to find him. He blended into the shadows with his dark jeans and T-shirt. Only his blond hair stood out in the faint porch light. Now he stepped through the door. He wasn't that much taller or bigger than Darren, but in that instant he dwarfed the other man.

"What the hell are you doing here, Browning?"

"I was coming to say thank you." Gibson's gaze slid toward Libby, his expression softening slightly. "My parents are with Allie. Her fever finally broke." He put himself between her and Darren, placing a protective arm around her shoulders.

His voice, when he spoke to Darren again, was thick. "Looks like I've arrived just in time. What are you doing here, O'Malley?"

"Libby and I have something to talk about. Private business, if you can take a hint."

Gibson shifted his eyes to Libby. "Is that true?"

"No. I asked him to leave. I *want* him to leave." To have Gibson by her side was such a relief, but how much had he heard of their conversation?

Gibson dropped his arm and moved forward, corralling Darren.

"We didn't finish our business," Darren said, leaning around Gibson to point at Libby, even as he stepped backward.

"Our business is more than finished. It never started."

"But if Nicole is my—"

Gibson grabbed hold of Darren's collar and tipped the other man's head so that Darren's cap fell to the ground. "I don't think you have the situation figured out yet, buddy. You committed a crime against this woman. If she wanted she could land you in jail. Think about how your wife and kids would feel about that."

The breath caught in Libby's throat. He'd heard enough. He'd heard everything. Pent-up rage hardened the planes of Gibson's face and she hoped Darren didn't push him to do something they'd all live to regret.

Although Darren was definitely in the weaker position, his eyes flashed aggressively. "She couldn't prove anything. Too much time has gone past."

Gibson tightened his grip, jerking Darren slightly forward. Libby noticed him clench his other hand into a fist, and prayed this wasn't about to disintegrate into a fight or worse.

"Well, I for one," Gibson growled, "am willing to back her story."

"And so am I."

Good Lord, it was her father, standing at the front door. The escalating noise must have woken him. In his arms he had a rifle. Pointed directly at Darren's head.

"Furthermore, I'm perfectly capable of pulling this trigger and saying that I only did it to protect Libby. Heard some noises out on the porch and found you attacking her."

"You're crazy," Darren whispered, but his cracking voice revealed his fear.

"No. I'm not." The older man stepped forward and brought the gun within inches of Darren's blue cotton shirt. "Maybe I was before. Hell, I must have been. Not to have protected her...to have kicked her out of the house when she needed so much help..."

His eyes flashed over to Libby, and she saw the full agony of his remorse. A sudden movement from Darren snapped his attention back to the present.

"Watch what you're doing there, O'Malley. Cause it would sure ease my mind to settle this score tonight. A few years too late, but better late than never."

Libby held her breath, praying he wouldn't pull the trigger. The men in her life were out of control, and she didn't know how to contain them. She tried to issue an order for her father to put away his gun and for Gibson to stop clenching his fists, but, as if she were paralyzed, the words wouldn't come.

"You're not going to shoot me," Darren said. Still, he backed off.

"I don't know if I would count on that if I were you." Gibson looked as though he would gladly take the gun from her father and finish the job himself.

Darren shifted widened eyes to Libby, silently pleading for her intervention. The sight of the man, frightened and humiliated, struck her as hilarious. Libby felt laughter break out from the back of her throat. Was she going crazy? She'd never seen anything less funny in her life. Yet she couldn't seem to stop the inappropriate convulsions as they took possession of her body.

Her laughter proved the final straw. Darren, too, seemed to draw the conclusion that she'd snapped. Like a victim in a horror film, a fearful revulsion reshaped his features. He took a few more hesitant steps backward, then turned suddenly and fled to his truck. Libby could hear herself still laughing hysterically as he swung the vehicle around and drove furiously back down the lane.

"WHY DIDN'T YOU tell me, Libby?" Gibson said about half an hour later, sitting in the rocker next to Libby. Her father had gone back to bed; they were finally alone, with only the stars and the slip of a quarter moon for company. "God, it kills me that you went through all that on your own."

"I was only seventeen and I was ashamed. I guess I thought it was partly my fault."

"Oh, Libby." That she could possibly have blamed herself for what Darren had done broke his heart.

"It was awful, but it happened a long time ago."

Maybe. He was only finding out now, though. And bad as learning out about the rape was, trying to understand Henry's reaction was even worse. "I still can't believe your father kicked you out because you were pregnant. Did he know you'd been raped?"

Her long sigh stabbed his conscience. "The signs were there. I guess he chose to ignore them."

God, his head hurt with the enormity of this. Darren had known Libby had just lost her mother and Chris. What kind of creep preyed on a girl like that?

Yet he couldn't heap all the blame on Darren. He'd been so hard on Libby since she'd come home, condemning her for leaving her father and not telling Darren about their child. Damn, the woman deserved a medal.

"Dad wasn't himself when he ordered me off the farm," Libby said. "After the accident he went a little crazy. I don't want you to blame him, Gibson. He needs you. You're his neighbor and his friend. Just about the only person around here who still talks to him."

"That's why you wouldn't tell me why you left, wasn't it? You were protecting him...."

"He has no one." Her voice choked. "At least, he won't when we're gone."

Here was the crux of the problem. Agitated, Gibson rose and paced the length of the veranda. Then he stopped in front of her, choosing his words with care. "But you don't have to go anymore, Libby. Don't you see?" He pulled her up beside him.

"How can you say that, after all you heard tonight?" She yanked her hands away and whirled out of reach. "Now that you know the truth, you must see I can't raise Nicole anywhere near that man." She stared out over the railing into the vast night sky.

Gibson came up from behind her, tentatively raising his hands to knead the taut muscles at the back of her neck. "I can understand why you were scared Libby, but if you look at it logically, you don't have to be afraid of Darren. He has nothing to gain and everything to lose if the truth comes out. His reputation, his wife, his children—they'd be the ones to suffer, much more than you or Nicole."

At his mention of her daughter's name, he felt her muscles tighten. "I can't take that chance. I can't have my little girl finding out that the only reason she's alive is that a man raped me. She's only seven, Gibson. When she's older she'll have to know the truth. But not now. And not like this."

"We can protect her together, Libby. You, me and your father." He pivoted her until she faced him. With one finger he tipped her face upward.

"I love you, Libby." He saw her bottom lip tremble at his declaration, but he didn't stop. He had a lot to get off his chest.

"I'm sorry for all the hurtful things I've said since you've been back. I figured that you'd suffered in the years you were away, but I had no idea how much."

"It's—"

"Shh. Let me finish. I also want to apologize for

getting angry when you criticized the way I was rais-ing Allie. I was lashing out at you because you were right, and I hated you for that. I let my guilt about what happened to Rita stop me from being the kind of father I should've been.''

He stopped when Libby pressed a finger to his lips. ''You're a good father, Gibson. Just a little blind occasionally.''

He caught her finger and kissed it. God, but she was sweet. And strong. And more beautiful than any-thing he could imagine. He'd spent the past week trying to pretend she was gone, steeling himself for the inevitable, but it had only taught him one thing: he couldn't let her go—he needed her too much al-ready.

He placed a hand behind her neck and dipped his head, pausing when his lips were just a hair's width from hers.

Her lips parted ever so slightly, and he captured them with his own. The warm, sweet kiss acknowl-edged that she, too, had needs. He welcomed her arms as they came around his neck and tightened his grip on her. Holding her like this was all he'd wanted for so long now.

''Gibson?''

He covered her mouth with another kiss, didn't want to let her talk—she'd only come up with more excuses why they couldn't be together. She was a physically strong woman, but in that moment she felt so frail in his arms.

He ran his hands up and down her, trembling at the gentle swell of her hips. He'd never felt an emotion to match this. So much desire and love, splitting and then merging, like two forks of a river.

"Trust me to take care of you, Libby. You and Nicole. I'll protect her like she was my own. Believe me, I'll never let Darren hurt her, in word or deed."

"Oh, Gibson." A sob choked her and he cradled her to his chest.

"I love you, Libby. We belong together."

"I l-love you, too. But I can't let people go on thinking Owen is Nicole's father. It isn't right."

"I agree."

"Then, what will I tell them?"

"That it's none of their business. You held out against my badgering long enough. A few nosy neighbors shouldn't be much trouble."

She laughed softly against his chest.

"Anyway," he said, smoothing the hair from her cheek with the back of his hand, "after a couple of years they'll be so used to thinking of her as my daughter, the question won't even come up."

"Your daughter. I like the sound of that."

So did he. Nicole, too, was precious to him, and he was more than happy that the woman and the child came as a package. He pulled Libby to his chest again, thinking she belonged on this land, just as he did. She'd left it only because she'd had no choice.

"So you'll stay?"

She looked up with tears in her eyes but a smile on her lips.

"I'll stay."

## *EPILOGUE*

LIBBY TORE OPEN the envelope. A single sheet floated down onto the kitchen table. Her high school diploma. She smiled slowly. The past couple of months had been eventful. First the wedding. Then her finals. And now... She patted her tummy gently. If she wasn't mistaken she was about six weeks' pregnant.

She and Gib had married on her farm, and a prouder father than Henry there had never been. The ceremony, with both daughters as attendants, had seemed perfect. There'd been no time for a honeymoon, of course. Not with harvest around the corner. Libby didn't mind, though. Her new life was honeymoon enough. She grinned, remembering their first time in Gibson's bed, then in the field behind the barn, and of course the back of his pickup when they'd been really frantic.

She and Nicole had moved easily onto the Browning farm. Nicole had gotten almost carte blanche to decorate her new room. She'd ended up plastering the walls with baseball posters. "She'll want to redecorate in about six months' time," Gibson had predicted, "When hockey season starts."

Libby hadn't felt funny moving into the house that

Rita had decorated. She appreciated the modern conveniences. And it wasn't as if they spent that much time indoors, anyway. She could hardly wait until the spring. She had big plans for the vegetable garden, and the perennial border needed major revamping.

Libby tucked her diploma in the back of one of the kitchen cupboards and went outside to hang laundry. Allie and Nicole were on the playground set, fighting over whose turn it was to use the swing.

"Work it out between you," Libby answered when they appealed to her to intervene, "or neither of you can use it." She recalled her initial fear that she'd favor Nicole over Allie. Nicole would always be her baby, but Allie was her daughter now, too. Libby knew she'd do anything for either of them.

The line squeaked as she pushed the clothing out into the breeze. In the distance she saw a cloud of dust rising on the road. Gibson, on his way home from selling grain. She tried not to smile. It was ridiculous how happy she felt whenever he was nearby.

"Daddy's back!" she called to the girls, but they were too busy playing to notice. Libby tucked her feathered hair behind her ears and ran to the front yard, in time to see her husband step out of the truck.

He grinned when he saw her and held his arms open. She ran to him and he pulled her close and gave her a kiss that was short but very sweet. When she tipped her head away from him, he touched her bottom lip gently with one finger.

"Sometimes I forget that the only reason I married

you was to get that cinnamon bun recipe of your mother's for Connie.''

''There is that proviso that it stay in the family,'' she agreed, ''but I never thought someone would marry me for buns.''

He kissed her again, his hands roving to her backside. ''They're awfully good buns,'' he whispered against her mouth.

''You should know.'' As she twined her arms around his neck, she felt the bottom of her T-shirt come untucked. She smiled, knowing the way that little sliver of bare midriff drove her husband wild.

''Good thing I unloaded the grain truck,'' he said, his voice suddenly husky. He picked her up and carried her around the back. ''Think the girls will notice if we disappear for a few moments?''

''I highly doubt it. But Gibson, the *grain* truck?'' The fine wheat dust would work into her hair and clothing and itch her for the rest of the day.

He whisked off his cap and blond hair tumbled over his forehead. Dipping low, he nuzzled her neck. ''I'll give you a bath. Later, when the girls are in bed.''

Libby sighed. She loved the way he washed her hair in the old-fashioned claw-foot bathtub that was big enough for two.

Gibson's hands were underneath her top now, even more persuasive than his words. She thought of the exciting news she had to share. The baby, her grade twelve certificate...

''Oh, Gib. Yes. Right there.''

But good news could always wait.

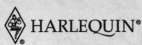 **HARLEQUIN®**

## makes any time special—online...

**eHARLEQUIN**.com

## <u>your romantic life</u>

### —Romance 101———
♥ Guides to romance, dating and flirting.

### —Dr. Romance ———
♥ Get romance advice and tips from
our expert, Dr. Romance.

### —Recipes for Romance ———
♥ How to plan romantic meals for you
and your sweetie.

### —Daily Love Dose———
♥ Tips on how to keep the romance
alive every day.

### —Tales from the Heart———
♥ Discuss romantic dilemmas with other
members in our Tales from the Heart
message board.

# Tyler Brides

## It happened one weekend...

Quinn and Molly Spencer are delighted to accept three
bookings for their newly opened B&B, Breakfast Inn Bed,
located in America's favorite hometown, Tyler, Wisconsin.

But Gina Santori is anything but thrilled to discover her
best friend has tricked her into sharing a room with
the man who broke her heart eight years ago....

And Delia Mayhew can hardly believe that she's
gotten herself locked in the Breakfast Inn Bed
basement with the sexiest man in America.

Then there's Rebecca Salter. She's turned up at the
Inn in her wedding gown. Minus her groom.

*Come home to Tyler for three delightful novellas
by three of your favorite authors: Kristine Rolofson,
Heather MacAllister and Jacqueline Diamond.*

### HARLEQUIN®
*Makes any time special™*

Visit us at www.eHarlequin.com

PHTB

# CELEBRATE VALENTINE'S DAY WITH HARLEQUIN®'S LATEST TITLE— *Stolen Memories*

Available in trade-size format, this collector's edition contains three full-length novels by *New York Times* bestselling authors Jayne Ann Krentz and Tess Gerritsen, along with national bestselling author Stella Cameron.

### TEST OF TIME by **Jayne Ann Krentz**—

He married for the best reason.... She married for the only reason.... Did they stand a chance at making the only reason the real reason to share a lifetime?

### THIEF OF HEARTS by **Tess Gerritsen**—

Their distrust of each other was only as strong as their desire. And Jordan began to fear that Diana was more than just a thief of hearts.

### MOONTIDE by **Stella Cameron**—

For Andrew, Greer's return is a miracle. It had broken his heart to let her go. Now fate has brought them back together. And he won't lose her again...

### *Make this Valentine's Day one to remember!*

Look for this exciting collector's edition on sale January 2001 at your favorite retail outlet.

**HARLEQUIN®**
*Makes any time special* ™

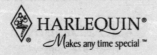

#1 *New York Times* bestselling author

# NORA ROBERTS

brings you more of the loyal and loving,
tempestuous and tantalizing Stanislaski family.

*Coming in February 2001*

# The Stanislaski Sisters

### *Natasha and Rachel*

Though raised in the Old World traditions of their
family, fiery Natasha Stanislaski and cool, classy
Rachel Stanislaski are ready for a *new* world of love....

*And also available in February 2001 from*
*Silhouette Special Edition, the newest book in the*
*heartwarming Stanislaski saga*

# CONSIDERING KATE

Natasha and Spencer Kimball's daughter Kate turns her
back on old dreams and returns to her hometown, where
she finds the *man* of her dreams.

*Available at your favorite retail outlet.*

*Silhouette*®

*Where love comes alive™*

# TEXAS CONFIDENTIAL

Penny Archer has always been the
dependable and hardworking executive
assistant for Texas Confidential, a secret
agency of Texas lawmen. But her daring
heart yearned to be the heroine of her
own adventure—and to find a love
that would last a lifetime.

And this time...
## THE SECRETARY GETS HER MAN
### by Mindy Neff

Coming in January 2001 from

HARLEQUIN®

## AMERICAN *Romance*